PRIVATE DANCER

KIMBERLY DEAN

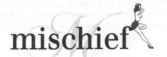

mischief

Mischief
An imprint of HarperCollins*Publishers*
77–85 Fulham Palace Road,
Hammersmith, London W6 8JB

www.mischiefbooks.com

A Paperback Original 2013

First published in Great Britain in ebook format by
HarperCollins*Publishers* 2012

A catalogue record for this book is
available from the British Library

ISBN-13: 9780007534777

Set in Sabon by FMG using Atomik ePublisher from Easypress

Find out more about HarperCollins and the environment at
www.harpercollins.co.uk/green

CONTENTS

Contents

Chapter One

The spotlight was bright as Alicia stood on-stage, pinned in its crosshairs. The light felt hot on her face and even hotter on her body.

Awareness blistered inside her.

There was nowhere to run. No place to hide. She felt like a bug under a microscope.

A vulnerable, prized bug.

The brightness made it difficult to see, but she could feel the attention focused on her. The hungry, lustful eyes of a crowd of men. If she listened hard, she could hear their short, panting breaths.

Around her, music began. Its hard-driving rhythm caught her in the chest and she gasped. The beat reverberated between her breasts, and her nipples tightened.

They felt hot and pinched. Shy. The bass started creeping through the floor and into her feet. It jumped higher and higher, grabbing her thighs and encouraging her to move. To dance.

'Come on, baby. Show us what you've got.'

It was time for her solo.

Her heart beat faster in her chest, excited and scared at the same time. She'd never done this before. Of all the solos she'd performed in her life, she'd never stripped off her clothes while going through the motions.

Yet that was what she was here to do.

Unable to fight the tug of the rhythm any longer, she swept her arms over her head. Her hips swayed back and forth timidly, and then with more vigour.

A wolf-whistle cut through the air. The male approval was clear.

She was here to strip. Just the word alone sent a flush of fire through her nervous system. She was going to end up practically naked, her body on display for the Satin Club's wealthy clientele.

She was going to end up dancing with a pole.

'Oh, man. Look at her,' someone groaned.

She couldn't see who was admiring her, but she could see that pole. The gleaming brass fixture stood at the end of the long runway in front of her. Her knees went a little weak when it glinted under another spotlight, almost as if winking at her. Daring her to come play.

Her palms became damp and she swept them over her undulating hips.

There was just something about that pole. Something hard, challenging and outright sexual.

'Enough with the teasing,' a rough voice growled from the darkness. 'We paid to see skin.'

That's what they wanted, wasn't it? To cut through the social niceties, straight to the need that drove mankind.

Sex ... or at least the simulated dance of it.

Obediently, she reached for the zipper at the back of her skirt. As she looked down, it seemed odd that she was still in her street clothes. But maybe that was what they wanted. The church secretary fantasy ...

The beat of the bass settled between her legs, warm and pulsing.

The heavy skirt suddenly felt too confining anyway. The cut was binding and the material couldn't breathe. She worked the ugly skirt over her hips and kicked it aside. It was only then that she noticed the stilettos on her feet. Definitely not the church secretary kind.

But maybe the sexy church secretary fantasy.

The naughty black shoes lifted her bottom and pushed her weight onto her tiptoes. Air swept between her legs as she widened her stance to retain her balance. A groan from her left caught her unaware, but the sound reminded her that she was supposed to be performing. Still unsure of the high heels, she did a slow bump and grind.

More groans joined in.

She fought to hold back one of her own.

Oh, the shoes felt incredible. They lifted her up, making her aware of the muscles in her legs and the point of her toes. They certainly drew the attention of the male species like a laser.

In that moment, she felt powerful. Sexy.

Her confidence soared as she strutted down the runway. The heels had ties that wrapped around her ankles. She could feel the ribbon tickling her Achilles tendons. The feeling was surprisingly sensual, like intimate kisses.

She opened the top button of her shirt – and then another to let in the cool air.

Which wasn't really so cool at all.

Alicia felt like she was going up in flames. She knew the point of all this was to arouse the crowd, but she was naïve enough that she was arousing herself.

And she hadn't even started in on the pole yet!

Her blood began to pump, warm and thick, through her veins. The tails of her shirt brushed against the back of her thighs and between her legs. Beneath the stiff cotton, her breasts felt achy and full. Her nipples were so tight, even the cups of her bra seemed rough.

'Take it off. Take it off.'

The chant started, low and steady. It grew in strength and volume as she reached for the remaining buttons on her shirt. The crowd of men was goading her, begging her. She toyed with them for a while, sashaying around on-stage, dancing as the shirt hung open. She wore a sensible white cotton bra and panties beneath it, but even they seemed to push the boys to the edge.

They loved it. The chanting grew louder and more raucous. They loved her.

Gathering her nerve, she swept the shirt off her shoulders and let it fall to the runway behind her. The almost complete bareness sent a shock through her – like ice had just been brushed over her skin. Her nipples became turgid, poking against her bra cups. Very few men had seen her like this. Only two, in fact. Now, an entire roomful of strangers was getting an eyeful.

Arousal gripped her as sure as a hand between her legs. It held her there as she walked determinedly onward, facing her greatest fear.

And possibly, one of her sharpest desires.

The pole.

Reaching out, she caught it with one hand. The brass was cool. Unyielding. A shudder went through her. Stepping closer, she leaned her forehead against its hard length. Her breasts plumped on either side of it, and her hips rolled forward.

When she softly kissed the hard metal, a hush went throughout the room.

They wanted to see her dance?

Kicking one leg high, she wrapped it around the brass pole. It gripped the back of her knee and the skin of her thigh pinched. That secret spot between her legs squeezed convulsively and then moistened.

Oh, heavens.

Alicia arched her back, letting her breasts thrust upwards. They felt trapped in her prim white bra. She was almost desperate to get it off. The sensation was making her lightheaded.

The confinement was too much.

Reaching back, she undid the hooks from the eyelets. She sighed when the cups loosened. The beat of the music intensified. She could almost feel the crowd leaning forward, wanting to see.

She wanted to show them.

She wanted to feel the freedom. She wanted to feel the nip of nakedness.

Using the leg that was wrapped around the pole, she pulled herself upright. Still, the straps of her bra and the cups remained in place.

In the distance, she heard somebody swear.

The frustration made her smile. Poor baby. She shrugged her left shoulder and the strap fell. She shrugged her right and the elastic snagged on the point of her shoulder.

The music reached a crescendo, and she couldn't tease any more. She whipped off her bra and threw it away.

The crowd went wild as her breasts were exposed. Her nipples pointed at her appreciative fans, pink and proud.

Not so shy anymore.

The act freed her, too. She spun around the pole, holding on to it tightly. Her breasts jiggled as she twisted and arched. She moaned aloud when her nipples bumped against the cool hardness. It felt so good. Her leg tightened, and the metal warmed from the heat of her skin. It pressed tight against her mound, smooth and insistent.

Arching back again, she spun and spun and spun –

***

'Sinners repent!'

The words blasted next to Alicia's ear. She jerked in surprise, and her surroundings changed in an instant. She was no longer in the cool confines of the Satin Club. She was outside, across the street, stuck in the crowd of protestors. An electronic squeal made her wince. Her head whipped around and she saw her father. He'd upgraded from a megaphone to a microphone with speakers. Loud, crackling speakers. She plugged her finger into her ear to stop the assault.

Confused, she tried to orient herself. She wasn't on the Satin Club's stage; the bright light shining on her was the sun. Her toes weren't pinching because she was wearing stiletto heels; her feet were sore from standing too long on a concrete sidewalk. And the hard pole she'd wrapped herself around?

Oh, dear Lord.

Her face heated to the point where it had to be crimson. The hardness pressing against her mound and biting into the back of her knee was the yardstick they'd stapled to the back of her sign – the one that said 'SATIN = SATAN' She quickly pulled it from between her legs and set it a good foot away from her. She pressed her hand to her face and hoped that nobody had noticed.

If they had, they didn't say anything. All around her, Sunlight Epiphany's parishioners were intent on waving their signs at anyone who dared to even pass by the Satin Club on the street.

'Deny these evil temptations! Cast out your demons and follow the one true light!' The words boomed from the speakers that had been set up in the back of a pick-up truck. Her father was on a mission and, when he got like this, nothing could stop him.

Alicia winced. She understood their cause, but she wasn't sure they should be harassing random pedestrians.

Besides, did they really know that the Satin Club was evil? None of them knew for sure what was going on behind that red door. That's what she'd been trying to figure out when she'd slipped into that fantasy.

Daydream, she quickly amended. It had been a daydream, a flight of a bored mind.

Not a fantasy.

She shifted her weight, trying to bring some relief to her aching feet. She couldn't help it. She had an affinity for dancers. She was just trying to understand.

What would it be like? she wondered.

She stared unblinkingly at the club across the street as those around her yelled at cars stopped at the light. What would it be like to work in such a place? To dance without clothes? To perform for the specific purpose of titillating those who looked at you?

Her body tingled, wrapped up in the idea, but her brain just couldn't comprehend. It was just so foreign to her, so *dirty*. She'd danced nearly all her life. She understood what it was to portray emotion through dance, to tell a story. The stories they were telling at the Satin Club, though … those tales were suited for the deep of night, in the privacy of a bedroom. What were they thinking, putting them out there on display for everyone to see?

It was disturbing and shocking – and, admittedly, a bit intriguing.

'Turn away from the devil!'

Alicia stepped further away from her father. The noise was just too loud. Instead of screaming at the club, shouldn't they be trying to talk with the people inside? To explain the dangerous path they were on? Her church was protesting against this place for a reason. How did those women feel about what they did? Did they hate it? Were they yearning for a better life and holier pursuits?

Or did they do it because it felt good?

'There they are!' someone behind her gasped.

'The devil rears its ugly head.'

Rapid-fire words started coming through the speakers. All around her, Alicia felt the energy of the crowd of protestors surge. She looked around, trying to figure out what was going on.

Her eyes widened when she realised that the door to the Satin Club had opened and two imposing men had walked out of it. Men in suits seemed to flock to this place, but these two were different. Their clothing might be expensive and impeccably cut, but it did nothing to civilise the men wearing it. The one on the left was shorter and leaner, with the body of a fighter. And the nose, she thought as he slipped on a pair of sunglasses. For all his ruggedness, he wore an air of gentility, a hard-won polish of money and power. The other did not. Big, muscled and intense, what you saw was what you got. And the big man was unhappy.

Sebastian Crowe and Remy Hunt, owner and operations manager of the Satin Club.

Her sore toes began tapping nervously against the sidewalk. She knew the two men on sight and she instinctively stepped further into the shade of an elm tree. As bad as it had been before, the conflict between her church and the Satin Club had just become more real.

And more dangerous.

Heaven help them.

* * *

Bas strode across the parking lot with Remy at his side, but his gaze was centred strictly on the crowd gathered across the street. Enough was enough. He'd been trying to turn the other cheek, but the assholes had upgraded from a megaphone to a speaker system. It was time to settle this.

'I'm sick of these religious nuts.' Remy cracked his knuckles, but his hands clenched right back into fists. 'Do we stand outside their church yelling at them on Sunday mornings?'

'They think they're saving our souls.'

'My soul is just fine. They're the ones who need to "do unto others".'

The corners of Bas's mouth curled. 'The Golden Rule? Really?'

'Even my grandmother would want their heads. This isn't spreading God's word. This is harassment.'

It was, but there was also that tricky business about freedom of expression and the right to assemble.

It was mid-afternoon. The Satin Club opened their

11

doors early for those white-collar good-ole-boys who still liked to conduct business the old-fashioned way – with booze flowing and skin flashing – but Remy was right. This irritant wasn't just a nuisance anymore. It was beginning to affect business, not only for them but for their neighbours. Hetty from the 24-hour diner next door had already called to voice her complaints. It was time to do more than sit back and take the high road.

Besides, he and Remy had always been more comfortable on the back alleyways, anyway.

Bas's eyes narrowed. They'd been watching the protestors from Sunlight Epiphany Church ever since they'd shown up a week ago. Reverend Harold Wheeler was the loud-mouthed leader of the bunch. From what they'd been able to gather, the rabble-rouser had moved to town from Birmingham a few years ago after his former congregation had found him elbow-deep in the collections plate. His new followers either had forgiven that little discretion or didn't know about it.

The decibel level rose when the crowd saw them, and Bas's jaw hardened. He had nothing against religion – until it was used against him. Then, he wasn't afraid to fight back.

And fight dirty.

His attention moved over the angry bystanders. As always, it settled on one trim figure off to the side – a feminine figure with soft, curling brown hair and a sweet innocent face – a silent figure with a body that *screamed*.

'What did you learn about the angel?'

'Her name is Alicia Wheeler.'

The way his operations manager drew it out, it sounded like something he'd like to taste. And savour. And lick all over again.

Didn't they both?

'The reverend's daughter and, as luck would have it, *a dancer*.'

Bas stared at her. Sweet little Leesha was a knockout. She wore boring, prim clothes and flat shoes, but that only made her all the more tempting. His gaze traced down her body, over her full breasts and along her trim waist to nudge at the secret spot between her legs. Did she really think it was hidden by the dowdy skirt she wore?

'A dancer,' he murmured under his breath. Now wasn't that interesting? 'Is she any good?' His gaze hadn't left that private spot. He could practically feel her lush, innocent pussy opening up to him, taking him deep. She'd be tight.

Would she be wet?

'Not our type of dancing,' Remy replied, 'but she can move – although she seems to have given it up since moving back to work at her father's church.'

Bas's mouth watered. Now wasn't that a shame? He could see that sensual body filling out a ballerina's leotard, her breasts stretching the fabric tight. His palms tingled, thinking of those trim hips rolling and her hair flying around her shoulders. He could hear her breaths panting as her legs flexed and her toes pointed tight.

He'd known there had to be an outlet for her frustration, because, whether she knew it or not, that was one frustrated woman. It radiated all the way across the street and through a security feed. She looked so buttoned up and tied down. She showed up every day at her father's side, but her expression always seemed calm and controlled. Almost distant. Was that because she was secure in her beliefs? Or was she there only because she was expected to be?

Everyone knew that preachers' kids could go one of two ways. They either toed the line or went a little wild. Being lashed down with rules and bound by strict expectations could drive anyone to act out, to rebel and experiment with the wrong kind.

He wondered which way Alicia Wheeler went.

'She's clean as a whistle,' Remy said, practically reading his mind. 'From what I could find, she's always been a good girl. A model of good behaviour, right down to those succulent toes.'

Her toes weren't what Bas wanted to suck on.

'Any vices or kinks? Anything we can use?'

Remy shook his head, but his gaze was locked onto the pretty brunette, too. He'd done the background checks on everyone in the crowd they could identify. He probably knew what kind of perfume she used, what size bra she wore and if there were any toys in her bedstand. 'She got top grades. She volunteers. Doesn't smoke or do drugs. She doesn't have so much as a parking ticket on her record.'

'Kind of makes you want to shake up her structured little life, doesn't it?'

A sound came from deep in his friend's throat.

'What about sex?' Bas pressed.

'She dates the Joe Schmo to her father's right. I doubt he's even found a way into her pants yet.' Remy shook his head. 'Makes you sad for the girl, doesn't it? Look at that body. She needs someone who can ride her good and long, someone who could make her moan.'

Maybe someone who could break the chains that were holding her back?

'Let me take care of this,' Remy said. 'I could have this crowd gone by tomorrow.'

Bas didn't think they were quite to that stage. Yet.

'I've got something else in mind.'

The operations manager sent him a quick look, but then followed his gaze back across the street. Back to sexy, repressed Alicia.

'Dancers need to dance,' Bas said softly.

15

He knew a weak link when he saw one.

The Satin Club was the classiest and most exclusive gentlemen's club in town. It was also his baby. He'd built it from the ground up, and nobody was going to tear it down, harass his clients or threaten his girls. Protecting it was his job, but he couldn't attack a church outright. There was no winning that kind of battle.

No, this might take a bit more finesse.

And that's where the sweet-looking Ms Wheeler came in.

She might not approve of the naked gymnastics their girls performed, but she appreciated art. She appreciated physical movement and expression. As a dancer, there would be empathy there.

Strip away the nudity and the voyeurs. Ignore the money that exchanged hands and all the extra-curricular activities that happened behind the red satin curtains. At the heart of the Satin Club was movement of the human body. The female body. The beat, the rhythm, the instinctual response to the sound of music.

The freedom.

Oh, yeah, as prim and proper as Alicia Wheeler seemed, she'd respond to the core of what happened here. Good girl or not, she'd respond to the dance.

'Let's go introduce ourselves,' Bas said.

It was time to see what would happen if all that repression was unleashed.

***

Alicia watched Sebastian Crowe and Remy Hunt approach like two black panthers stalking their prey. Whenever her father decided to stage one of these protests, she always made sure to do her homework. She studied up on the city's laws on assembling and permits. She determined the most effective, yet safest places to gather. Most importantly, she learned all she could about the people they were about to aggravate – because people were always aggravated when her father started one of his campaigns.

What she'd learned about these two had made her antennae go up.

Despite appearances, she didn't like confrontations. She hadn't wanted to tangle with these two, but her father had insisted. A den of iniquity, he'd called it.

The lion's den was more like it.

'Heathens! Lust worshippers! Bow down and repent before the Saviour!'

Grimacing, Alicia worked her way through the crowd towards her father. She wished that Paul hadn't bought the speakers. They had her teetering on the edge of a migraine. 'Dad, stop yelling. They're coming to speak with you.'

He ignored her completely. 'Admit your sins! Beg for forgiveness!'

17

She cast a glance at Colin, silently asking for help, but he lifted his hands in defeat. She sighed. If anyone disliked confrontations more than she, it was her boyfriend. If she wanted to even call him that.

That was another problem, but this one was more pressing.

She wrapped her fingers around her father's shoulder. 'Please stop.'

A frown momentarily settled on his face. He'd become thinner in recent months. The gauntness almost made him look fragile, but there was a glint in his eyes when the two representatives of the Satin Club began to cross the street. Eight days of this, and he'd finally got a response.

Alicia clutched the top edge of her sign. Please be civil. Everyone, please be civil.

'God knows,' her father spat at the two men. 'The Lord sees what you do in that depraved –'

The words were cut off abruptly when the bigger of their two visitors reached out and simply took the microphone out of her father's hand like a parent taking a toy from a naughty child. He shook his head and made a show of turning the device off. Alicia looked quickly at her father. Red was starting to creep up his neck. He opened his mouth to speak.

'Reverend Wheeler.' The man in the sunglasses shoved out his hand in greeting before he could get out another word. 'I'm Sebastian Crowe, owner of the Satin Club.'

The words were pleasant, but there was enough steel underneath to make a shiver go down Alicia's spine.

Her father looked at the outstretched hand in distaste. If he took it, he'd be consorting with the enemy. If he denied it, he might lose the chance to convert the misled. Conflict was clear on his face, but he accepted the handshake. It lasted all of a second before contact was broken.

Sebastian Crowe folded his arms over his chest. 'I understand you've taken an interest in my club.'

Alicia edged further away, but froze when Remy Hunt's dark gaze snapped to her. She stared at him, surprised and breathing a bit too hard. He was even bigger up close. Big, shadowy and daunting. She was unsettled that she'd captured his attention. There was something untamed about the look he was giving her, something primal and overtly ... *sexual.* Her fingers tightened until the cardboard sign scraped her palms.

Instead of moving on, his hungry gaze swept boldly down her body to settle on her breasts. She sucked in a shocked breath. Her nipples were still tight from her daydream. She hoped her bra hid the fact but –

His gaze dropped lower to the sign and one dark eyebrow lifted.

Alicia froze, that familiar sense of fire and ice sweeping through her. Oh, dear Lord. Had he seen her? All the way from across the street?

Had he seen her – *humping* a stick of wood?

19

Mortification washed through her, but he wasn't even trying to hide the way he was looking at her. His intimate gaze was sleepy but steady, and a muscle ticked in his jaw. She might not have a lot of experience, but her feminine instincts recognised the prickling of her skin and the weight in the air between them. The look was one of lust. Pure, unbridled and white-hot. She swallowed hard when she felt her body respond. Heat settled in her breasts and her nipples beaded tightly. Low in her belly, she felt a clench.

'Free to demonstrate,' she heard vaguely. 'But realise that there are other businesses you're disturbing ...'

The conversation continued around them, but Remy Hunt just continued ogling her, practically making love to her with his eyes. Only he wouldn't call it that. Something warm and heavy coiled tight in Alicia's belly. This man hadn't said a word, but she'd got the message loud and clear.

This stranger wanted to fuck her.

The word sounded coarse in her ears, but her body liked the rough sound of it. Her skin sensitised and thighs squeezed. She was so surprised by the intimate reactions it gave her the power to look away. Shaken, she stepped back.

Only he took a step forward until he was only an arm's-length away.

Her heart skipped, and she cast a glance at Colin. Pink dotted his cheekbones, but he averted his gaze. A tight sound squeezed out of the back of her throat. She sent a beseeching look towards Paul, Steve, Jeanne – nobody seemed to notice what was happening between her and the club's manager. They were intent on Sebastian Crowe and seemingly ready to pounce.

What was an uncomfortable encounter was turning unstable. She needed to pay attention and defuse the situation – although she had no idea how to defuse a situation like Remy Hunt. The words 'noise ordinance' crept into her consciousness.

'Father, they're right.'

The words were hoarse when they passed her lips. Out of the corner of her eye, she could have sworn she saw the Hunter smile.

She cleared her throat. She'd warned her father about this. 'Anything above sixty-five decibels and we can get ticketed.'

Her father's mouth worked. 'They can ticket me all they want. I follow the law of God.'

'And they'll impound the sound equipment.'

Those words got through to Paul, at least. He'd borrowed the sound system from a friend. Her father's new follower leaned over to whisper in his ear.

Alicia flinched when she felt a hot touch to the back of her hand. She whipped her head around and found Remy Hunt still watching her, but now holding out the microphone.

She looked at it in his hand. As she watched, his thumb moved suggestively up and down the side of the moulded plastic. It swirled around the silver knob atop the device and her lips flattened. There was no mistaking that gesture.

She snatched the phallic symbol from his hand, but was horrified when she heard him chuckle. She looked at the death grip she had on the microphone and nearly dropped it. She hadn't wanted it because he'd made her think of his cock. *A* cock, she quickly amended. *Any* cock ... penis ... manhood ...

Her cheeks flared and she quickly hid the microphone behind her sign.

That only drew his attention back to her breasts that were now hard and feeling twice as heavy.

Alicia licked her lips.

And regretted that, too.

Damn the man. What was he doing to her?

Determinedly, she focused her attention on the discussion going on between her father and the Satin Club's owner. Reverend Wheeler looked flustered and upset, while Sebastian Crowe looked controlled and relaxed. With his sunglasses in the way, she couldn't see his eyes. As she watched more closely, though, the lines around his mouth deepened.

For some reason, the subtle reaction made her shiver. It was an intriguing mouth. Firm, yet lush for a man. With that nose, the contrast was sexy.

Sexy. The word rang in her thoughts and she tried to push it aside.

These two did offer temptation, she realised. A dark temptation she'd never encountered before so up close and personal. They were both attractive, in a wicked, forbidden way. Her spine stiffened in defence even as her hand turned a bit sweaty against the microphone.

Her father was right about these two.

'I'm simply saying you should know all the facts before you start to judge,' Crowe said, his voice reasonable and calm. The line at the corner of his mouth sharpened, though, and Alicia felt that hot, tight sensation in the pit of her stomach slide even lower. 'Have you or any of your people experienced my club?'

'We would not set foot inside that devil's lair!' Paul snapped.

'And you couldn't, because you aren't a member,' Crowe continued, unfazed. 'We screen our clientele. This is a gentlemen's club. We offer a respite for businessmen looking for an escape from today's pressures, emails, phone calls and negotiations.'

'You have whores stripping and showing their wares.'

Alicia gaped at her father. When had the focus changed from the men who paid to enter the club to the women who danced there?

Crowe pulled himself at least an inch taller and that calm composure slipped away to expose a grittier underbelly. 'My employees are not whores. They are dancers. Artists.'

'Showing their naked bodies is not an art form.'

'Are you saying that the female body that God created is not beautiful?'

Her father was taken aback. 'I ... I ...'

'Praise his name with dancing,' Crowe quoted. 'Is that not what the Bible instructs?'

Alicia blinked.

'Don't you quote the Bible to me,' her father snarled. 'It is an abomination coming from your lips.'

Crowe slowly turned his head and Alicia felt pinned. Hunt's gaze hadn't moved from her either. She'd felt it stroking over her, hot and slow, even as she'd hid behind her sign. But now she'd drawn the attention of both men. Both stalking panthers.

'Isn't your own daughter a dancer, Reverend Wheeler?'

Her father sputtered in surprise before slashing his hand through the air. 'She doesn't do that anymore.'

Alicia sucked in air so hard, it hurt her tight lungs. She didn't know what surprised her more. Crowe had obviously studied her as intently as she'd studied him, but her father ...

She'd expected him to say, 'Not that kind of dancing'. But he hadn't.

His tone had been so cutting, so disparaging. Had her dancing been an embarrassment to him? Was he really condemning expression through all movement of the female body?

'That's a shame,' Crowe said. 'I heard she was very good.'

'Don't you miss it?' Hunt said quietly.

They were the first words the big man had spoken and, like his gaze, they were directed at her. The question was so unexpected; Alicia didn't know what to say. She did miss dancing. She missed it desperately.

'Don't you miss the music flowing through your veins?' Crowe asked, double-teaming her. 'The rhythm beating in your chest? The passion pulsing?'

The hot knot inside her lodged directly between her legs, and she could feel it throbbing.

Had these two seen her get caught up in her fantasy?

He'd made it sound so basic, so elemental, so ... so *carnal*. She licked her lips and her skin heated in discomfort. She'd never considered it sexual before, but she did miss the way dancing made her feel. Strong, in control and *desired*. She'd loved becoming one with the music, letting it enter her, thrill her and soothe her. She craved to put her body through the exertion again, to feel her muscles straining and air stroking over her skin as she moved.

Her nerve-endings tingled.

Had her dancing been about more than she'd known? She'd loved the attention of the crowd. She'd savoured their eyes upon her as she'd revealed her innermost self.

'My club and patrons appreciate our dancers,' Crowe said. 'The Satin Club values women.'

'You objectify them,' her father said.

'We empower them. I'd be happy to give you a tour of the place anytime so you can see for yourself.'

Alicia's gaze flicked up reflexively, only Crowe wasn't looking at her.

'Anytime.'

The word was practically whispered in her ear. Remy Hunt was.

'Come see our stage,' Crowe offered. 'We have more than poles. Our dancers pride themselves on their routines. We allow expression that the strip clubs you lump us in with do not. Hell, one of our most popular performers never takes off a piece of clothing.'

'Hell is right,' her father snarled. 'Hell and damnation. We will not set foot inside that viper pit.'

'Yet you'll judge it.'

'We'll fight the devil wherever we find him.'

But had they? None of them really knew what went on inside that building, Alicia thought. Shouldn't they learn more before they cast the first stone?

Crowe's words had struck a chord within her. He'd verbalised her feelings in a way she'd never been able to. This man knew the heart of a dancer and he allowed grown women to do what they loved for a living.

Was that so wrong?

'So be it,' he said. His eyes were still hidden, but the chill radiating from him told that they'd gone cold.

As if on cue, a police car crept into view behind them, parking along the curb. Seeing that he had backup, the Satin Club's owner stepped away and wiped his hands.

Of them? Of the possibility of working towards a truce?

'When any of you are willing to have an adult discourse about this, let me know.'

This time Alicia knew his gaze was on her. She was the only one who'd tried to keep the discussion polite and open.

'My offer stands,' the enigmatic man said before turning and walking away.

A sandy-haired cop passed him, coming towards them. His ticket pad was already out and he was frowning at the size of the speakers that were perched in the back of Paul's pick-up truck. It was clear that he'd been called about the noise. If only they'd listened when Crowe had warned them.

'So does mine,' Hunt said quietly.

Alicia shivered when the words were practically whispered in her ear. When she glanced up, she found the man's gaze settled suggestively on her hand. She realised that the microphone was snuggled into her palm, and her thumb was worrying the shiny knob atop it. Round and round, the pad of her thumb went. Over and across. Flicking against the edges.

She dropped the microphone like a hot potato and Remy Hunt chuckled as he walked away, leaving her flustered.

Alicia looked around worriedly, but her group's attention was on the police officer now.

She let out a shaky breath and eased the vice-like hold she still had on her sign. She felt like she'd just escaped danger – or more precisely, that it had just let her go.

She knew about the devil and the temptations it put in good people's paths. She'd listened to the sermons and read the texts herself. She forced herself to take another step back, only to bump into the tree behind her. The rough bark bit into her shoulders and buttocks as she watched the two black panthers glide away, their strides masculine and confident. Temptations were dark, attractive and hard to ignore.

Her gaze dropped to the microphone that sat propped up suggestively in the grass.

She'd just never realised how sharply temptation could bite. Or how strongly curiosity would pull.

Chapter Two

She shouldn't be here.

Alicia knew that. She stopped even as her fingers wrapped around the knob on the door to the Satin Club.

This was a mistake in the making.

For a moment, she stood still, just staring at the red wooden door. When she crossed its threshold, would she be crossing the line? Or would she be broaching the divide?

It had been over a week now since the stand-off between Sebastian Crowe and her father, but things hadn't got any better. What had been tension between the two groups before had stretched to a high-wire level of strain. She was afraid that something would soon pop and she'd be left to clean up the pieces. Wasn't it smarter to stem off the problems now? To try to reach a compromise before things spiralled out of control?

Deep down, she believed that it was.

Only she knew she wasn't the one who should be knocking on the door to the lion's den.

Her fingers turned slippery.

Nobody knew she was here. Sunlight's protesters had left soon after rush hour traffic, and the day was at that lingering stage between sunshine and darkness. She glanced back to her car, knowing she should hop into it and drive away before the night came out to play. But now was the perfect time to accept Crowe's invitation. She scanned the parking lot. Few of the other spaces were taken. If she was going to reach out to the Satin Club's owner, this was the time to do it. She wouldn't have the nerve once the sun went down and the place got busy.

Besides, she was curious what lay behind this red door.

Her fingers curled again, obtaining a tighter grip.

She'd been staring at it for the better part of a month. She knew what others in her group thought went on behind it – or she thought she did. The whispers and innuendo were hard to follow, and her imagination only went so far. But Crowe and Hunt had left a definite impression.

They'd also made her painfully aware of how sheltered a life she'd led.

A breeze blew across the parking lot, ruffling her hair and brushing against the back of her neck. The sensation made her shiver, and she jumped reflexively.

She also inadvertently opened the door.

She was caught before she could close it again. A bouncer leaned against a tall stool just inside the entryway, and he'd already caught a glimpse of her. A long glimpse. She felt the caress of his hot look as it stroked over her hair and down her body all the way to her high-heeled shoes.

The door suddenly became her shield.

'May I help you?' the man asked.

From his polite tone, she could tell he thought she'd made a wrong turn. Her cheeks heated. He was probably right about that. She cleared her throat. 'I'm here to speak with Mr Crowe.'

His eyebrows rose and the interest in his eyes sparked. There were questions on his face as his gaze swept over her once again.

Alicia couldn't help it, she edged another inch behind the red door.

She'd vacillated on what to wear for this meeting. What she'd worn the other day had seemed so stiff and *church-like*. Definitely not appropriate for the Satin Club – despite her twisted daydream – yet she hadn't wanted to dress up to the level in which she saw the businessmen and their lady guests entering the club. She didn't own any sparkly cocktail dresses, and she didn't want to show the club that kind of respect until it earned it.

So jeans and a trendy knit top were it.

She tugged the neckline up towards her chin.

'Your name?' the man asked.

'This is Ms Alicia Wheeler, Charlie,' a low voice drawled.

She looked sharply to her right and discovered the infamous club owner walking towards them. She frowned. How had he seen her?

He extended his hand and she found herself in the predicament her father had experienced – only for very different reasons. Sebastian Crowe was an extremely attractive man and this evening he wasn't wearing dark sunglasses. His eyes were green, a deep forest colour that somehow made them even more intense. He was only an inch or two taller than she was in her heels, and it left her with nowhere to hide. She pressed her palm against his, and he kissed the back of her hand.

The gesture disarmed her. Her stomach gave a funny twirl, but her knees nearly unlocked when the tip of his tongue darted into the dip between her knuckles. She tried to pull her hand back but, instead, found herself pulled forward.

'I've been waiting for you to join us,' he said, a hint of a smile on his lips.

She was surprised when the door shut behind her. The soft click shouldn't have been audible, but it was like a time mark in her brain. She'd crossed the line, and she didn't even remember doing it.

She glanced over her shoulder and tugged discreetly at her top again. 'How did you know I would come?'

The hint became reality when the corners of his mouth curled. 'I just knew.'

He cupped her elbow. 'Let me show you around my club.'

He steered her past the coat-check desk and into the open room. The feel of his hand on her bare elbow was distracting, but Alicia was curious. She'd been on the outside looking in for so long. She was here to talk, but she found herself looking around, trying to take everything in at once. Half of her cringed at what she might discover. The way her fellow church-goers went on, she expected to be subjected to lewd acts and wild music.

It was just the opposite.

'This is our main show floor,' Crowe said, sweeping his hand over the expanse. 'Things are quiet now, but Chanteuse should be starting her routine in a few minutes. What do you think of our stage?'

'It's ... *beautiful*.' The word wasn't something Alicia had expected to use, but it was true. She looked around in wonder. The stage was at the far end of the room, but it was much larger than she'd expected. They could perform shows there. A dancer could do runs and leaps. The floor looked professional, sturdy and immaculate. The polished grain made her toes curl hungrily inside her shoes.

Curse him and Hunt. Their talk last week had made her yearn to dance again.

Her gaze followed the runway out to the obligatory stripper's pole. Her heart beat faster, and she couldn't help but stare at it. Despite her imaginings, she'd only seen glimpses in cable TV movies of how dancers actually twirled around such a thing. It stood there, gleaming under the soft spotlight. It was a prop like any other a dancer might use – although a suggestive prop. Her teeth nibbled at her lower lip. Just how creative did some dancers get?

Crowe urged her deeper into the room and she had to tear her gaze away from the centrepiece of the performance area. Her heels sank into deeply padded carpeting.

The room was sumptuous. There was no other word for it. Everything was a lush deep-burgundy colour. The wood was dark oak, and the pole that had captured her attention was brass. Or make that poles. Her eyes widened when she realised there were three scattered around the room. It wasn't the set-up she'd expected to find. The room had a feeling of a classy dinner club, with half-circular tables directed towards the stage. She'd pay money that the fabric covering all those oversized chairs and settees was velvet.

'I designed everything to speak to comfort,' Crowe said as he led her to the bar. 'And pleasure.'

His thumb brushed against the back of her arm and she fought off another shiver. 'I believe that's what we need to speak about.'

'I'd be happy to talk about your pleasure, Ms Wheeler.'

His comeback was so smooth and so soft, her mouth went dry. 'Not ... not my pleasure.' She squared her shoulders. 'Your definition of pleasure. It goes against God's teachings.'

'Does it?'

She nodded. This was the solid ground she needed. 'What goes on here should happen privately between a man and a woman.'

'And what do you think happens here?'

She licked her lips. She had to admit that the feel of the place, the ambience was different from anything she'd anticipated. The Satin Club was clean, classy and, above all, sensual, but she couldn't forget the darker side of what surely happened here. 'I really don't want to get into specifics, but –'

'I think we should.'

'But –'

'Relax, Alicia. You came here for answers to your questions. Let me give them to you.'

Her solid ground suddenly felt uneven. He'd said he was willing to talk, to have an open discourse. 'We need to work out a compromise.'

'We will.'

The pulse in her neck fluttered. She hadn't planned on spending any amount of time here, but curiosity had got the best of her. Now that she'd got past that red door, she didn't know how she was supposed to negotiate with this man. Her fingers curled around her clutch. The sun had been so close to the horizon when she'd come in. She didn't want to be here when –

Music came through the speaker system. It wasn't the soft, piped-in music that was a constant under-beat to the place, but a bluesy number. It started with a slow, grungy beat that picked up with a soulful wail of a guitar. The lighting system swung up and into life, and Alicia's gaze locked on the stage. She was caught when a beautiful woman with the longest set of legs stepped out from behind the curtains. The redhead was dressed in a man's tuxedo jacket, stiletto heels and not much more. She looked classy and sexy and perfectly in tune with the club and the music.

Alicia watched with laser-like attention as the woman did a slow pirouette. The dancer found her spot and did another whip turn, stopping on a dime when she faced the audience again. She then went into an exaggerated hip swivel and the game was on.

A whoop went up from the crowd and Alicia couldn't stop her smile of delight.

This wasn't random hip gyrating and boob shaking. The woman on that stage had classical training. More importantly, she was doing a choreographed routine. Alicia watched as the dancer performed, becoming more and more animated as the drive of the music became heavier and the crowd became more vocal. There weren't many customers there at such an early hour, but those that were in attendance were attentive.

How many dance recitals had she performed at where people spent more time checking their watches than watching the hard-practised show?

This dancer had her crowd in the palm of her hand, and Alicia felt her toe begin to tap. It had been so long since she'd felt the thrill of that kind of power. At long last, the beautiful redhead started up the catwalk and she realised why it was there. So dramatic. So commanding. With a flourish, the dancer whipped off her jacket and Alicia gasped.

The woman's body was amazing. Strong and toned, with such fluid control. She wore tiny scraps of material that covered her breasts – or really, just her nipples – and her … other private places. Warmth settled in Alicia's face, but she couldn't look away. There was nothing repulsive in the scene before her. On the contrary, it was captivating … and somehow *right*. The dancer's moves fit the music, and her body was something to be admired.

The way she *moved* ...

Alicia's jaw literally dropped when the dancer gripped the tall pole and stepped up close ... and then ...

The heat in her face suffused her entire body.

Oh, so that was how it worked.

She watched in fascination at the way the dancer used the pole, or, in some cases, let it use her in return. When the woman straddled the hard brass fixture and suggestively rubbed her crotch against it, Alicia froze in surprise.

And felt a somewhat ashamed arousal.

Erotic dancing, indeed.

A glass of white wine was pressed into her hand, and she blinked. Sebastian Crowe. She'd nearly forgotten he was still there, but he merely nodded at her and turned his attention back to the stage.

So did she.

She took a deep drink of the cool alcohol, but she was more aware of her surroundings now. The air in the club had definitely got thicker and closer. It was as if everyone was breathing in rhythm. Deep and slow. Hearts steadily picking up speed.

Crowe's hand settled low on her back, and her breathing fell out of sync with the crowd's. The touch felt personal. Polite, but too intimate. She tried to discreetly separate herself from it, but his fingers spread wider and his thumb stroked against her spine.

It was then that Alicia realised her hips were rocking in time with the music.

Her wine sloshed in her glass.

'Don't stop,' Crowe murmured. Again, that thumb stroked against her spine, so warm even though her knit top kept the contact from being skin-on-skin.

She gave a quick shake of her head, embarrassment running through her.

'But you were enjoying yourself,' he said. 'It was giving you pleasure.'

Pleasure. There it was again, that dangerous word.

'Mr Crowe –'

'Call me Bas.' That thumb moved again, seemingly harmless, but oh-so-attention-demanding. 'Why don't we go into my office where we can speak in private?'

That sounded like a very bad idea. On the other hand, she might be able to regain her composure there. She could put a desk between them and organise her thoughts. She nodded mutely.

That hand at the base of her spine turned her towards the far side of the room. She followed along, but her steps hitched when she saw the nook on the other side of the bar. Still out in the open but tucked in the corner was another dancer, one she hadn't noticed – but several of the patrons had.

The woman was also dancing on a slightly elevated stage.

Only she was in a cage.

All the air left Alicia's lungs. A gilded, very pretty cage, but a cage nonetheless. The dark-haired brunette was wearing a tiny G-string, stiletto heels and a smile. Her body rocked in time with the music, but her style was more aggressive. Blatantly sexual. She gripped the bars of the cage in a way that could only remind Alicia of fingers wrapping around a headboard. The woman's hips ground and her breasts bounced, their tips beading up tight and red. What was most shocking of all, though, was the hands on her.

'They're touching her!' Alicia gasped.

This! This was what her father had warned her about. This was the debasement of women, the objectification.

The hand at the base of her spine rubbed in soft circles. 'Only because she's letting them.'

'What?' She snapped her head towards Bas and found him much too close. Instead of standing beside her, he was behind her now, his mouth only inches from her ear. She could feel his hot exhales on her neck and goosebumps spread down her spine.

'Look more closely,' he said softly. 'She's the one in control.'

Uncertainly, Alicia looked back, her chin swivelling in jerky increments. Once she took in the picture again, she couldn't look away. He was right. The dancer was in charge. Men circled the platform, looking up at her. They could reach inside the bars any time they wanted, but the dancer could stop their caresses by simply moving to the centre of the cage. Yet she didn't. With a gleam in her eye, the seductress kept her curvy body all but plastered against the bars where her admirers stood. She rocked and swayed in time with the music, but her lips trembled when a hand thrust inside the cage and stroked over her calf and ankle.

The dancer was letting the men touch her, and she was enjoying it.

Alicia was flabbergasted. She knew a lot about performing and she knew a fake smile when she saw one. This one was not for show. This was about …

Pleasure.

There it was again.

The hot, tight feeling in the pit of her belly drifted lower.

'The Petting Zoo is only for dancers who want to enter it,' Bas said into her ear, 'but I must admit, most of our girls do. In fact, they're the ones who came up with the idea.'

Alicia let out a shaky breath. 'They did?'

That one hand at the small of her back became two as his hands fell lightly on her hips. Her lashes fluttered downwards. Her body was moving again, dancing in time with the sultry tune floating in the air.

41

'It's not only the gentlemen who become aroused by exotic dancing.'

No. No, it wasn't. She took another quick drink of her wine and discovered it nearly gone.

'Some of the girls felt frustrated by the all-look-no-touch model.'

'But what … what if …'

'If things go too far, there's always someone watching out for them.'

Someone …

Her gaze lifted and she found herself pinned by a familiar stare. Remy Hunt lounged in the corner, his arms folded over his muscled chest. A flash of heat went through her and the tightness low in her belly throbbed, pulsing in time with the music. The thought of him watching while other men touched her … The idea of him looking at her while a stranger's fingers plucked and pinched …

Oh, dear Lord.

She had to go. Her hand trembled, spilling the rest of her wine on the expensive thick carpet. She had to go now.

She turned but nearly ran smack dab into Bas's chest. He took the wine glass from her and passed it to a waiter.

'My office is this way.' He turned her and Alicia found that Hunt had moved as well. Silently, swiftly. The operations manager pressed against a door that blended so well into the wall, she hadn't seen it. It swung open on oiled hinges, and Bas gave her another nudge. Hunt gave her no space as she walked by him and her shoulder brushed against his chest. Heat spread down her arm, making her fingers tingle.

She was playing with danger here.

Her feet moved fast, and she separated herself from the two powerful men. She looked around for an escape, but instead saw a wall of television monitors. She took a step closer. One was trained on the spot across the street where her group of protesters stood every day.

Her body flashed hot. They had seen her! They'd been watching her for days.

She shouldn't have come here. This had been a very bad idea. She was in over her head, and she knew it. Her hands shook as she opened her clutch and searched for her keys.

'Please,' Bas said, 'have a seat.'

'I'm fine,' she said. 'Really, I should be going now.'

He continued around his desk as if he hadn't heard her and took a seat in the leather chair. 'I'm glad you came here today, Alicia. I've been trying to be patient, but I'm not quite sure what it is that the Sunlight Epiphany Church wants from us.'

Her chin jerked upward. Once again, he'd shifted gears on her.

Her fingers finally wrapped around her keys, and she looked at the door. Once again, Hunt stood silently watching her. He leaned against the wall, seemingly at ease, but that image of a lounging black panther returned to her mind's eye. She could feel its intense gaze upon her as its tail swished back and forth.

'Leesha?'

The soft sound of her nickname had her looking back to the desk. There were two panthers here, she had to remember. One somewhat domesticated, the other not.

'I'm sorry. You really should talk to my father about this. I could set up a time and –'

'Do you want to close us down? Because there are families who depend on paychecks from the Satin Club to survive. We pay our employees very well.'

'Our intent isn't to make anyone want,' she said immediately.

A grunt came from the side of the room, the first sound that Hunt had made. When she threw a worried glance his way, she found his gaze raking down her body. With *wanting*.

She shifted uncomfortably.

His look finally settled on her breasts, hot and blatant. The crisscross design of her top was fashionable and not all that exposing, but it did dip lower in the neckline than she normally wore. The bodice was fitted and complimentary – if she wanted to showcase her breasts, she finally realised. She wore a bra, but she could feel her nipples stiffening and swelling.

Unable to stand his attention, she sat in the chair facing Mr Crowe. Bas. She swept her hair over her shoulder. These two unsettled her, but she needed to get the situation back under control. She'd come here to speak to them and, although she was distracted, that finally seemed to be what the club owner wanted, too.

'Would a donation to the church help?' Bas asked.

She shook her head. 'Money isn't the issue.'

'Then what is?'

His gaze was solidly on her face, but as Alicia settled her clutch in her lap, even she was aware of her body's response to what was happening around her. Trying to be discreet, she pulled at her top.

And nearly moaned.

Her nipples were so sensitive.

'The sexual ...' Her words were so soft they were nonexistent. 'The sexual nature of what goes on here.'

'Do you consider sex a bad thing?'

His words were steady and clear, not embarrassed at all.

She cleared her throat. 'Not between a married man and woman, but –'

'But you've had sex, haven't you?'

If her embarrassment had been bad before, it went white-hot now. She stared at her lap, unable to meet his green stare. She couldn't answer that question, not from a man she didn't even know. It was private. Confidential.

And with what her father and church preached, she shouldn't be able to answer yes.

'Yet you're not married,' Bas continued. Her lack of virginity was a foregone conclusion to him but here it wasn't an issue. Outside, in her world?

She cringed.

'Sex is not evil, my dear. Sex is about gratification, for both men and women and any combination thereof. God gave us the wonder of sex in order to procreate. It's only man who made it complicated.'

Well, they'd done a doozy of a job. Alicia crossed her legs, but that only increased her tenderness. Her private woman place felt so hot and achy. This kind of talk was so foreign to her, so taboo. Pressing her legs together helped, but she wanted to rub. She needed to rock against the chair, something, anything, hard.

'Couldn't you change the style of dance?' she suggested hopefully. 'Make it a dinner club with shows and performances?'

Behind her, Hunt made a sound that sounded like a scoff. It was quiet, but it reminded her he was there.

As if she could have forgotten.

Sex with him wouldn't be complicated. No, it would be straightforward, raw and hungry. Why had she given him her back?

'Dinner theatre wouldn't be financially feasible,' Bas said, shaking his head. 'The production costs would go up for staging, lighting and music. We'd have to drop our exclusivity clause for members and open up to the public. Even then, with our location, we wouldn't draw a large enough crowd to keep us in business for more than three months.'

'Don't forget wardrobe costs,' Hunt added.

Bas laughed at that, and the low rumble made Alicia rub her thigh. They were being so pleasant and respectful, but the undercurrents in the room were tugging at her. Sloshing her to and fro.

'Wardrobe costs would definitely skyrocket.' Crowe leaned forward, balancing his chin in his hand as he watched her. 'So again, I'm at a loss as to what I'm supposed to do to satisfy your church.'

The questions he was asking were valid. He was running a business. Admittedly, it was a business some might not like, but he had employees who depended on the incomes they made here.

'Would you consider apologising?' she asked. 'Admitting your indiscretions?'

'What indiscretions?' For as polite as he was being, his voice had an edge now that she'd only heard arise when he'd spoken to her father.

'The dancing …' she said weakly.

'You like the dancing.'

She jolted in surprise. The edge in his voice had become a lash.

'You enjoyed what you saw out there,' he said, challenging her to deny it. 'You thought it was beautiful and intriguing. I saw it.'

He had. She hadn't been able to keep her body from responding to the rhythm of the music. 'That doesn't mean I approve.'

'Bullshit.' His hand slipped from under his chin and slapped against the desk. 'I'd lay money on the fact that you liked it so much, you want to try it.'

Her gaze jumped to his. 'I do not.'

'Thou shalt not lie, honey cakes.' Those green eyes of his sparked, and his stubborn chin jutted forward. This was the fighter she'd seen, the uncivilised scrapper. 'You don't follow your made-up rules any better than I do. I felt your hips working out there. I could feel the rhythm taking over your body. You want to dance.'

'Of course, I do. I'm a dancer, but not like –'

'Exactly like that.'

Her mouth clamped closed. She couldn't argue like this. She did want to dance again. They'd set off something inside her last week. She'd been all around town looking for a studio where she could train again, shake off the cobwebs and wake her body up. All she'd found were prima donna studios that catered to pre-teens. She didn't need to learn how to do an arabesque, she just needed the floor space and time to practise. But she didn't want to move like –

Thou shalt not lie.

He'd trapped her again with her own beliefs.

She had been fascinated by what she'd seen on that stage. The sensuality the redheaded dancer had displayed had shocked her at first, but then she'd sensed the honesty in the movements. It was the one overriding theme she'd noticed when she'd first walked in the door. This place was open and honest about sensuality, something she'd never been allowed to, or had the audacity to, explore.

'I could never –'

'You could. I invited you here, and you accepted.'

'I wanted to talk.'

'And we're talking. I'm trying to understand why you and your people feel the need to repress what others want to do. Why do you ignore your own needs? Why is pleasure such a bad thing to you?'

'It's not a bad thing.'

'But sex is?' He sighed. 'You want to dance, Alicia. Let's just start with that. Why don't you dance for me?'

Her eyes went so wide, they went dry. 'What? No, I couldn't.'

'For yourself, then. On the stage, any style you want. You pick the music. Our customers would love you, and I can't stand the thought of you holding yourself back. All that talent going to waste? It's a shame.'

Her toes curled again, remembering that floor. That pole!

His eyes narrowed and the spark turned into something more calculating. 'All right, here's my deal. If you dance and you don't enjoy it, we'll close down the club for a month.'

Her breath caught. 'A month?'

'Bas,' Remy warned from behind her.

Crowe held up his hand. 'Will that settle the gripe with your church?'

Alicia's lips moved, but nothing came out. It was more than she'd expected and she wasn't sure how to respond. Her father would be thrilled with the outcome – as long as he didn't know the means she'd used to achieve it. A month would give things time to quiet down. Church members would move on to other issues, hopefully not so volatile.

'Yes.'

The word was out of her lips before she knew it. Before she could take it back, Bas's chair rolled back and he stood. Behind her, a sound came from Remy as if he'd been punched in the gut.

She knew how he felt. She'd just agreed to dance for these men.

She lifted her shaky fingers to her lips. She was horrified at her impulsiveness, yet suddenly so excited, the proof was in her panties. All that heat and tightness had finally let go. She was wet.

'Excellent,' Bas said, moving around his desk. 'Let's go to wardrobe and find you something to wear.'

Her hair flew over her shoulder as her head whipped towards him. 'What? Now?'

'No time like the present. I want this disagreement solved.'

Hunt finally pushed himself away from the wall and was in their space. Alicia rose, not wanting to be in a submissive position next to him, but standing wasn't much better. He towered over her and his mood buffeted her. He was not happy about this.

'What do we get out of the deal?' he growled.

'If she enjoys herself, Alicia will get her father to close up shop and move on.'

She nodded mutely. That was reasonable. It would be a fight, but she could do it.

'And she'll dance at the club for a month.'

Her lips parted on an exhale. She couldn't agree to that. One time was a risk, but she couldn't dance here full time. Others would find out. The scandal would be horrific.

'No risk, no reward,' Crowe said with a steely smile.

Oh, he was a tricky one.

Alicia felt her heart pounding against her ribcage. Her breasts were still peaking against the soft fabric of her top and the wetness in her panties was threatening to seep into her jeans. How had she got herself into this situation? What was she supposed to do?

Dance. Nervous as she was about it, that was the one

thing she knew she could do. At least once. The rest would just unfold as it would.

But the pole!

She couldn't lie about this. She'd already seen how the dance worked, and honesty was above all else. They would know if she'd enjoyed herself.

And so would she.

'All right,' she agreed, steeling her spine. 'I'll dance on your stage.'

'Fuck that,' Hunt said, stepping into her space and stealing her air. 'For a month, you're going in the cage.'

Chapter Three

Alicia stared at herself in the mirror, horrified and trans-fixed in one improbable moment. What was she doing?

Her hand trembled as she pressed it against her stomach. Thank goodness Chanteuse had helped her with her wardrobe. She doubted she could have handled trying on the Satin Club's skimpy outfits in front of either Bas or Remy. Still, the costume she'd ended up with was little more than a bikini. Make that a little *less* ...

Her fingers brushed against the low-riding edge of the bottoms. They barely covered her pubic hair, and she'd tried on several pairs before she'd found ones that would.

Her face flared, indescribably hot.

She kept herself tidy down *there*. She just didn't realise that most of the dancers waxed. She bit her lip. The mere thought of letting some aesthetician touch her, see her private area and *groom* her ...

Her fingers pressed against her throat. Oh, things were spiralling out of control so fast, her head was spinning.

She turned to see herself from behind. The G-string fit her like a glove, but covered much less. The tiny bands of fabric that lay against her hips continued around to the small of her back. The stretchy fabric outlined the top of her buttocks, but left them bare. She'd never, ever, displayed so much skin. Her butt looked rounded and firmed, muscled from so many years of disciplined exercise, but the thong design let a thin strap of material part her rounded cheeks and delve into the crack between them.

That intimately placed strap of fabric bit. And rubbed.

She shifted in discomfort, but the binding material only moved with her.

How was she supposed to dance in this? She'd already used the bathroom to clean herself up once. With this intimate caress following her around, she'd be in a constant state of distress.

And arousal.

Oh, heavens.

She faced the mirror again. She couldn't go out there where everyone could see her like this! Her breasts looked plump and firm, overspilling the tiny pink cups of the bikini top. She tugged at the fabric, trying to cover more of herself. She'd always been self-conscious about how full she was up top. For as sleek and toned as the rest of her body was, her curves were generous. Almost too generous for a dancer.

But that's what they wanted her to do – dance. Dressed like this. In that dreadful, conspicuous, tempting cage.

She pressed her legs together so tightly, her ankles rubbed and her knees ground.

'I can't do it,' she whispered. She couldn't stand it. Dancing was one thing, but the touching? By strangers? Men with sexual intent?

Her private area clenched, threatening to dampen again.

She doubted she'd be able to step out of this room in this get-up.

But she'd agreed to a deal.

The thought whispered through her mind. She didn't give her word lightly, and there was a huge reward waiting if she lived up to her part. There was a reason she was here, stripped down bare. Her fingers clenched. She had a fundamental disagreement with the two men who stood somewhere outside the dressing-room door. What they called 'pleasure', she called 'sin'. They might enjoy the things that went on in this club, but what about the dancers? Did they feel objectified? Ashamed? Dirty?

She hoped her church's picketing had caused some

self-analysis, but the situation had become stalled. Something needed to be done before a peaceful protest turned into something ugly. Bas had given her an opportunity to push past that barrier.

She just had to dance.

In these tiny strips of sparkly fabric.

That left her virtually naked from the back.

Her stomach twisted. 'But you'll get your way ...' she insisted to her reflection.

There was no way she was going to enjoy this. It was so much more than in her dream. More nerve-wracking. More scary. More immoral. Her palms were damp and her pulse was racing. The thought of walking out into the main room sent a wash of cold through her. And climbing up into that cage? She felt like she was going to be sick.

The end was worth the means, though, and the end was a foregone conclusion.

Now. She had to do it now before she lost her nerve.

The heels of her borrowed shoes clicked against the floor like a countdown clock as she walked to the door. Bas would be there to accompany her to the stage. She had to think of it as a stage, because that was what it was. Once she started thinking of it as a cage, she would lose it.

Her fingers were tremulous as she opened the door. When she saw the man waiting for her, her nipples pinched just as surely as if he'd reached out and nipped them himself.

Remy.

He was leaning against the wall again, his shoulders taking his weight, but he stiffened when he saw her. Her self-preservation instincts kicked in and she tried to close the door. He stopped her with one hand spread wide against it. Taking one step, he entered her space. His heavy gaze chafed as it moved down her body.

Alicia quivered.

The air had become charged, staticky and ready to spark. Goosebumps popped up on her skin and her breasts ached. Their tips were unbearably tight, pressing against the thin fabric and catching his attention. A muscle in his jaw worked.

She let out a surprised whimper when he rubbed the back of his hard knuckles over an engorged nub. That was it, just a nudge, a hard bumpy caress and her breast felt like it was on fire.

Unlike Bas, he didn't smile. If anything, the line of his jaw only hardened.

The door swung open as he pressed on it harder and Alicia had to accept the inevitable. It was time. She had to dance.

If she didn't, she knew she'd be flat on her back on the dressing room floor with this big, intimidating man rutting into her.

Her private area clenched again, and this time wouldn't relax.

Hunt's hand settled on her lower back as he accompanied her down the hallway. It felt hot and huge, his fingers tickling the line of her thong. She folded her arms over her stomach. Her breasts felt full and they bounced with every step she took. Her butt felt exposed and that insidious strap of fabric between her cheeks was driving her mad.

Too soon, they were out in the main room.

She sucked in a hard, nervous breath and felt every man's gaze in the room turn to her. She felt vulnerable then. There was nothing between them and her. Their lecherous hands, those hungry eyes.

Instinctively, she moved closer to the big man at her side. His hand slid from her back to settle at her waist.

'They're looking at you because you're hot,' he said softly. 'Dance, and they'll be begging at your feet.'

Her breath hitched. She'd been told she was beautiful before, both in body and spirit, but being hot was something else entirely. It made her feel feminine. Womanly. Powerful.

'I'm ready,' she whispered.

The cage would protect her, put some solid bars between her and the crowd.

And deep down in that secret place inside her, she wanted to be trapped inside it. On display.

Alicia was vividly aware of her nakedness as she walked across the room. There was no place to hide and she felt the stares on every inch of her bare skin. Too soon, they were at the cage. A series of steps lifted her to the small enclosure. Hunt held her hand as she climbed, her thigh muscles quivering with every step. Her fingers wrapped around a bar as she stepped inside. It felt solid and sturdy. The door clicked shut behind her and she spun around.

Had it only been a short time ago that she'd walked into the front door of the Satin Club? Fully dressed with good intentions?

She watched the crowd as it started to gather around her.

She'd definitely crossed a line.

Silence boomed around her, and her fight-or-flight instinct kicked in. She wanted out. She needed to run.

But the music started then, and her eyes drifted closed. 'Feel Like Makin' Love' by Bad Company. Her belly clenched. Oh, that was so not the song she needed, with its grungy groove and insinuating rhythm.

It got to her just like every other time she'd heard it.

The beat of the song awakened her muscles and the sensuality flowed through her veins. Still, she stood frozen. There were so many eyes upon her, so many men gathered round her tiny, elevated stage. Bold eyes, lustful eyes.

A steady green gaze caught hers. Bas. She looked at him, her panic mounting.

'Dance,' he mouthed.

Dance. Right. That was their agreement.

Her hair brushed against her back as she looked nervously from right to left. The club's patrons had gathered around her and she was fully circled. Her skin tightened. She felt self-conscious and uncertain. Indecent. A high wolf-whistle permeated the air, competing with the soulful song, and her face flushed.

Dance.

She had to dance.

Five minutes and it would be over. She could get dressed, the club would go on hiatus and she could get her father and his followers to move on. Hopefully, somewhere far, far away.

Her hips gave a little twitch.

'Ooo, baby. That's right.'

She nearly laughed, she was so nervous. Really? That was all it took?

She closed her eyes and let herself slip further into the music. She'd always been able to vanish into its midst. Her hips started rocking, though her legs were still pressed together tightly. She made her arms drop from where they were wrapped around her waist.

The song really was wicked. It pulsated, advancing and retreating with clever guitars and a booming bass line. A groan sounded somewhere behind her, and her body loosened. All she had to do was listen and move. And it felt good to escape, to go somewhere else in her head and become someone entirely different. Suddenly, the music had her. She was in the song, in the moment.

Instead of growing louder, the small group of men around her went quiet, almost as if holding their breaths.

That was when she truly began to dance.

Staying firmly in the centre of her cage, she let the music take over. Her hips swung with the beat and her hands reached out to catch it. Her hair flew and her breasts swayed. The sensation made her bite her lip. She'd always had to lash her breasts down when she danced, to the point where her flesh couldn't move. Here, today, her breasts were moving. They were swaying, jiggling and jouncing. She lifted her arms over her head and her head dropped back.

Mmm, it felt good.

'Oh, sweetheart,' someone said in a rough voice.

That's right, honey, she thought. Her legs spread as she found better footing. She'd never tried to dance in heels so high, and they made her very conscious of her legs ... and her bottom. The feel was unnerving. So bare, so perky, so –

Available.

She'd strayed from the safe zone and the tips of a stranger's fingers glided over her left buttock. Alicia jerked so hard, her breasts nearly bounced out of the string bikini. Her body flashed hot and then cold – and then hot again. She spun around, her hair flying around her shoulders.

They couldn't touch her there! They'd only stroked the other dancer's legs. Below the knee. She could deal with that. Nobody had told her they could do more.

A young businessman stood with his arm outstretched into the cage.

She looked at him, wide-eyed and uncertain.

'Come on, sweetie,' he said. 'Let me pet you.'

The Petting Zoo. Her panic flared, but somewhere in there was excitement, too. Her gaze searched the crowd, and she connected with an intense green stare. Bas's eyebrows lifted.

It was her decision.

She was in charge.

She sucked in a hard breath. Someone swore, and her excitement mounted. So did her self-confidence. They could touch her – but only when she said so. And if she did this, nobody could argue that she'd dodged the bet. With her legs spread, she did a deep squat, almost a plié, before rising again with an exaggerated grind of her hips.

Her gaze connected with the man who'd touched her. He looked so boyish. Harmless. His fingers curled towards her, almost begging.

Power solidified in her chest. Remy had been right.

She held the crowd's attention in the palms of her hands, and they were all attracted to her. They liked what they saw. Her body and the way she used it pleased them.

It pleased her, too.

After so many years of rules and chastisement, the feeling was surprisingly freeing. A link or two of the chain that bound her broke and slipped away. Hesitantly, she turned, giving the man her backside again. Her skin prickled when she felt him and others staring. They could see every flex of her muscles, every shiver of her flesh.

She edged back one step and then another.

She shuddered when those strong fingers stroked her cheek.

Oh, this felt good.

Sinful.

Her breath went jagged when another hand cupped her right buttock. Cupped her and squeezed. Hard.

Oh, dear ... dear ... *heavens*!

'Baby, you're like velvet.'

Her eyes shut tight. Her body was suddenly guided not only by music but by touch.

More hands braved to reach through the bars. One lone finger traced the line where her bottom met her leg. Another stroked down her spine while a bold, calloused hand reached between her legs and stroked her inner thigh from her knee all the way up to –

She gasped, and her eyes flew open.

Her gaze connected this time with Remy's.

His dark eyes were steady as always, hot and intent. And mocking?

The hand on her right buttock squeezed again, making her muscles bunch. He was watching the whole thing, just like she'd imagined.

Just like she'd fantasised.

Her breaths went short, and her ... her womb pulled tight. She was suddenly so aroused, it hurt. Taking a bigger step back, she put herself fully into these strangers' hands. Her body vibrated, threatening to spiral out of control.

'Come on, honey. Give it to us. You know you want to.'

She did. With everything inside her, she did.

The music poured over her, while countless hands touched her. She watched Remy watching her and her anticipation mounted. She hadn't known she'd wanted this, needed this. She danced and was rewarded with admiring hands, fingers and dark whispers.

She gripped the bars of the cage as her hips worked. Not being able to see the men helped her courage, but it made their touches more unsuspected. More shocking. Just when she thought she was getting used to them, a thumb slipped under the band of her thong.

'Oh!' she gasped.

It was the masterful hand that still clenched her right

butt cheek, the one that had refused to let go. That firm thumb stroked up and down, up and further down … Her butt clenched when it slid between her cheeks, rubbing flesh that had never seen the light of day, much less felt a caress.

'I don't –'

'You do.' The voice was gruff behind her.

She looked over her shoulder and was surprised to find an older man with silver hair at his temples. He was handsome, fit and carried an aura of authority. Somebody's boss, no doubt. Her gaze shied away. She couldn't look at him. She couldn't look at any of the men touching her. Not yet. But she didn't move away as she looked to Bas for support. His eyes were hot and curious. He lifted his shoulders. *It's your decision*, she could practically read.

The thumb stroked deeper into her crack, and her body shuddered, all thoughts of dancing gone. Move away. The decision should be easy. Just say no and step forward. The thoughts were just a whisper in her mind. They paled to the roar in her ears.

'Bend over,' the gruff voice said.

The silver-haired businessman. She couldn't get the look of him out of her head. His instructions were simple, but devastating. She couldn't. She shouldn't –

But her body was no longer her own. Her motions were no longer guided by her training. They came from the gut, were driven by nature.

'Bend. Over.'

And sexual need.

Another hand spread wide across her spine and pushed her forward. Alicia bent at the hips. The hand on her inner thigh pulled her leg outward and she widened her stance. She gripped the bars in front of her to retain her balance and to try to keep herself together.

Her fingers turned white when the thumb underneath her thong began wiggling. Her toes curled inside her shoes. She waited for that insidious touch to delve deeper between her legs. She was ready for the stroke, craving it, but she was stunned when instead that thumb flicked.

Every muscle in her body clenched when the crotch of her tiny panties was pushed aside. Another flick tucked it up in the notch between her vulva and her inner thigh, and she was exposed completely.

She squeaked in distress. That tiny placket of material hadn't been much, but she'd relied on it to protect her modesty. Now it was gone. Her private womanly area was bared to all the strangers' eyes. Her pink flesh. Her dampness. Her curls.

She wanted to die.

Behind her, there was a chorus of groans and moans.

'Now that's a pussy.'

She went white-hot at the word, but she remained bent over, frozen and trembling.

The tremble became a shudder when that masterful

thumb slid over her, finally touching her. Her back arched hard. 'Oh, please. I – I can't –'

'You're so soft and gorgeous.'

It was the baby-faced businessman who'd first asked to pet her. A finger glided over her swollen flesh and slipped into a crevice. Her spine stiffened. Was that him?

More touches came, and her head bowed. How many were back there? How many were touching her? She couldn't look again, any more than she could control her hips. The movement they were following was natural, guided by need and something more.

Desperation.

Oh, stars, she'd never felt like this. Her body was spiralling upwards, clenching tighter and tighter. Her skin felt hot and prickly. Her – her p-pussy was fluttering and so, so achy and wet.

A moan ripped through her lips when a determined finger circled her sensitive opening. Round and round, it stroked her until her hips were pressing back, the bars biting into her flesh.

'Fuck her,' someone growled. 'She wants it bad.'

The finger penetrated her, going deep.

'Ohhhhhhh,' she cried.

From then on, everything circled in her head. The music, the thrill, the hands, the fingers, the *kisses*. Lips touched her butt as the one finger inside her became two, and she sighed in delight. She hadn't expected gentleness.

She didn't get much.

The pressure increased and her brow furrowed. Another finger had penetrated her, but was it from the same hand? They worked inside her, pumping like pistons until she didn't care.

Someone played with her clit. The touch was shocking and intimate. She flinched away, but strong hands clenched her hips and offered her up. That touch was ruthless. Alicia looked down between her legs and watched as fingers tugged on her pubic hair and a thumb worried her overly sensitive nub.

'God, look at her.'

Her eyes flew open and, in that moment, it was as if cold water had been thrown over her. No, not God. God couldn't see this.

But Remy could.

Her gaze locked with his, and her nipples tightened until they threatened to poke right through the sequined material of her tiny bikini top. He'd touched her there, rubbed her briefly with his knuckles. The way she was bent over, her breasts were on display for him. They swung and juddered with every move she made.

And she was moving faster, almost jerkily now. Her breaths sounded harsh in her own ears.

'That's a hungry pussy,' someone said.

Another tug at her curls. 'I like that she doesn't shave.'

'I want to suck her.'

Her ears felt hot from talk like she'd never heard, but that didn't stop the desire moving through her. The overwhelming need.

'She's close,' another man said.

'She wants this bad. Fuck her harder.'

No, not harder!

'Yesss,' Leesha groaned when the fingers inside her became rougher.

They weren't moving in sync, and it felt like a hundred fingers were filling her. When they found their rhythm, her knees nearly buckled. The pressure was thick, and the fingers at her clit teased round and round. She lurched hard, though, when the pad of a foreign finger pressed directly over a place she hadn't expected.

Her most secret place.

Panic washed through her. 'Remy!'

It was Bas who came to her rescue. 'No anal penetration,' he barked at her side.

The crowd behind her went quiet for a brief moment.

'Her ass is mine,' Remy finally growled.

Someone behind her chuckled, and the momentary reprieve was gone. Her ass was his? Alicia felt herself going under as the finger-fucking intensified. Her pussy was theirs. Nobody was stopping them. Not Bas or Remy.

And not her.

She was so wet, her dampness dripped from her. Her hips were working. Fingers were plunging. A touch stroked over her inner thigh, picking up her wetness. It lay deliberately on the bud of her anus again. Shocked, she looked at Remy, but the finger obeyed the rules. It pressed firmly against her tender opening, touching her in a shocking way. Wetting her.

And it wouldn't go away.

Was it the young businessman? The silver-haired boss? The black man she'd seen?

'Oh ... *Oh*!'

Her lungs worked like bellows, and her blood thundered through her veins. Her hips began to jerk hard and then the orgasm hit.

Like a tidal wave.

Right there in public, in front of a bunch of strangers who now knew her intimately, Alicia reached her sexual peak. A hoarse cry left her lips, reaching above the music that still wafted through the air. The fingers inside her stilled, grinding deeply and she shuddered again. That insidious touch on her anus swirled, and she dropped helplessly to her knees.

Pleasure.

She'd thought she'd known what it was.

She hadn't had a clue.

She let it settle over her as another tremor clutched her and then gently left. The fingers slipped out of her as she rested in the middle of the cage, out of their reach. She was almost sorry when the hot finger on her anus left her, too. Her body felt warm, replete. Heavy. She let her hair fall forward to hide her face. Her muscles were relaxed and her womb was positively glowing. She'd never felt like this before. She'd never come like that, not in private. Not with someone she cared for.

A dark, scared feeling fleetingly passed through her chest.

What had she just done?

The door to the cage clicked as it opened. Another mark in time.

She felt herself lifted into strong arms and she curled against a muscled chest. She pressed her face into Remy's shoulder as he carried her from the room. He wasn't safe, but he was protective.

Alicia swallowed hard.

There was no argument to be had here. They had a deal, and they all knew how things had turned out. The Satin Club wouldn't be closing down for a month; she'd just become their star employee. The truth couldn't be hidden. Not here, not out in the open where everyone had laid witness.

They'd challenged her to dance and not like it. How could she have enjoyed it any more?

She'd just come for a group of complete strangers.

Chapter Four

'Dad, do you think we could skip the protests today?'

Alicia sat on the edge of the wooden chair in front of her father's desk. They were in his office at the church. The room was sparse with white walls and stern furniture. A Bible sat on his desk and a picture of a lost lamb graced the wall behind him, but the room was so quiet – in colour, in warmth and in volume. A radio sat on the shelf to his left, but no music came from its speakers. The only sound to be heard was that of the air-conditioner, and it was working overtime.

'It's supposed to get into the high nineties this afternoon,' she explained, latching on to the excuse. 'I don't want anyone to overheat.'

'It's hot in hell,' he muttered, not looking up from the

paper on which he was scribbling. A computer sat at his side, but he rarely turned it on. He was an old-school man, in thoughts and in actions. He viewed the Internet as a playground for degenerates, and the only use he had for it was his email. 'We will not let the devil push us away simply because we're uncomfortable.'

Alicia toyed with the ledger in her lap, lining it up against the hem of her skirt. She was certainly uncomfortable, but not because of the heat. Tonight was her first night dancing at the Satin Club. She was nervous, scared and queasy over the situation she'd got herself into. She'd barely slept all night as she'd tried to think of a way out of this mess. Step one had to be getting her father to stop his boycott.

'We've had some elderly parishioners showing up. I'm worried about heat exhaustion.'

'Then bring bottled water and fans.' He slapped the desk in annoyance. 'We're making progress, Alicia. We can't stop now. Crowe and his depraved minions are on their heels.'

Hardly. Leesha pressed her thighs together tightly. Bas wasn't backing down. No, he was a fighter, just like she'd pegged him. He might use unusual tactics, but he'd stand his ground. Just look at what had happened to her when she'd tried to go toe-to-toe with him.

Her face heated and she pulled her skirt and the ledger further over her knees.

73

She still hadn't got over what happened the other night. The feelings were still so close to the surface: the embarrassment, the horror – and the astonishment, the adrenalin and the bliss. She still couldn't believe what she'd done, but dancing like that? Feeling those strangers' hands on her? They'd brought her to such a sharp state of ecstasy, she still had to be careful how she walked or sat.

Even this hard wooden chair was getting to her. She shifted in distress. She'd been so sensitive ever since it happened. It was as if an awareness had been lit inside her. She had a sexual side, a side that needed gratification.

Apparently it had been starved for too long.

'Please, you need to reconsider.' She opened the ledger determinedly. 'The number of worshippers in attendance on Sunday mornings has dropped significantly.'

He waved off her worry. 'We don't need the meek or the non-believers.'

'We need their offerings.'

His blue eyes finally met hers. They were watery, but steely with fire. 'Are people not tithing?'

'Well ... yes,' she admitted. As far as their numbers had dropped, the actual dollars in the offering plates had gone up. The believers were showing their faith where it counted. 'But we've got several comments on how radical we've become. We haven't had any new attendees in weeks.'

'*Radical*?' That one word brought her father to his feet. 'We're fighting against evil.'

Leesha rocked slowly in her chair. This was not how she'd wanted things to go. She'd hoped to approach this logically, to have a straightforward discussion, but she could see it was too late for that. He was committed to his cause.

He rounded his desk, his blue eyes narrowing. 'Has Lucifer touched your thoughts? Are you wavering in your commitment?'

She wasn't wavering. Her commitment was just to peace and understanding. She'd already lost one battle to keep that. 'No, I'm just … Father, we haven't worked on the bulletin yet for this Sunday's service. You haven't signed the checks for the gas or electricity bills. You haven't spoken to Jeanne about the hymns you'd like her to play. Have you even thought about your sermon?'

He bristled with indignation. 'I will speak as the spirit moves me.'

Which wasn't a good thing. He could be a powerful speaker when he planned his services, so eloquent and moving. She hadn't seen that side of him for a while now. He'd become so myopic. 'I just think we need to spend less time at the Satin Club and more time here.'

He stood over her, frowning. 'Did those men at the club get to you? Are you fearful, child?'

Fearful, uncertain, excited – it was hard to tell which way the adrenalin was pulling her.

He knelt before her, taking her hands. 'Evil can be frightening when you stare it in the face, but we must be strong together. We can't tremble or let them separate us.'

'Dad, you know I'm on your side.'

There were still questions in his eyes, worry for her. She took hope in that worry. For the first time in a very long while, he was looking outside himself. Vesting himself in something other than hate and vengefulness.

'Let us pray together,' he said.

She bowed her head, warmth filling her chest.

'Father in heaven, help strengthen our resolve in the face of darkness. Help us cast out the demons. We are your servants, Lord, your soldiers. We will be strong in your stead.'

He gripped her hands so tightly Alicia winced, but then he was pushing himself to his feet. He bobbled slightly when his arthritic knee seized up, but grabbed the back of the wooden chair and pushed himself upright. He lifted his Bible high. 'Let us be off to meet with our fellow soldiers.'

Stand on the picket line with Bas and Remy watching her through their security cameras?

'Maybe I'll stay here, just for today,' Alicia hedged. 'I have a lot of work to do.'

'Nothing is more important than standing tall against your fears.' He grasped her by the arm and pulled her upright.

She caught her ledger before it tumbled onto the floor. This wasn't working. Instead of getting him to back down, she'd got him charged up.

There was a spring in his step as he pulled her towards the door. 'We will win this fight, you and I together. In a few weeks' time, the Satin Club will be no more.'

* * *

The Satin Club was hopping by the time Alicia made it there that night. She could see the cars in the parking lot and hear the muted beat of music. She was nervous and uptight as she parked her car at the diner next door. They'd instructed her to park behind the club, but she couldn't be caught there. She didn't want anyone to know where she was. How could she ever explain?

For a long moment, she sat in her car just staring at the building. The desire to run was so strong. They had to have seen her on the picket line with their security cameras and spies. Would Bas be angry with her? She hadn't got her father to budge, although there'd been no microphone or speakers today. She hadn't lived up to her end of the bargain on that, but she was here.

She was going to dance.

Her stomach clenched. Just dance. Without any clothes, perhaps, but she was not getting back into that cage. There would be no extra-curricular activity tonight, even though her nipples were pinching and her hips were loosening. She was here to entertain … visually, with no touching allowed.

She blew out a breath. 'A month of this?'

There was no way her nerves could take it.

Before she could chicken out, she got out of the car. She could feel the eyes upon her as she made her way to the club's back entrance. She keyed in the code she'd been given, but hesitated when she opened the door. On the other side of those red satin curtains, the place wasn't so lush. The hallway was dark and intimidating. It was industrial with hard floors and metal shelves. The music had a melody now, but it sounded hollow. She wrapped her arms around her waist. Really, it was like the back-stage of any other theatre where she'd performed, but she wasn't comfortable here.

She stayed near the exit as she contemplated what to do next. She couldn't just walk out into the performance area. How could she show her face? The last time she'd been here, she'd exposed herself, physically and emotionally. Footsteps suddenly echoed over the beat of the music, and she stiffened.

'Alicia, welcome.'

She struggled not to blush when Bas turned the corner.

He was dressed in black, the panther in all his sleek glory. He tucked a hand in his pocket as his gaze skimmed over her. If he was gloating, she couldn't tell. His green gaze was indecipherable in the dim lighting.

He frowned as he looked up at the burned-out fixture on the ceiling. 'Sorry it's dark back here. I'll get someone to work on that.'

He held out his hand. 'Come.'

She had no option but to take his hand again, a willing sacrifice. He led her down the hallway to the changing room she'd used before, and it brought up mixed emotions. She was used to getting ready for performances in places such as this. Bright bulbs of lights surrounded big mirrors. Make-up was strewn about the tabletops, and lockers lined the far wall. There were the familiar tools of the trade: legwarmers, liniment and wrapping tape. It was the dance world she was accustomed to.

But, oh so very different.

She chose a spot, set down her bag and clutched her hands together. They were shaking. 'I'm sorry about the protesters today. I know I promised, but –'

He cupped her shoulder. 'It's all right. I knew you wouldn't be able to stop it in a day.'

His touch was warm and firm, but not angry. He trailed his fingers down her bare arm. She'd worn a sleeveless top to try to stay cool. The heat had been beating down on her all day, but somehow she knew she'd be shivering once she hit the stage. There was already a chunk of ice in the pit of her stomach.

'Sit,' he said. 'I want to go over the rules with you.'

Rules? Really? She'd thought this place was about breaking them.

She was too antsy to sit, so she leaned her hips against the make-up table and wrapped her fingers around its edge.

Bas's expression was stoic as he watched her. He was so different from Remy. With Remy, she knew exactly where she stood and what he wanted, shocking as it may be. Bas was more calculating, and it put her off-balance. What did he expect out of her this month? Was he trying to prove her wrong? To show her that the club wasn't depraved and sinful?

Because she'd got a taste of the darker side in that cage. Although she'd been a willing subject …

'You look like you're about to face a firing squad,' he commented. 'Relax.'

'I don't think I can,' she said honestly.

He frowned. 'I want you to enjoy yourself here, Leesha. This isn't a punishment. It might not seem like it now, but this place could be your sanctuary.'

Sanctuary. Her stomach turned. 'I already have one of those.'

He bowed his head apologetically. 'Poor choice of words. I just want you to know you can do anything you want here. You can explore things you're curious about, delve into things you like. You can try new styles of dance and expression. Nobody's going to judge you or hurt you. You're safe here.'

She nodded slowly, not quite trusting him. 'What if I don't want to take off my clothes?'

The lines around his eyes deepened, and she stilled. It was the one sign she knew that signalled his displeasure.

'That's the one thing I won't allow,' he said. 'You will not hold back on me or this bet. The gentlemen who visit this club pay for certain privileges. Seeing your beautiful body is one of those. Besides, this experiment is supposed to push you outside of your boundaries, to get you to experience the pleasure that you've denied yourself.'

Pleasure, again. She couldn't hold his gaze.

'Clearly, that's something you need to do.'

There it was: the reference to her time in the cage. She'd been waiting for it, but her reaction wasn't quite what she expected. She'd expected shame, but instead she felt confusion. He'd watched her lose control, but he was encouraging her to do it again. Demanding it. The idea was so bizarre. Her whole life had been about control and denial.

She bit her lip as that place between her legs pulsed, and she crossed her thighs to try to ease the sensation. 'But you said that one of your most popular dancers never strips.'

81

He grinned like a hungry crocodile. 'That's because she's sixteen. Once she hits eighteen, I won't be able to hold the little minx back.'

'Sixteen?' Alicia gasped.

This place was *unseemly*. Even as she cringed, she felt a spark inside her. Maybe that was why she'd been sent here – to help change the club's ways from the inside. The Lord did work in mysterious ways.

Bas shrugged. 'She's like you, the girl loves to dance.'

'But –'

'But unlike you, dance is all she's allowed to explore here. This is your time, sweet Leesha. Nothing's holding you back here. I want to see how far you can go.'

'With dancing,' she stressed.

'Sure, with dancing.' His gaze dropped to her breasts and then the way her legs were rubbing together.

Alicia felt a prickle at the back of her neck. He was so careful in his wording. He'd said he wanted her to feel safe here. Somehow that was one thing she didn't think she'd ever feel inside the walls of this club. Safe from him? Maybe. He was so controlled, so in charge.

But from herself?

She wasn't sure. She was experiencing desires she hadn't even known she had.

The door to the dressing room suddenly sprang open, and Chanteuse strode in, all long legs and streaming red hair. She was flushed and breathless. A big grin was on her face, but she stopped when she saw the two of them. 'Oh, sorry. Should I come back?'

Bas waved her in. 'I'm just going over the rules with Angel.'

'Angel?' Alicia said.

'Don't look so stricken. Every dancer here has a show name.'

'But ... *Angel*?'

Chanteuse patted her on the knee as she passed. 'It's a good fit. The guys the other day certainly thought you'd fallen from heaven.'

Alicia balked and felt her face flame. 'You – you saw that?'

'Saw it and heard it. Honey, you were spectacular.'

Alicia wrapped a hand over her mouth, utterly horrified. She hadn't thought about anyone other than Bas or Remy, but this dancer had seen her in the cage. What must the other workers in the club think? The bouncer and the bartender? What about the men who'd touched her? The men who'd played with her and brought her to orgasm? Would they be in the crowd tonight?

She felt woozy. Of course they would. Bas was a smart businessman. He would have advertised that she was coming back.

Oh, she couldn't do this. God might have sent her on a mission, but she wasn't up to the challenge. She pushed away from the table and began to pace.

'You can come here any time you want,' Bas continued, 'but your performance hours are from eight to twelve. I know you have a day job, so I'm willing to let you pull an early shift. On weekends, you'll dance from ten to two. We have beds if you want to spend the night.'

'As in sleep?' Chanteuse let out a laugh. 'Yeah, right.'

Alicia turned on her heel. 'I can't work on Sundays.'

He watched her steadily. 'It's one of our busiest nights.'

She looked towards Chanteuse, who shrugged in agreement.

Bas leaned back against the wall with both hands in his pockets now. 'Once their wives release them from their church obligations, a lot of men come to me. Here, for what you'll provide.'

Leesha looked to the ceiling, trying to find strength. She'd had no idea. This had to be why she'd ended up here. Determination started to build inside her chest. Maybe that's why she was being allowed to dance again, to experience the pleasure she'd left behind. She was here to minister, to bring back those who'd strayed from their faith. It was like that lost sheep in her father's office.

'You'll be on the main stage once every hour,' Bas continued. 'When you're not the main attraction, you'll be expected to work the crowd and dance the off-stages.'

'Work the crowd?'

84

'They can't touch unless they make special arrangements. You have the final say.'

'Say yes,' Chanteuse whispered. 'The tips are awesome.'

'Tips.' Bas snapped his fingers and nodded as if that was something he'd forgotten. 'There might be some touching if you're willing to accept those.'

Alicia stared at him, not understanding.

He grinned softly. 'You are an innocent one. They slide the bills into your G-string.'

Her eyes widened. 'But –'

He chuckled. 'And sometimes there, too.'

Her mouth dropped open, and this time both he and Chanteuse laughed out loud.

'I meant that they're so tiny,' Alicia protested. 'The G-strings, I mean!'

'Speaking of which …' His gaze slid down the zipper to the crotch of her jeans. 'Did you wax?'

Her breath was knocked right out of her. How could he say these things out loud? She sent a worried look to Chanteuse, but the woman was changing. The redhead was literally stripping out of her costume and putting on her street clothes – right in front of God and her boss.

Amazingly, Bas's attention was still on her. 'Well?'

'I shaved,' she hissed. She wrapped her arms around her waist and hugged her elbows. Everything was so out in the open here. Nothing was forbidden.

Or looked down upon. Or considered shameful.

That took her aback. People weren't made to feel bad here – about anything.

He cocked his head, his gaze considering. 'Let it grow back in a bit, and I'll spring for a visit with Ricky.'

'Ooo, Ricky.' Chanteuse slipped her feet into comfortable flip-flops. 'That's a treat.'

Finally, Bas pushed himself away from the wall. 'That's about it. Did you bring an outfit?'

'Yes.' Alicia's pacing had brought her back to the table. Reaching out, she set her hand protectively on her bag. She'd brought her own clothes, but now she didn't know if that was such a good idea.

'Have you chosen your music?'

She nodded and that calculating smile pulled at his lips again.

'You've been practising.'

It wasn't a question, because they both knew the answer. Of course, she'd been rehearsing. She couldn't get on that stage without a plan this time. She was here to dance and she'd been choreographing all day long. In her office and on the sidewalk across the street ...

Why not? She was being given a chance to dance again. Why not do things the way she wanted? She couldn't make a fool of herself again. She couldn't let others take the lead. When it came to her dancing, she was going to be in charge.

'I make the rules on the dance floor.'

He clicked his tongue, apparently happy with what he saw. Alicia was surprised when he set his hand on her waist and brushed his lips across her cheekbone. 'There's only one rule I'm really going to hold you to, Leesha angel. You enjoy yourself.'

***

'Did she show up?' Remy asked when Bas stopped at the bar.

'She's here.'

Remy nodded. He was busy balancing glasses one atop the other, with the finishing touch being a shaker of salt. As much concentration as it took, he knew that old Henry had fallen asleep again at Table 5 and Joaquin from the lawyer's office was getting a bit rowdy. If the counsellor grabbed his waitress's ass one more time, Remy was going to have to escort him to the door. He was aware of everything that happened in this place.

The one person he hadn't seen yet, though, was the angel. He'd been waiting for her. 'She cut it close. I was beginning to think she didn't have it in her.'

Bas leaned back against the bar. His attention was just as honed, but it was on other things – like how much they were bringing in with alcohol sales tonight and how much higher they could turn up the air-conditioning. It was a squelcher out there tonight, but it was good to keep things a bit warm inside the club. It fit the mood. Nobody wanted to be frozen out, especially when things were getting hot on the stage.

Bas signalled to the bartender for a water. 'She's shaking in her shoes, but her nipples are showing right through her top. She was awfully squirmy, too.'

So a lot was going on down below, too. That surprised Remy. He hadn't thought she'd have the courage to come back here after her experience in the cage. The fact that she did told him she was made of sterner stuff than he believed.

For a holier-than-thou type, that intrigued him.

The salt shaker was balanced just so. Carefully, he let go and stepped back from his creation. It would take more than a puff of air to knock that tower down.

He wondered just how much pretty little Leesha could withstand.

Turning, he leaned back against the bar next to Bas. 'Her father isn't cracking.'

'No, but she is.' Bas took a long drink of his water, the muscles in his throat working. He nodded to the stage when the lights went down. 'I think we're in for something special, Remy.'

The lights flickered and went on low, signalling that the next performance was about to begin. Over the loud-speaker came a deep, crooning voice. 'Ladies and gentlemen, please welcome to the Satin Club stage our latest featured performer, Aaan-gellll.'

The beat of the music started, and Remy frowned. It was a timid piece, not something the crowd would go for at all. When the spotlight swung up, there was a lone figure on-stage. A prim, tightly-lashed figure in plain, frumpy clothes. 'What the hell?' he muttered.

Even so, his cock stirred.

Her hair was up in a bun, she wore glasses, and her skirt hung all the way down to mid-shin. She looked so subdued, crisp and clean in her best Sunday go-to-meeting clothes. His teeth clenched. Was she going to preach to them from up there? There was absolutely nothing sexy or come-hither about her at all.

Except for the shoes.

His gaze focused on them like a soccer player's on a net. They were black and sky-high. Still, he might not have noticed them if not for the ribbons. They wrapped around her feet, circled her ankles and crisscrossed up her shins. They finally tied somewhere up under that long skirt. He could see the tail ends hanging down, tickling her Achilles tendons.

He reached down to adjust himself. Oh, sweet mercy.

She *was* preaching – preaching to the choir.

All alone up there on the stage, she held the attention of every man in the room and she hadn't even started to move yet. She was covered from neck to shin, but they could see her shape in the harsh spotlight. Her

89

breasts were high and full. Her waist was nipped in, and her hips were sleek.

She looked like the church secretary she was, the woman who'd given him boners just standing across the street and waving that saucy sign. Remy found himself salivating at the thought of all those clothes coming off, piece by piece.

But then she started to move and he nearly swallowed his tongue.

Holy balls.

She was incredible.

Her hips started rocking first, back and forth, and then she added a twitch. That ugly skirt swished, inching up only a little, teasing him and hiding her. She walked forward on the stage, seemingly hesitant and out-of-place, but then a high note pierced the air.

All hell nearly broke out when the music went into a serious rut, grungy and dirty. The sweet church secretary changed with it, whipping off her glasses. They went flying into the crowd and bounced off old Henry's forehead. He awoke with a start and nearly fell out of his chair when he realised what he was missing.

Remy's fingers clenched into fists as she let her hair down. It was amazing hair, long and brown and wavy. It flipped and bounced as she moved and suddenly all he could think about was wrapping it around his cock as she sucked him dry.

Did she even do that? Would he have to teach her? Given what he was seeing on that stage, she'd be a quick study.

The crowd was suddenly on its feet. Beside him, Bas had gone still.

This wasn't normal, even in their line of work. Remy had seen dozens of naked women gyrating on that stage. So had most of the men in the room. This one was completely dressed, hardly strutting, and yet his dick was already poking at his zipper.

His buddy had been right. She was something special.

He folded his arms over his chest as she finally started working that butt-ugly skirt over her hips. A much nicer butt was exposed. High, firm and rounded. He shifted his weight against the bar. That ass was so his. He couldn't wait to grab it, hold her in position and pound into her as she squirmed and squealed.

'Lord almighty,' Bas breathed.

Her shirt was undone now, and they could all see the body underneath. She was wearing white cotton, something Remy was pretty sure wasn't even in their wardrobe collection. The bra and panties were plain and unadorned, but they didn't need to be pretty. What they were hiding was spectacular in and of itself.

A muscle under his ear panged and he rolled his jaw to ease the tension. God, he wanted to see her breasts. He'd watched them dangle and jounce as the boys had

91

fingered her yesterday, but he hadn't yet seen them bared.

The shirt hit the floor and there she was, twisting and grinding in her prissy little bra and panties – and those naughty, naughty shoes. The crowd was now gathered around the runway and bills were being waved at her left and right. She seemed shy about that, hesitant to let those hands touch her again.

But her gaze kept drifting down the runway to the pole.

Remy stood upright. She wanted this, the little vixen. She wanted to be dancing here, just like this, in those clothes and with that pole.

The bra. He wanted it off. His nuts were already so tight, they were like billiard balls. He was ready to march over and tear that stupid bra off with his teeth when she finally went for the tab at her back.

Around her, the breathing of their customers went ragged. The music was hard and driving, full and grubby. The mounds of her flesh bounced and jiggled as she danced, and then gradually they were released. She took a deep breath of air and her chest expanded, pushing her breasts high. Her eyes drifted shut in that moment and she arched her back. She swept her hands up her belly and covered the jiggling globes. Almost with curiosity. Definitely with pleasure.

A shudder went through her that wasn't choreographed.

Oh, fuck! Remy was staring so hard, his vision started to blur around the edges.

Her nipples were big and pink, reddening with excitement. She felt herself up and enjoyed it, but then her chin snapped down and her gaze focused on the pole. Like a woman possessed, she charged down the stage towards it. When she finally came into contact, she wrapped herself around it, her delight evident. She rubbed it between her bare breasts and Remy bit the side of his cheek as her pink nipples stood out, turgid and hungry. She pressed her mound against the brass fixture and humped unabashedly. From where he stood, he could see the wet spot spreading in the crotch of her panties.

But no dark shadow. Had she waxed? His boner twitched, ready to fire off.

She spun around the pole until she had to get dizzy. When she finally stopped, she arched back. Her naked breasts lifted high and her hair brushed against that tight little ass. Kicking one leg up, she pointed her toes and rubbed against the brass pole some more.

He'd seen exotic dancers with a lot more technique, but never one who was so enthusiastic. She wasn't quite sure what to do with that lucky-ass pole, but nobody in the place was about to stop her as she experimented.

Unfortunately, the song was only so long. It had to come to an end, and it did before she came to hers. She seemed surprised when the beat stopped, but she'd trained as a dancer her whole life. She ended with a pirouette beside the pole, and dropped dramatically to her knees.

Her face was hidden by all that luscious hair, but her entire body bobbed as she sucked in air, trying to catch her breath. When she finally rose, the applause lifted with her. For someone so confident before, she now seemed shy and unsure. She covered her breasts with her hands, but let them fall in increments when Bas shook his head.

Remy swallowed hard. God, she was gorgeous like that, naked and visibly aroused. Her breasts were high and heavy, her stomach was quivering and her cheeks were dotted with pink.

All around her, dollars waved. He sent a quick look over the crowd to make sure nobody got over-anxious. She knew what to do, didn't she? One of the regulars showed her, shoving a bill down the front of her wet panties. She swivelled away in surprise. Others soon followed, and some of her bravado returned. She thrust out a hip for a dollar here, meekly offered her backside for a fiver there ...

When she finally walked offstage, her straight-laced panties were bulging with tips. Dollar bills were crammed into every nook and cranny. Her walk was a bit funny, but her shoulders were back and those amazing tits were held high.

Remy's eyes narrowed to nearly slits. He wanted to fuck her so bad, he couldn't see straight.

'Shit,' Bas exhaled. It sounded like the first deep breath he'd taken in minutes. 'We've got a star on our hands, Rem.'

Remy didn't know about that. He just wanted to get his hands on her.

Chapter Five

Alicia was exhausted by the time her shift ended. Exhausted, thrilled, self-conscious and more than a little turned on. In truth, she had a sneaking suspicion that she was *horny*.

Embarrassment twinged inside her.

She'd heard the word, but she'd never understood what it meant. She'd been aroused before, yes, but she'd never walked around in such a state of sexual need. All that concentrated male approval had affected her more than she'd anticipated. She'd expected to be ashamed and uncomfortable, but she'd never thought her sensual nature would be provoked like this. She hadn't even realised she had a sensual nature.

But it was stirring now.

Stirring, churning and coiling.

She accepted one of the employees' hands as he helped her down from a side stage. Her breasts bounced as she climbed down the steps, and there was nothing she could do to hide her response. Her nipples had been stimulated for hours now. They were so tight and achy. Her body was reacting so strangely to all of this.

And so powerfully.

She could feel the hot male gazes upon her as she made her way to the hallway back to the dressing room. On her bare ass, gliding down her legs, caressing her breasts, tugging at her G-string. She'd been virtually naked in this room with these strangers for hours. It hadn't begun to seem normal, but she'd stopped trying to cover herself long ago.

Bas wouldn't allow it.

And to be honest, she got a thrill out of the attention. The attention on her body, the attention to her dancing; the attention simply on her.

Her eyelids got heavy. Oh, she wanted to be touched so badly.

Her fingers curled and they brushed against her hips as she walked. Trying to be surreptitious, she slid them up to the band of her G-string. She traced its lines over her hipbones and down her legs towards her crotch.

What was wrong with her? She was practically trembling with need. Had the other day done something do her? Was she like Pavlov's dog now that once she danced, she needed to be rewarded? Her thighs were clenching as she turned the corner.

She came up short when she saw Remy waiting.

Big, muscled and looming. He was lounging casually in the darkened hallway, his shoulders pressed back against the wall and his legs crossed at the ankles. He looked lazy, dangerous and ready to pounce.

Alicia couldn't help it. Her hands came up to cover her breasts.

He smirked at the move, but unlike Bas he didn't order her to expose herself. A shiver went through her. No, that wasn't Remy's way. If he wanted to see her breasts, he'd make her show them in a much more physical way.

She edged back a tiny step. And then another.

'How was your first night, Leesha?'

Her stomach clenched. The way he said her name was like a lick across her skin. Beneath her hands, she felt her nipples pinch. They poked into her palms, begging for manipulation.

'Fine.' The word came out as a hoarse whisper.

His gaze drifted down her trembling belly to her G-string. 'Looks better than fine from where I'm standing.'

Her buttocks clenched. Even with all the bills tucked inside, the thing barely covered her down there.

'You enjoyed yourself on that stage.'

It wasn't a question, and she didn't know quite how to answer. 'I was scared.'

'You don't have to be. Nobody's going to get to you. They'd have to go through me first.'

His dark eyes sparked and he pushed himself away from the wall. The movement was fluid and unhurried. Alicia was so transfixed by the sight of all that strong, muscled flesh coming at her that she froze like a deer in the headlights. When she finally reacted, it was too late.

He trapped her against the wall, leaning in until his body brushed against hers. So hot. So threatening. So tantalising. She swallowed hard and her hands tightened on her breasts. Her feet scurried to move her out of the way, but they only inched her back until her bare butt was pressed against the cold wall.

She was caught.

He braced a hand aside her head and encroached on her personal space even further. 'You were beautiful up there.'

Something fluttered inside her chest. Beautiful, not sexy or slutty.

'I got hard watching you dance.'

Her heart began crashing against her ribcage and her thighs rubbed uncontrollably. She'd never attracted a man like him before. He was so ruggedly male, so handsome she couldn't help but stare. Those eyes – the way he watched her.

Her nerves began to sing. He was catching her at

precisely the wrong time. She knew she should stay far away from this man. He wanted to do things to her that she couldn't fathom. He scared her and fascinated her and excited her in ways she didn't understand, but in her purest heart she knew she should run in the other direction whenever she saw him.

'I shouldn't like it,' she whispered. 'It's dirty and improper.'

'But that's what makes it feel so good.'

She let out a squeak when he caught her by the waist. He moved in that fluid way of his again, lifting her until she was pinned like a bug against the wall. Instinct had her clutching at his shoulders, but then she remembered her nudity. Her hands clapped back over her breasts, and she shivered at the look of disapproval that crossed his face.

'Seriously? You've been showing them off all night to anybody who will look.'

Yes, but she'd been safe on the stage, out of reach, and he intended to do more than look.

His hips were hard as he used them to hold her in place. With the wall immovable behind her, Leesha wriggled in distress. There was no way to fight him off when he caught her hands and dragged them away from what he wanted to see.

'Remy,' she whispered when he pinned her wrists against the wall next to her ears.

'Wrap your legs around my waist.'

She squirmed like a worm on a hook. He was so much bigger than her, so much stronger. And heaven help her, her body was melting and quivering before him.

She looked down the hallway, back towards the main room. It was dark and secluded, but anyone could catch them here.

Could *save her* here, she meant. Why wasn't she calling for help?

'Wrap. Your. Legs.'

The bite in his voice sent a nip through her system. Shakily, she swung a leg around his hip. The wrap-around ties of her shoe dangled. It took some dexterity to hitch herself up and clench him with her other leg, but she managed it. Still not letting go of her wrists, he worked his hips higher into the notch at the juncture of her thighs. Shifting, thrusting and lifting until she was riding on him right where she wanted.

Leesha arched her neck and ground her head against the wall. Oh. Oh, goodness!

She shuddered when he raked his teeth over her jugular vein. 'I don't get it,' he said, almost angrily. 'So naïve and better-than-thou, but I wanted to fuck you in that church-lady outfit as much as I do with you standing here with your tits out and begging for it.'

She sucked in air. The coarse language stung her ears, but her body felt like one exposed nerve that needed petting. What was wrong with her?

'Do you want it, Angel?' His teeth dragged over her collarbone and his tongue dipped deep into the hollow at the base of her throat. 'Do you need me?'

No. Absolutely not. She couldn't let him drag her down.

'Yes,' she groaned.

A rough sound came from deep in his throat and his head dipped. He latched onto her breast like a man starved for sustenance and she let out a cry. His rough tongue lashed against her nipple, rasping across it like heavy sandpaper. When he pressed it against the roof of his mouth and began to suckle, her entire body arched. In distress or pleasure, it was hard to tell. They were so interchangeable in the otherworldly realm where she found herself.

'Let go,' she said hoarsely.

His mouth opened more widely over her breast, plumping it as he refused to give up his prize.

'My hands,' she panted. 'I meant my hands.'

He turned her loose, and she wrapped her arms around him, one hand cupping the back of his head. His tugging was so intense; it was like he wanted her milk. She wondered what it would be like if she had any to give to him. She could feel her womb clenching as it was.

'Is this the way it's going to be?' he asked when he finally turned her loose. His breath was warm and wet against her skin. 'You dance and I fuck you?'

She squeezed her eyes shut. That sounded wonderful to her.

'Innocent little dancer.' He nudged his nose against her other aching nipple. 'I'll make you a naughty girl yet.'

Alicia groaned. She didn't want to be naughty – but she'd always wondered what a girl had to do to get that label.

'Is that what you want?' he asked.

'No.'

'Liar.'

That hot, suctioning mouth clamped on, and her shoulders rolled. She felt each tug deep down in her core, and she was already so needy. So desperate. Her hips began twitching against the bulge filling out his jeans.

His hands were on her then, plumping her breasts for his mouth and grabbing her butt. One worked its way deeper between her legs. Dollar bills rubbed, but she let out a moan when he cupped her.

'You like men touching your pussy, don't ya, babe?'

Just the sound of that wicked P word made her belly squeeze.

His rough fingertips worked aside the stretchy fabric until they rubbed against her private flesh. She was slick and plump. 'Aw, yeah, you do.'

She shuddered as he probed and investigated her.

'Do you like to have it sucked and tongued? Do you like it when a big fat cock pushes inside you?'

Oh, her ears were burning, but his wicked words were setting her body aflame. She'd known it would be like this with him. She'd known it from the way he looked at her.

Her breath caught when two of his thick fingers burrowed deep, stretching her.

'You're sopping. Have you been wet since that first dance?'

She had. She'd made fantasy become reality and it had aroused her more than she could have ever dreamed.

'Shit, you're virgin tight.' His fingers moved up and down inside her, wiggling and tickling. He pulled back to look into her face, and his dark eyes got heavy. Dangerous. 'What are you like back here?'

Back where?

Alicia arched like a bow when his fingers abruptly pulled out and slid back. They trailed fire over her sensitive skin, but then one was pressing against her anus. She clutched at his shoulders, trying to push him away, but the pressure on her back door only intensified. Her sphincter muscle was no match as his thick finger penetrated her.

A gasp left her mouth, and then a low moan. 'Ahhhh!'

His finger stiffened and worked deeper, going one knuckle deep and then two. Leesha sucked air into her lungs. The sensation was overwhelming, dark and biting. She felt vulnerable and debased, but the pleasure was shocking. So wrong. His finger seated deep and she let out a cry.

He caught it with an open-mouthed kiss. A mind-blowing, dangerous kiss. He worked himself closer to her until her breasts were plumped against his chest and her ankles were locked high against his back.

That devilish finger slowly retreated. It dragged against sensitive flesh, stimulating her in places she'd never felt before. She was relieved when it exited, but her thrill shot back up when the pressure started again. Harder this time. Thicker.

She jerked her mouth away from his.

'Too much?' Those eyes of his were entrancing. He slid his fingers back to her pussy to pick up more lubrication. 'Now, let's try.'

The penetration started again. Two fingers, Alicia thought desperately. It had to be. The pinch was hotter, the sense of fullness more scandalous, and he'd only started.

Her nipples raked against his hot chest and she dug her nails into his shoulders. She hadn't known people did this. It certainly wasn't normal, was it? It felt so wrong. She shouldn't let him do this. She didn't like it … maybe. Fear shot through her because she wasn't sure. Her hips began to move, to try to find an escape. She had to get away from that insidious touch. She was afraid what would happen if she didn't. Instinct had her internal muscles pushing down, trying to expel him.

Instead, those insistent fingers disappeared into her. 'That's right, baby.' He leaned his forehead against hers. 'Take me in. Take it all.'

She wasn't prepared when his thumb slid into her pussy and he squeezed from both sides. A sharp cry left her lips and she twisted in his arms.

'God, baby. You're hot for it.'

She was so close to climaxing, it hurt. This shouldn't make her feel this way. This shouldn't make her want it so much.

'God, I want to be inside of you. Unzip me.'

Leesha was nearly too far gone to hear, but one thing penetrated the sensual haze clouding her head. One word made its way through the mists of dark, seedy pleasure, and it was the one word guaranteed to make her go cold – the one name that would make her realise that she was succumbing to temptations that were impure. Unholy.

God.

She tensed. She hadn't listened to the warning the other night, and she'd regretted it. Somewhat. The pleasure had been overwhelming, but afterwards? The questions and self-recriminations had eaten at her. She couldn't give in again. She held herself stiff as she pushed at his shoulders. 'No. Stop.'

He looked at her in surprise.

'Please.' Her legs flailed and she reached for his forearm

that circled underneath her. She clutched at his wrist and tugged. 'Stop touching me like that.'

'You want my fingers in your ass,' he said, his voice low.

'No.' Not anymore. She'd remembered why she was here. She was supposed to be showing them the light – not exploring the dark enticements of the flesh.

His fingers curled, making her bite her lip, but she didn't have to ask him again. He stared at her, his face carved in stone as he retreated. She expected him to jerk his touch out of her. Instead, he drew it out, making her feel every spark of friction, every delectable millimetre.

She unwrapped her legs from around his waist and her toes reached for the floor. She was gulping for air now, but for entirely different reasons. She'd promised herself she wouldn't do this. She'd told herself she would dance, but she wouldn't let anyone touch her while she paid her thirty days of dues. Yet he'd barely had to look at her and she was offering herself up to him.

Her nakedness chilled her now. Uncaring of the rules that had been set for her, she wrapped an arm across her breasts. She was off the clock. She'd been heading to get dressed. Why hadn't she just walked past him and gone home?

He caught her by the waist. 'What's wrong?'

His eyes were hard, but his hands didn't hurt her. She just hurt on the inside, deep where her principles and beliefs lived. 'I have to go. I can't do this.'

A muscle in his jaw ticked. 'Sure you can. You were doing it quite well.'

She shied away, unable to look at him. 'It's wrong, immoral.'

'Who says?'

'I'm sorry.' She dipped her head. 'I'm not built for this. I wasn't raised this way.'

He moved then, making her flinch. Once again, he was leaning over her, his hands propped on either side of her. His breath was hot in her face. 'You are built for this. For me. Once you let go of your prejudices and condescending attitude, you come find me.'

He caught her by the chin and kissed her. Sexily, intimately. Her lipstick was on his mouth when he pulled back. He wiped it off on the back of his hand as he stepped away from her. 'Maybe then I'll show you just how good we can make each other feel.'

* * *

Alicia was wound up tight. She paced around her bedroom, confused and uncertain. She'd done the right thing, she knew, but it felt so wrong. Her body was strung so tight she ached. She was still aroused, more so than she'd been after just dancing, but she didn't know what to do to ease her distress. Her nipples were raw and her lips were swollen. Her womanhood – pussy

– was throbbing and her bottom? Remy's not-so-casual play had left her feeling aware and hungry.

She'd had to make him stop. She would have regretted her actions if she hadn't.

But she'd been so close to finding that dark, consuming pleasure again.

She clenched her hands together. Even the brush of her nightgown had been too much. She kicked it out of her path and revelled in the feel of being completely naked. No G-string bound her and no shoes strapped her in.

But she needed something. Someone.

Colin.

He was her boyfriend. They had a committed relationship. Intimacy was OK if it was wrapped in love, wasn't it?

She pounced on her bedside phone before she could rationalise any further. She hit his number on speed-dial, but it took several rings before he answered. His voice was groggy when he spoke. 'Hello?'

'Colin? It's Alicia.'

He cleared his throat. 'Is something wrong?'

'No.' She looked at the clock. It was after one. 'I'm sorry, I didn't mean to wake you.'

'What's going on? Do you need something?'

'I need you,' she said bluntly.

She heard sheets sliding and envisioned him sitting up

in bed. 'Did you hear something outside? Did your A/C break down?'

She didn't need a handyman, although once that thought sank into her head, she nearly groaned. Her thighs clenched hard, and she dropped onto the bed. 'Can you just come over, please?'

She heard him fumbling for his glasses. 'Sure. Just give me twenty minutes or so.'

'Ten,' she insisted.

'All right. I'm coming.'

But she wasn't and that was the problem!

She wrapped her arms around her knees and rocked back and forth. She was so horny, so aroused, so out-of-her-mind. Was this what it was like to be possessed? By the devil? By impure thoughts? If saying no was the right thing, why was she suffering? If she'd let Remy do the licentious things he'd wanted to do, she knew she'd be feeling better right now.

And by better, she meant fantastic. Blissed out. Satiated.

But morally bereft.

She sprang back to her feet and began pacing again. It was twelve long, gruelling minutes before she heard a car outside. Headlights lit her room, but then faded as the sound of an engine disappeared. She ran to her front door and yanked it open.

Colin's eyes nearly bugged out of his head when he

saw her standing stark naked and backlit by the light from the living room. 'My gosh, Alicia.'

He looked around the apartment complex in horror and gave her the bum's rush inside. He locked the door behind him, averted his eyes and hurried over to her couch, where he grabbed the afghan draped over its back and tried to swing it around her shoulders.

She was already reaching for the fly of his pants. 'Make love to me, Colin.'

He jerked as if she'd just plucked his string. 'Leesha!'

She kissed his neck and nipped at his earlobe. He didn't tower over her like Remy did. He was just her size, and he didn't make her feel meek or vulnerable. Or sexy or trembly. She shook off the thought. They were equals. They were a couple.

Although they weren't married.

She pushed Bas's whispered comments to the back her of mind. She just needed to feel close to someone. She needed to be held and comforted and screwed hard.

Oh, she wasn't thinking right, but Colin was so much safer than anyone down at the club. He cared for her, and they shared the same belief system. He'd never hurt her or push her to do inappropriate things.

She kissed him and tugged up his T-shirt. 'I want you.'

He went up on his tiptoes when she softly kissed his nipple. 'Whoa, sweetheart. What's gotten into you?'

He didn't want to know that. He didn't want to know

the who, the what, the where or the how. She pulled his T-shirt off and caught his hand. He followed when she led him to her bedroom.

She understood why he was concerned. They didn't usually have booty calls. When they slept together, it was usually at the end of a date with dinner and a nice wine. Their relationship was about mutual respect, and she felt warmly towards him.

Not feverish and off-kilter. Not crazy out of her mind in need.

But she needed him now to work off the edge. Remy had left her hanging right on the precipice – or she had left him there.

The bed hit the back of her knees and she let herself fall onto the mattress. She bounced when she hit, but she was already pulling Colin down atop of her.

He fell clumsily and she winced.

'Sorry,' he mumbled. His hips were twisting as she tried to get his pants off. He reached down to help push at his briefs. 'What's the rush?'

She kissed him and he wobbled before falling down on one elbow.

'OK, OK.'

Leesha spread her legs wide and offered her hips up to him. Her breasts shuddered as she waited for him to situate himself. His cock was still limp when he pulled it out. Impatient, she reached for him.

His eyes went wide when she gave him a few jerks. 'What are you – oh, my!'

She didn't know what she was doing, she was just going on instinct now. She wished he would just take over, roll her back on the bed and thrust into her, but he was nearly as inexperienced as she was. That wasn't what she needed right now.

'I want you inside me.'

'Alicia!'

As shocked as he sounded, his boner popped up, straight and hard. She scooted down on the mattress, trying to get him where she needed him most. He wasn't nearly as big as Remy in this way either. The provocative bulge in that man's pants had felt huge when she'd wrapped her legs around him.

She did the same with Colin, but there wasn't as much to cradle. He was wiry, whereas Remy was built like a Mack truck. She squeezed her eyes shut. She couldn't compare the two. It wasn't Remy she wanted making love to her.

She sighed when the tip of Colin's penis found her nook. He thrust and she let out a pained yip.

'Not like that.' She adjusted the angle and bore down. He slid in and she dropped back against the mattress. 'Like thaaaat.'

He wasn't thick and he wasn't long, but she was tight. It was a good fit, a comfortable one. He began to thrust and she pulled his head down to her breasts. He flinched when he found her nipple in his face, but he kissed it politely.

Alicia groaned. No, she wanted him to suck her. She wanted to feel his teeth and tongue. Like Remy's...

Ohhhh. She needed, but he wasn't quite – *Agh!* Frustration rolled through her. She didn't want comfortable, orthodox love-making. Drawing her legs up, she dug her heels into the mattress and lifted her hips. Instead of pounding into her, though, Colin pulled back.

She clawed at the sheet beneath her. 'Harder,' she begged.

'I don't want to hurt you.'

'Faster.'

'Honey, take it easy.'

She didn't want it easy. She wanted it rough and tumble. She wanted to be pressed against a wall and fucked like there was no tomorrow.

She wrapped her fingers around Colin's wrist. He was holding her hips, trying to keep her at his pace. She guided his hand to where they were connected. She blushed and was thankful the room was dark. She just needed his fingertips to brush her there. If he even toyed with her a little, she knew she would come.

He yanked his hand away and braced himself on his elbows. His weight rubbed back and forth over her. Alicia tried to pull him down on her. She wanted to feel his weight press her deep into the mattress. They'd found a rhythm now, with her lifting as he bore down. Still, it was a careful, if rushed, rhythm and she just couldn't get where she wanted to go.

'You shaved,' he panted. His glasses were steaming over.

She squirmed beneath him. Yes, she had. The sensation of his male parts against her female ones was stunning, more intimate, but even so, it wasn't enough.

She clutched at his back. He was thrusting now like a pint-sized jackhammer. The thrusts were short and shallow, making her crave all the more. 'Colin!'

The muscles in his neck went taut.

'Sorry.' His body was straining, but he jerked out of her, leaving her empty. She clawed at him, trying to get him to come back, but the feel of her nails scraping along his butt was too much for him. His body arched, his cock rose and he ejaculated all over her belly. 'A-leee-shaaaa.'

Leesha rolled her head on the pillow, groaning at the loss. Her hips were now hovering above the mattress as she tried to rub her mound against him. Just a tweak of his fingers. Anything.

He fell atop her with a winded 'oof'. 'Wow, that was just – wow.'

No, it wasn't! It wasn't even close.

115

She tried to push him off of her. If she rolled him over, maybe she could ride him and make herself come.

He misread that message, too. 'Oh, gosh. I'm sorry!'

He bounded off the bed, straightened his glasses and scurried to the bathroom. When he returned, he had a washcloth in his hand. He looked like a skinny teenager as he rushed to her bedside, his little dick hanging limply between his legs. With jerky moves, he started cleaning her up. 'I know you don't like to get dirty that way, but you know we can't have premarital sex.'

Alicia's fist bounced off the mattress. They'd just had sex – only one of them hadn't come. She pushed the rough washcloth between her legs. 'Rub me there, for God's sake.'

'Alicia!' He jerked his hand away. 'Don't take His name in vain.'

She couldn't take it anymore. Was she breaking rules or being prudish? What was worse, pleasure from the intimate touch of a near stranger or frustration from the lack of touch by a loved one?

Did she even love him? Or was he just a suitor her father considered a good worshipper?

She rolled off the far side of the bed, her body aching. Her legs were wobbly as she rushed to the bathroom and locked the door behind her. Bracing her hands on the counter, she bent over the sink. What was she supposed to do?

What was right?

What was right for her?

Were they two different things?

She looked at herself in the mirror. Her hair was mussed and her eyelids were heavy. Her breasts swung, free and full, with her nipples engorged. Was this how everyone at the club had seen her tonight? Were those red marks left by Remy's whiskers?

Colin knocked softly on the door. 'Honey? Are you OK?'

No, she wasn't OK at all.

Her gaze locked on her reflection in the mirror. Hesitantly, she lifted one hand from its spot beside the sink. Her fingertips brushed over her belly, moving gradually downward. The moment they slid over her clit, she saw stars. Glimmers of satisfaction ran through her, long overdue.

She fell back against the wall, both hands diving between her legs. 'Ahhhhh!'

Masturbation was nearly as forbidden as premarital sex, but she couldn't hold out any longer. She needed this. Her pussy was so plump and sensitive. She stroked her fingers through her wetness and played with the tender nub that could make her explode. She plunged her fingers into her pussy. They weren't as thick as Remy's or as long, but it was something.

Just not quite enough.

Her gaze landed on her travelling toothbrush holder sitting by the sink. It was long and cylindrical, hot pink and plastic. Longer than her fingers. Thicker. And harder. She was grabbing for it before her scruples or narrow-mindedness could kick in.

She was trembling as she lined the plastic tube up with her opening. She'd never done anything like this and fear and self-loathing were lurking nearby. The threat wasn't enough to make her stop. She pressed hesitantly and felt herself opening to take the foreign intrusion. She was wet and slick, and her internal muscles clung.

Taking a deep breath, she pushed harder.

Her knees nearly melted when the hard plastic delved into her. It went deep, deep, deeper than she expected. Deeper than Colin had gone. The ridge where the two halves screwed together was thicker. It rubbed against her, making her feel every stroke.

She shuddered and squeezed her eyes shut.

Her shoulders ground against the wall as she thrust the make-do phallus inside her over and over again. The toothbrush inside rattled about like a stowaway on a very unsuspecting trip. Her free hand played with her clit, plucking it and rubbing it fiercely. In five minutes, the plastic dildo managed to achieve what her boyfriend hadn't.

She came, a long moan erupting from her lips.

'Leesha?' There was concern in Colin's voice as it came through the door.

Her knees wobbled, and she let them fold. She dropped to the rug in front of the shower and felt all the tightness inside her spring loose and gradually relax. Gasping for air, she bent forward, bracing her hands against the side of the tub. The toothbrush holder was hard inside her, still buried deep. She could see only an inch or so of the pink end sticking out between her legs.

Colin pounded harder on the door. 'Alicia!'

'I'm fine,' she said tiredly. Finally gratified.

She swept her hair out of her face and sat back on her haunches. Carefully, she reached between her legs and extricated the pink phallus from her pussy. Her legs were unsteady as she pushed herself to her feet. When she looked at herself in the mirror, the desperation was gone.

But not the concern.

What was becoming of her?

She snagged a washcloth from the towel rack and vigorously washed the stickiness off of her thighs. She bit her lip as she cleaned more sensitive areas, areas her own lover had been hesitant to touch. She scrubbed the toothbrush holder until it squeaked, but then tossed it away from her.

When at last she unlocked the bathroom door, she had a towel wrapped firmly around her naked body. It was the most she'd had on for hours, but she felt self-conscious as she faced her boyfriend. He was already dressed and sitting on the bed.

Dressed. When she'd called him over for sex.

It made her decision easier.

'Colin, this isn't going to work out. We should see other people.'

Chapter Six

'How's the crowd?' the voice on the cellphone asked.

'Pretty good.' Bas walked around the floor of his club, looking over things and making sure they were the way he liked them. They'd only opened their doors half an hour ago, but they already had a good-sized gathering. Not bad for late afternoon. 'Word must have got out about our new dancer.'

He smiled softly. Little Leesha's first night had gone well. Very well. He just might be able to kill two birds with that stone.

'Don't get too cocky. You know how you are.'

Yes, he did, and he fought it every day. 'I'm just trying to make sure we stay in business.'

He checked that the tables had been polished, the

carpets had been vacuumed and the light near the back entrance had been changed. A vase of fresh flowers was waiting in the coat check area for Lucy, who was celebrating a birthday. All in all, things looked clean, sophisticated and sexy. Just like they were supposed to.

'If you need me, let me know. I can come down there.'

He rolled his eyes. They weren't to that point yet. 'I've got this.'

'OK, I'll talk to you later then. Say hey to Remy.'

'Will do.' He disconnected and walked up to the bar. Instead of building a glass tower, today Remy was nursing a beer. 'Sam says hi.'

Remy just grunted.

Bas stopped. He tried again. 'I see you've got Luther on the door. Where's Charlie?'

'On the cage. You got a problem with that?'

Bas let one eyebrow lift. 'Just asking a question.'

His operations man had been in a piss-poor mood ever since he'd shown up for work. Something must have got in his craw, but there was only so much leeway he'd give him.

'The guy deserves some eye candy, too,' his friend muttered.

Bas supposed he did, although the bouncers weren't supposed to ogle the talent. They were there to protect the girls and the club's other assets. But Remy knew that. He was the one who'd set the rules.

'You get some salt in your sweet tooth, Rem?'

The man threw back his drink, draining it. 'None of your goddamn business.'

All right. Bas signalled the bartender for a beer of his own, but frowned when the line sputtered.

'I'm on it, boss.' The barkeep set the chilled mug on the polished bar top and flipped his towel over his shoulder.

Bas's eyes narrowed as the man kneeled to fiddle with lines and connections. The last thing he needed was for the equipment to malfunction when he was expecting big business. 'Speaking of God damning anything, have you taken a look recently at our admirers across the street?'

Remy grunted again, only this time it sounded more like a growl.

He'd take that as a yes. Bas turned and leaned back against the bar. The main stage was empty, but Chanteuse and Ivy were keeping the customers entertained. Chanteuse was rubbing a whip back and forth between her legs while Ivy was wrapped around one of the side poles like her namesake. 'Couldn't be our angelic new attraction that's gotten your dick in a twist, now could it?'

'Drop it.'

So Alicia Wheeler did have something to do with Remy's foul mood. Bas wasn't surprised. His friend had been jonesing for the pretty brunette ever since he'd started surveilling the fanatics across the street. Yesterday, though, she'd surprised everyone. He'd nearly had an aneurysm when she'd pulled that sexy church-secretary stunt, and Remy hadn't reacted much better. He'd been moving towards the stage like the girl had her hand on his dick.

Damn, but that sweet thing could move.

Bas frowned at the amount of foam on his beer. 'I noticed her boyfriend wasn't out there today.'

Remy held out his empty glass so the bartender could give the tap another try. 'Think she got to him?'

Bas shrugged. She seemed to get to everyone with a working penis. 'Maybe.'

'Yeah, well, one little freak isn't enough. She needs to work faster. I don't like her standing across the street acting like she's Miss Hoity-toity when we all know she'd prefer to be over here getting down and dirty with us.'

Bas sent his friend a look out of the corner of his eye. He wasn't so sure about that. Ms Leesha was only starting to walk on the wild side. She hadn't taken any trips down their darker, more warped roads yet. She simply loved the dance, the art and the emotion. Exotic dancing played right into that, although the emotions and art of sex probably weren't quite what she'd had in mind.

He took a drink of his beer. Yes, their Angel liked being just a little bit rebellious, but how far did that daring streak go?

'You might be right,' he mused. 'Getting her to stop the protests is a lot to ask.'

'That daddy of hers still has his microphone.'

Yes, he did and Bas wasn't happy that Doyle had let the loudmouth keep it. He'd remember that the next time the sergeant visited for a lap dance with Marguerite.

He drummed his fingers along the side of his chilled mug. Maybe it was time to give Remy a project, something that would help focus all that bad attitude. 'She might have started to whittle them down, but we can't let these displays go on much longer. Are you still interested in having a go at them?'

'Just give the sign.'

Bas held up a finger. 'Only one. Let's start small.'

'Divide and conquer?'

'And on the down low. Nobody can know that we're behind anything.'

'Then I'm a ghost.'

Which didn't seem possible, but Remy could move and strike like the wind. He folded his arms over his chest. Tension was still thrumming in the air, but it had some direction now. It wasn't running around, bumping against everyone and making customers nervous. Anxious customers were tight with their cash. Bas wanted everyone here to feel loose and free. The looser, the better.

'Which one?' the operations man growled.

Bas tilted his head to the side until he felt a satisfying

pop in his neck. Rolling his shoulders, he considered the question. 'That microphone is fucking annoying.'

'Then maybe I'll just have to fuck over its owner with it.'

'Fine by me.'

Whatever the guy's perversions, Remy would ferret them out. He was good that way – finding people's weaknesses, temptations and kinks. The people across the street might think they were holier than the people who crossed the threshold of the Satin Club's doors, but Bas had come to learn one thing.

Good or bad, innocent or jaded, everyone had kinks.

* * *

Bas was waiting for Alicia when she showed up for her second night's shift. Things at the club were rocking and he wanted to touch base with her before they both got too busy. They hadn't had a chance to talk after her premiere last night. Every time he'd seen her, though, she'd been wide-eyed and breathless.

And hard-nippled.

She'd taken to her new assignment like a mink to sex, but there were lines of tightness around her mouth when she came through the back door. She took a step back when she saw him, but then relaxed. 'Bas.'

Her shoulders dropped an inch or so and she sent a

quick glance at the new light on the ceiling. It glowed 150 watts strong. Still, her gaze darted to the side wall and then down the hallway behind him. Dots of pink coloured her cheeks.

Interesting.

'Welcome back,' he said.

She hefted her bag higher on her shoulder. For some reason, she wasn't meeting his gaze. Instead, she concentrated on the floor and nibbled on her lower lip. He stared at that wet, plush flesh. He could think of better things she could do with those lips – and that mouth.

'Yesterday went very well, I thought,' he said. She was in a T-shirt and jeans, not the prim clothing she'd worn on the picket line. She was sexy in just about anything, but he doubted he'd ever see her in her church clothes again without wanting to rip them right off of her. 'We've got a good crowd tonight.'

At that, her gaze flicked up, hesitant and alarmed. 'To see me?'

'Word of mouth travels fast. You put on quite a show last night.'

She winced. 'I probably shouldn't have done that.'

'The good-girl-gone-bad routine?' He frowned. 'The hell you shouldn't have. With what you took home in tips, you should be able to pay your rent for the month. You had some of our regulars so wound up, they paid you instead of buying another round of drinks.'

She squeezed her eyes shut. 'About that ... I was wondering if instead of performing – like that – could I maybe serve drinks or...'

What the hell?

He closed the distance between them fast. He didn't like the direction this conversation was going. He didn't like it one bit. 'That wasn't the deal, Alicia.'

'I know, but last night ...' She squirmed. 'I don't think this is right for me.'

He was dumbfounded. Not right? Last night had been a revelation. He'd given her the chance to dance again, and in return the Satin Club had seen its best business in weeks. This could be a huge win for both of them.

He began counting. First Remy and now this. People were starting to ruin his calm.

'I don't give a shit what you think is right in here.' He tapped his finger against her forehead. 'You can't tell me it didn't feel right here.'

He laid a hand between her breasts and felt her heart jump.

'And here.'

He cupped her between the legs, and she sidestepped him fast. Oh yeah, she'd liked it there all right.

He pulled his shoulders back and stood like a wall in front of her. She was not going to back out on him. He held true to his promises, and he expected others to do the same. 'We had an agreement. You strip. One month.'

'But I just can't …' Her voice went tight. 'I can't stand it.'

'Stand it? You loved it. Hell, we had to clean your "happiness" off the pole before Marguerite could start her act.'

Those pink cheeks turned red.

Bas was getting impatient. 'I told you, the one thing you have to do while you're here is enjoy yourself. Maybe I need to add another requirement. No lying to yourself.'

'I'm not. The dancing was fine, but … afterwards …'

'You mean after you started to think about it.' He caught her chin and slowly brushed his thumb over that swollen lower lip. 'Look at you. When you left here last night, you were on a high. Now, you're all messed up again.'

He raked his gaze over her. He could see the outline of her nipples, just starting to harden. Why was she fighting herself so hard? She wanted this. 'Damn it, Alicia, I don't have the time to talk you through all these silly little crises of conscience. What you did last night was fucking amazing and, by now, all our customers have heard about it. They want to watch you, naked and writhing on that stage.'

'But …'

'But nothing. Get over it. They want to see you and, deep down, you want to show them.' He cupped her

129

breast and pinched her nipple hard. 'Here's the proof. Get out of your own way, sweetheart.'

He turned her towards the dressing room door and gave her butt a sharp swat. 'Now get in there and get ready. You're on in fifteen minutes.'

***

Alicia closed the door to the dressing room behind her and took unsteady steps towards her table. She'd been afraid to come back here and run into Remy, but she hadn't even thought about Bas.

She wouldn't make that mistake again.

She cringed with embarrassment as she put her bag inside her locker. Her butt was still smarting and she reached back to rub it. That hadn't been a soft tap he'd given her. It had been a rebuke, and it stung.

He was right. They had a pact and she couldn't go back on her word. Then, she'd be no better than –

Them?

Her chin dipped. That wasn't fair. They'd been utterly truthful with her from the start. She was the one getting confused and worked up.

She lifted her hair off her hot neck. Her breast ached and her mound still throbbed where he'd touched her. The truth collected in her chest, right where he'd poked her. This was what she feared most about coming back here – her own feelings, her very private reactions. She could feel the telltale dampness start to wet her panties.

She rubbed her thighs together, but the denim just didn't hit her where she needed it. She had to put a lid on all these emotions. She couldn't allow what happened last night to happen again. She had to remember why she was here – the reason she'd forced herself to come back to the club tonight.

She needed to get through to the lost. Whoever that might be …

'Angel, better hurry up. You're on in ten.' Chanteuse was changing into her street clothes. Her shift was just ending, while Alicia's night had only begun.

'Right,' she said nervously. 'Thanks.'

She reached for the tab of her jeans and slowly slid down the zipper. If she'd thought her first night as a stripper had been stressful, the second was a thousand times worse. The newness was still there, but she had a better idea now of what to expect.

And that was what scared her.

Even so, her body was warming, certain muscles tensing as she put on a skimpy costume from the rack. No more chaste work clothes. They apparently played into too many men's fantasies.

Which was another thing that had shocked her.

Was she really that naïve? Had there always been so many sexual undertones in the world around her?

She tugged at the cups of the bikini top, trying to get her nipples to lie flat. She was concerned about the way they were showing, how eager they looked.

She was anything but eager to be here. Last night, she'd been excited to dance. Tonight, she was scared, anxious and so physically uncomfortable she didn't know what to do. She'd got herself off. She'd played with herself. Why was her body still so achy and hungry?

A knock came at her door as she was slipping into her sky-high heels. They were pink tonight, with no straps winding up her legs. 'Two minutes, Angel.'

'I'm coming.' Summoning her courage, she rose and headed to her fate. She'd arrived late and she'd prepared nothing. She just hadn't been able to bring herself to do it.

Her knees were stiff as she walked to the back of the stage. She was still behind the curtain, but she could hear all the chatter behind that satin veil. There were more people here tonight, people who'd come to see her and what she was rumoured to do.

The beat of the music began, but she didn't recognise the song. She'd relied on the DJ, only the tune he'd chosen didn't sound slick and sexy. It was slow and leaden. When the curtains went up and the lights swung onto her, Alicia panicked. Slow took more control, but she felt heavy and clumsy.

'Just feel the rhythm,' she told herself. 'Just disappear into it.'

Only that didn't happen, not this time.

All she felt was self-conscious.

She danced around the stage. She had no choreography, so she fell back onto old tricks and familiar steps, but nothing felt right. The lights were too hot, and her lines were too tight. She was all too aware of the crowd hovering around her. They were all there – the stern boss man, the innocent young gun and the tough-looking black man.

Worst of all, Remy stood at the back.

She missed a step when she spotted him and had to bend over to catch her balance. The move threw her butt into the air, and the crowd finally let out a cheer.

'That's what we want to see, baby.'

She ripped her gaze away. The man terrified her. So big, so intimidating, so surly.

So downright cream-inducing …

She felt him staring at her, but she couldn't look at him. She didn't dare. The panther still looked ready to take her, but then tear her limb from limb.

It threw her concentration off-kilter, and she stripped off her top too early. Alicia bit the inside of her cheek with chagrin. She had to spend nearly the whole song with her breasts bouncing and juddering. It was good for the audience, but not for her. The confidence she'd had last night was gone and the attention on her body felt like a pointed knife. Last night, lust had slid across her skin like a scintillating blade.

Now, it was poking her, prodding her, frightening her. The crowd started chanting. 'Pole, pole, pole, pole.'

A shiver gripped her spine. That gleaming brass pole waited for her down at the end of that long runway. She didn't know why it disturbed her so. It would stand strong as she wrapped herself around it, contorting her body into all kinds of positions. It would warm to her flesh and cool when she left it alone. It would support her, pinch her and throw her on a wild ride.

It could also hurt her if she didn't learn how to handle it correctly.

'Pole, pole, pole!' They were starting to get impatient.

She began the long journey, breasts jouncing and tummy tightening. Even once she made it to the end of the runway, she didn't dare get too close. She knew from experience what that hard brass could do to her. She settled for grabbing it and leaning away as she swung about it.

'Aw, baby.' Disappointment settled over the crowd like a wet blanket.

In the end, there was applause, but way fewer tips. When the grumbling began, she knew the club's customers were disappointed.

And that hurt just about more than anything.

Alicia felt tears prick at her eyes. She loved to communicate with people through dance, and she had so much to express. But tonight, she'd given them less than her all.

Charlie was waiting for her when she got backstage and she covered herself with her hands. 'Bas wants you in his office. Now.'

The tightness in her stomach cinched into another knot.

'He's not happy,' the bouncer warned.

***

'The guy has a record,' Remy insisted. 'Trespassing in a women's bathroom. We could use that.'

Bas tapped his finger against his temple. 'It's good, but it's not enough.'

'Not enough?'

'Repentance. Redemption. The church is big on those, you know. He's probably told them he just got confused. Hell, we already know that Wheeler himself embezzled from his followers, but that's not keeping new ones away.' No, they needed something bigger on Mr Paul Simonsen, owner of the world's loudest speaker system.

A knock sounded on the office door.

'Come in,' Bas said absently. He turned back to Remy. 'Dig deeper. Get us more.'

The operations man tidied up his file, but glanced over his shoulder when he heard someone enter. When he felt it, was more likely. Even with those high heels she was wearing, Alicia was moving about like a timid mouse.

'I can come back if that would be better,' she said softly.

She stayed tight to the wall and Remy took a step back. His hand curled around the manila folder until it bent in half. Bas glanced from one to the other. Alicia was looking everywhere in the room but at the other man, while Remy's gaze, conversely, was drilling a hole right through her.

Bas's jaw tightened as understanding hit. Was *that* what the problem was?

Well, shit.

He raked his hand through his hair. He'd start with her first. 'What the hell was that out there on that stage?' he barked.

She stiffened so abruptly, the tails of the ties on her robe swayed. That didn't make him any happier. She'd stopped in the dressing room first, instead of coming straight to see him. They were going to have to talk about how she should follow his orders.

She glanced at the monitor where Marguerite was on-stage and wove her fingers together. 'A dance.'

'That was crap.'

Timid as she was, she still took offence at that. Those interlaced fingers turned white and her shoulders

136

stiffened. Everyone had their pride and he'd just struck a direct blow at hers.

Good, he wanted to get her attention.

'Are you going to argue with that?' he asked.

'No.'

'What happened? Where did my magic dancer go?'

The tension that was shimmering all around them rose in tone and in volume. It was as if a piano wire strung between the other two people in the room was stretching tighter and tighter.

'Did something go down between you two?' Bas asked bluntly.

'Wrong question,' Remy said, his voice low. 'It's who didn't go down that's the problem.'

Bas stood slowly, bracing both hands against his desk. Now he was getting somewhere. Remy's skulking mood … Alicia's cat-on-a-hot-tin-roof act. 'What happened?'

'Leesha and I were getting to know each other,' Remy said, 'when she suddenly decided she didn't want my cock in her pussy.'

Her gasp was the loudest sound she'd made since she'd stepped inside the room.

'Although she seemed to like my fingers in her ass well enough.'

'Stop it!' she demanded as she took a sharp step forward. All the colour had washed out of her face. 'It's not proper to … to … to kiss and tell.'

'We did a hell of a lot more than kiss, baby doll.'

Her hands clenched into fists. 'I know. I just – I should have stopped you before it went that far.'

This time, it was Remy who stepped forward, only his one step took him twice as far as hers. The file in his hand was not only bent now, it was crumpled in his fist. 'Why stop at all? You were getting off.'

She folded her arms tightly over her waist and looked away. As closed in as her body language was, her body itself was singing an entirely different tune. Her nipples were rubbing hard against the satin, tenting it and creating waves in the fabric that went all the way down to her cinched-in waist. 'It was wrong.'

'Felt pretty damn right to me.'

'Sinful,' she hissed.

'Son of a bitch.' Bas let out an angry hiss of his own. Sexual tension was supposed to bring customers in the door, not drag down his club. 'Rules again, Leesha? How many times do we have to go over this?'

She squared against both of them now, still within sprinting distance of the door. 'You can't make me do that. That wasn't in the agreement.'

'I'm not talking about the agreement.' The outburst made Bas aware of how far he'd let his control slip. He rubbed a hand over his forehead, trying to find the reins. 'You're supposed to explore things here, explore yourself.'

'I won't become a whore for you.'

'A whore?' Remy's tone was so low, it was practically sub-bass.

Bas looked at her in bewilderment. He'd never met anyone who was more determined to cut off her nose to spite her face. 'So let me make sure I've got this right. You and Remy made each other feel good and that somehow makes you a whore for the Satin Club?'

She shifted her weight, but didn't answer.

'It makes her a tease. Nobody was making her do anything.'

Her face fell at that accusation, but she didn't deny it.

'Alicia,' Bas snapped.

She jumped and the tails of the belt of her robe swung high.

'Everyone in the place knows the two of you want to screw, so why deny it?'

She blushed so hard, even her ears flared red. 'I didn't mean to … I don't know how to …'

She swung her hands into the air, but when the neckline of her robe gaped open she hurriedly tugged it closed. 'This place makes me feel things I shouldn't. The dancing, it affects me differently than other styles do.'

'Meaning it makes you hot?'

Her colour turned even brighter.

'Is that why it looked like you were dancing the robot

out there on that stage?' he asked, pointing to one of his display monitors. 'Because you were afraid you'd get aroused?'

'The robot?' she winced.

'Slutty robot,' Remy muttered.

'Stiff, uncomfortable and not sensual at all. Hell, you didn't even go anywhere near the pole.'

'I don't know what to do with it!' she blurted.

'Then get Chanteuse or Ivy to show you some tricks.' Bas pounded his fist against the table and then spread his fingers wide. He didn't like losing it like this. His temper was something he kept on a very short leash. He took a deep breath and followed it up with another. 'That's what those men in the crowd paid to see. They want to see you lose yourself in the dance. They want to see your lose control. If you turn yourself on while you're doing it, all the better.'

She looked physically pained, but her nipples were tightening and tenting the fabric higher.

'Is that the real issue here? Are you afraid to be aroused, Alicia?' he asked softly.

Her hands fisted at her sides, and she bit her lip.

Watching her standing there, fighting with her baser instincts, Bas felt his temper turning to something just as smouldering. If she looked at him like that one more time, he was going to be the one doing the biting.

'It ... hurts,' she admitted.

He tilted his head. 'So you didn't let Remy help ease the tension. Didn't you get yourself off at all after you left here last night?'

She looked like she wanted to crawl under a rock. 'Yes, but –'

Remy tossed the file onto the nearby sofa. 'But it wasn't enough, was it?'

She took a hesitant step back towards the door.

'It only hurts when you don't feed that need, Leesha.' Bas sighed. What a naïve, sexually starved creature. She needed them even more than they needed her. 'Remy, go get her.'

Her hands came up, palms out, as she stutter-stepped towards the door. 'Wait. What are you doing?'

'Giving you what you need. Hell, what I need. I've got to have the sexy dancer back, Angel. I need you relaxed and refreshed.'

'Bas,' she pleaded.

'Remy,' she squeaked when his big hands spanned her satin-clad waist.

Bas felt his cock stir. Remy already had the robe off her and she was down to the tiny bra and G-string she'd worn on-stage. 'Get on with it already, Remy. Fuck her.'

Chapter Seven

Alicia's pulse began racing when Remy started coming at her like that big black panther on the scent of prey. She took a nervous step back, but then he was there, hands on her hips and breath in her hair. She caught his shoulders reflexively. 'What are you doing?' she squeaked.

The belt of her satin robe snaked down her legs and onto the floor. When she reached to catch it, he pushed the garment off her shoulders entirely and tossed it halfway across the room. It billowed like a pink parachute before gently landing on the floor.

Something about that slow-motion freefall made Alicia even more aware of her exposure. She was left nearly naked in only the teeny outfit she'd worn on-stage. There was something acutely different about performing in bits of fabric under the spotlight than standing face-to-face, one-on-one, vulnerable and touchable.

His big hands settled onto her waist and turned her away from the door. 'What do you think?' he said low and soft into her ear.

He couldn't be serious. They couldn't do it here. They shouldn't do it at all! Bas was standing right across the room. Was he going to watch? The idea was horrifying, scandalous – and exhilarating.

Her high heels snagged against the carpeting as Remy bore her back, back, back. Her lungs began working like bellows, but they lost their rhythm when his mouth settled on her jugular vein. She tilted her head away, yet one lick and her blood began rushing.

'Now?' she whispered, shocked and so excited, her voice wouldn't work.

'Shoulda been last night,' he growled.

Her heel caught. She flailed, but he plucked her up and set her on Bas's desk like she was a doll. So light and pliable, there for his enjoyment.

Alicia pulled her knees up towards her chest, self-conscious and unsure. So many things were rushing at her – emotions, questions and possibilities. He was crowding her, hovering over her looking intense and serious.

What was serious was the bulge pushing at the zipper of his jeans. She tried not to stare, but sitting where she was, it was hard not to.

'Bas?' she asked worriedly, looking over her shoulder.

He met her gaze, and his expression was as solemn as the man touching her.

Astonishment gripped her. He was just standing there, watching. Waiting. Doing nothing to stop this. And why should he? He'd ordered it.

Her fingers wrapped around the edge of the cool, polished mahogany. 'We can't do this,' she insisted.

But a sharp, biting thrill went through her. What if they did?

'Watch us.' In a swift move, Remy pushed one hand under her legs and cupped her crotch.

Alicia arched like a rainbow. In trying to protect herself, she'd left the most vulnerable part of her wide open. She twisted and tried to push off the desk, but he had her.

And he wasn't letting go.

He ground the ball of his hand against her pubic bone and she shuddered. 'Ahh!'

She pushed at his chest, but he was immovable – except for his heart. She could feel it thrumming under her fingertips.

'Remy,' she gasped.

He fisted his fingers into her panties, and Alicia's thighs quivered. She didn't know what to do, how she was supposed to act. Her brain was saying one thing, while her body was shouting another. She tried to kick out, yet when she did, her thigh found a natural resting place around his hip. 'Please,' she said hoarsely.

Please, what? Please stop? Please don't stop? Please hurry?

She felt all of those things and more.

Bas's presence was unseen, yet heavy behind her. Like all those spectators in the crowd who watched her. And got excited …

Was that his thing? Did he like to watch? She was appalled.

And so electrified, her nerves snapped like hot wires.

The strips of her G-string dug into her hips as Remy pulled. The fabric stretched like a rubber band, lifting away from her freshly shaved pussy and exposing her to the cool air of the air-conditioning – and to the hot stares of two sexual men.

Alicia squirmed, bracing one hand against the desk and catching Remy's forearm with the other. His muscles bunched as the fabric refused to give way. She panted and rolled her hips. The spandex was biting and chafing. Much more of this and she'd want them off, too.

But she didn't. She didn't want to be naked down there. She didn't want to have extramarital sex with a virtual stranger – while another one watched.

Her hips rolled again, this time in something other than distress. It was shameful and belittling, but the idea was so hot.

Bas's breaths sounded rough behind her.

'Fuck,' Remy cursed. 'Damn thing won't give it up.'

Every gaze in the room was centred on her bareness and his fight with one of her few remaining pieces of clothes. He twisted his grip in a sudden motion and there was a harsh, resonating rip.

Alicia jerked back, her thighs clamping together and her ankles crossing as she defended herself.

She felt bare down there, chilled when she was so unbearably hot.

Without her G-string there was no keeping him away. His hand was still underneath her, privy to anything it wanted to touch. He parted her folds brazenly as his other hand fisted in her hair. He pulled her head back and his mouth covered hers in a hot, voracious kiss. His tongue dove deep as a thick finger penetrated her down below.

Alicia moaned. Oh, stars. It felt so good.

She squeezed her eyes shut and saw flashes behind her eyelids. The kiss went on and on as his finger investigated her recesses, prodding, rubbing and circling hard. Her thighs burned from the tension. She hadn't opened to him, and it made the penetration all that tighter. That one, intimately placed finger felt better than Colin's penis, fuller than that hard toothbrush holder.

She groaned when he pushed another into her.

'Ah, Angel. Why did you fight this when you need it so bad?'

She tore her mouth away from Remy's when the voice came from behind her, along with another touch. A cooler, more refined touch.

Bas.

He was still in the room!

She'd known it. She'd felt him back there. She'd known he was watching and the kinkiness had her belly twist. She just hadn't thought he'd *participate*.

Yet the clasp at the back of her bikini top had just given way, loosening the cups that strained to cover her breasts.

'Bas!' She gasped when his cool hands slid under the loose fabric and squeezed.

Pure sensation poured through Alicia and her thoughts splintered. She couldn't think. Right and wrong went straight out the window. Two men were touching her, fondling her. The idea was so surreal, so forbidden, her brain couldn't process it.

Her body could. Pleasure simmered along her skin.

She whimpered when Remy pulled her hips right to the edge of the desk, unbalancing her. She fell back against Bas. His chest supported her shoulders as he wrapped his arms around her possessively. He had her breasts in his hands, and he was working her in sharp tugs, rough pinches and deliberate rolls. Her nipples felt like they were on fire, but Alicia was mesmerised by what was happening below.

Remy's hands were on her thighs and he was pushing them open, wider and higher. When he dropped to his knees, she let out a nervous cry.

He was staring right into the heart of her. No man had looked at her like that before, other than maybe the men who'd toyed with her in the cage. Pulsations went through her at the memory, a totally inappropriate reaction to what had happened.

Remy saw it all, the shivers and the clenching. 'Mmm,' he murmured.

He pressed his face into her pussy and Leesha's entire core seized up. She was so shocked, she forgot to breath. So energised, she could feel the electricity snapping along her skin. Waves of hot tension coiled inside her as his lips played and his tongue –

Oh, heavens!

His tongue was raspy and strong. He laved her tender flesh, coaxing more dampness from deep inside her. He was merciless as he prodded at her opening and alternately flicked at her clit. Freshly shaved, the sensations were unusual and intense.

Leesha's thighs closed and opened, closed and opened wider.

There was nothing she could do to dislodge him. He wasn't letting her shyness get in the way of what he wanted. Finally, she reached down to thread her fingers through his dark hair. Her brain told her to push him away. What he was doing was so taboo. She'd never let any man do this to her. Colin had never showed any interest.

But Remy was lapping her up like a cat eating cream. She held him to her, not wanting it to stop.

Bas's breaths were hot in her ear, and Leesha arched, pushing her breasts into his controlling grasp. Remy's hands slid under her butt, lifting her for his mouth. After the frustration of the night before and the way she'd held back during her dance, the sensations were overwhelming. She couldn't take them. The orgasm hit her fast and yanked her into the deep end like a riptide.

She gave herself over to it, not fighting the current.

'That's it, baby.'

'Damn, she's so fucking hot.'

Remy bit her inner thigh in a careful love nip. Alicia felt another tremor go through her, but her heart jumped when the big man pushed to his feet. He was crowding her again, not letting her close her legs. Her nakedness was startling, especially after her climax. She felt plump down below, wet and sensitive.

And he was still looking at her.

The back of his fingers bumped against her as he unzipped his jeans. He made quick work of it, yanking the denim over his hips.

He wore nothing underneath, surprising her once again.

Her gaze went to his cock and she swallowed hard. She'd known Colin had been on the small size, but this man's swollen member looked perverse. Abnormal.

Huge.

Was he really going to push that thing into her?

Her legs instinctively curled up again, but he looped his arms under her knees, encouraging the position. Her feet dangled, clad in her sassy pink stiletto heels. Alicia let out a worried mew when he positioned the head of that angry-looking cock at her opening.

One nudge, and she felt herself stretching wider than she'd ever stretched before. Wider than was comfortable.

'Easy,' Bas murmured into her ear. 'You just came, baby. You're wet and relaxed. Don't tense up again.'

Remy was rubbing the tip of his cock in and out of her in sharp, little thrusts. 'Damn, she's tight.'

'Here, Angel, sit up.'

Alicia had no choice when Bas propped her shoulders higher, tilting her up. With her hips balanced right on the edge of the desk, the effect was that she bore down on Remy's thick prick, impaling herself further. She let out a sharp cry.

'Watch him disappear into you.' Bas's voice was rough in her ear. 'Watch as you eat him right up.'

Remy hefted her higher, tilting her up to just the right angle. He thrust his hips forward again and the pressure built inside her. Alicia's pulse crashed in her ears, but she couldn't look away from the place where they were connected. With Bas's words ringing, she watched as that big fat penis penetrated her. She felt every inch, every shiver.

And she creamed again.

He slid in deeper and grunted.

Alicia moaned. It was more than she'd fantasised. Bigger, harder, sweatier and grittier.

She was panting by the time he made it halfway into her. 'I don't think I can.'

'Baby, I haven't even started yet.'

And with that, Remy showed her how much he'd been holding back and how much she really could bear. The pressure doubled as he began to thrust and push; making her take him deeper and deeper. Her body undulated. She felt surrounded with Bas behind her and Remy between her legs. In a flash, it all became too real. Too far outside her comfort zone.

'Do what comes naturally, Angel,' Bas whispered into her ear. 'Dance with him.'

Dance? Like this?

But she felt the motion of Remy's hips, and she instinctively matched them like a partner on the dance floor. Thrusting and parrying, moving as one in a passionate paso doble.

'Ooohh,' she groaned.

The pleasure of this dance was incredible.

'Christ,' Remy hissed as he ground deep.

The blasphemy flew right by Alicia. He'd gone all the way in and was holding himself there. Circling and swaying, making her adjust to him.

It all fell into a rhythm then, the three of them finding pleasure in each other. Remy began fucking her without holding back, his fingers biting into her hips. Alicia rose and fell, loving the sensation of him filling her. Learning the moves instinctively.

He wasn't gentle and hesitant like Colin. He fucked her like a man. A hungry, demanding man.

And she was taking him like a woman, not a timid little virgin.

Bas let her settle back on the desk and he cast a shadow as he leaned over her. He kissed her, upside down as his hands settled over her breasts.

Alicia's whole body was throbbing and shaking.

Below, her pussy was being plundered. Above, her mouth was just as taken. Bas's tongue thrust in and out of her mouth. She sucked on it and felt him shudder. It gave her a sense of achievement. She was doing something she'd never dreamed she'd do. She was making love with two men, and she was holding her own.

She gulped in air when his lips left hers, but felt boxed in when he leaned over her further to tongue her nipples. They were so worked up and stimulated, she felt every lash. Then he began to suckle, and she was lost.

She clutched at Remy and fisted her hand in his shirt. She wished it was skin. Her other hand splayed wide on the hard mahogany desktop. Wet slurping sounds filled the office. It was shocking. It was overwhelming.

And it tripped her trigger again.

When she came, her toes pointed sharply and her nails dug into Remy's chest. Her other arm thrashed and something heavy from the desk crashed onto the floor. She paid it no attention as she caught the back of Bas's head and pulled at his hair.

She was straining, caught up in rapture when she felt Remy jerk between her legs.

He lodged that big cock inside her and she felt it spurt, hot and wet. The overflow dripped onto her thighs and she loved the sensation. For once, she had hot come inside her.

Remy's head fell back and the veins in his neck throbbed. His jaw clenched, but then he sagged forward, bracing himself heavily on the desk.

Alicia felt him more than saw him. Bas was blocking everything. She couldn't see anything, could barely breathe. She just felt his weight hovering over her, his mouth suctioning at her nipples. She couldn't move or even talk. She lay limp beneath the two men until Remy pushed at his friend's shoulder.

Bas gave up her breast about as readily as a hungry dog gave up a bone.

Spreading one hand wide over her belly, Remy slowly pulled out of her.

'You want some, Bas?' he asked.

Alicia's ears twitched, shocked at the invitation, but she was too tired to try to stop it.

And too curious as to what that would be like – to take two men in succession – to become such a sexual being that nothing mattered but the pleasure.

Bas was upside down in her view of things, but she saw the muscle that worked at the base of his jaw. She saw the way he smoothed his tie over his chest and took a deep breath.

She was hoping. She was dreading.

But then he shook his head no.

And her heart fell.

'I think we've done what we needed to do.' He stepped back from the desk and straightened his suit. 'Get her cleaned up, Remy. She's going back on the stage.'

Alicia's eyes popped open and she struggled to lift herself up onto her elbows. 'You want me to dance? Now?'

She felt like a wet noodle, wrung from the inside out.

'Yes, now. This is exactly how I want you. Free, sexed up, with nothing hindering you. Go show off, baby. Go dance.'

***

154

She'd never danced better in her life.

Alicia sat on a church pew in the middle of the sanctuary as she contemplated all the things that had happened the night before. She looked at her hands in her lap, but she wasn't praying. Sunlight streamed through the stained-glass windows and blue light draped over her. For the first time in a long time, she didn't feel guilty about anything. Just puzzled.

Last night, after she, Remy and Bas had *done what they'd done*, she'd had the performances of her career. Not just once, but every time the spotlight had settled upon her.

It was as if a power source had been lit inside her. She'd felt energised and inspired. Free. Baring herself had felt normal, evocative. She'd just let the music overtake her and the response from the audience had flowed through the floor, up through the stage and right into her core. Dancing had always been an outlet for her, but she had so much inside her now, dying to get out. Her lines had been pristine, as always, but there'd been such power and emotion behind her movements.

For once, she hadn't been afraid to show her sensual nature. She knew she had one now. It was an integral part of her, and she didn't want to hide it anymore. Why did some people think it was such a bad thing? With her insecurities left behind, it had seemed as natural as breathing.

Her hands clenched in her lap. Why had all this been held back from her? Why was sexuality so denigrated? She loved her body. She loved what she could do with it. Dancing ... and otherwise.

A blush warmed her face.

She loved the male body, too. It was pure art, in movement and in form. She just wished she'd seen more of it. She'd been naked, while both Remy and Bas had been fully clothed. And Bas hadn't even –

Why? Why hadn't he wanted to be with her?

She lifted her chin and finally saw the altar. The whole turn of events had left her conflicted and confused. She knew what she'd been taught. She knew what people labelled as right and wrong. Was she just being tempted away from goodness and light? Had she begun down a slippery slope?

Because being 'bad' had made her feel so much better.

Unclenching her fingers, she ran her hands over her lap, smoothing her dress. Her body felt different. Awakened. Excited. She could sense it in the way that she moved, in the very way she breathed.

Was it just the fact that she was dancing again? Could she have felt this way if she'd continued on the path she'd originally planned for her life?

She sighed as she looked up at the cross hanging on the wall.

She was strong in her faith, but this had never been

her intended career choice. She'd never planned to work at her father's church. She had a degree in business and a minor in dance. It had only been after her mother had died – and that unfortunate confusion about her father's former church's finances – that she'd moved back to help him. She'd been the one to inherit the family funds, after all. She hadn't been able to leave him destitute.

Especially when he was so passionate about his cause.

She knew what it felt like to be passionate now, but it troubled her that her needs and her father's goals were at such odds. She didn't know if she could go back to her strict, joyless, boring life anymore.

'Ms Wheeler?'

The scratchy voice made her spin in her seat. 'Oh, Paul. I didn't hear you come in.'

'I wasn't sure it was you, sitting there in the blue light. You look … *different* somehow.'

She hurried out of the cast of that hazy lighting. It wasn't showing, was it? Her doubts and her new-found attitude? Because this was one man she wasn't interested in sharing all that with. She exited into the main aisle so he didn't have her trapped. 'Did you need something?'

His gaze stroked over her much too slowly. 'That's a pretty dress you're wearing. Is it new?'

She smoothed the skirt and was happy it covered her down to her knees. It was a lightweight summer dress that was much more sedate and conservative than the deep-purple lingerie set underneath it. She bit the side of her cheek, happy he couldn't see that. She'd bought the new clothes with the tips she'd earned from her first night at the Satin Club. The dress was soft and flowing and felt good against her skin. The lingerie felt even better. She didn't think she'd ever be able to wear starched cotton again.

'Yes, thank you.' She folded her arms around her waist.

Paul Simonsen was one of her father's newer followers. Tall and gawky, he'd first shown up at one of her father's revival meetings. That had been when they'd still been meeting in a tent on the outskirts of town. Paul had agreed with her father's message and had stuck around. He'd helped convert this building from a run-down theatre to the little independent church it was today – with lofty goals of being so much more.

She should be thankful for his help.

Instead, she found him cloying and a bit creepy. He was one of those people who couldn't read body language, even though he watched it with unblinking eyes. She could never seem to shake him once he started talking to her.

'Are you looking for my father?' she asked, trying to move him along.

Those grey eyes of his were still wandering. Did he seriously think she couldn't see them doing that? She flipped her hair forward. Her dress wasn't low-cut at all, but she didn't like showing any skin in front of this man.

She supposed that was a good sign. She hadn't totally been corrupted. It wasn't every guy who turned her on or made her want to strip down to her birthday suit.

She brushed her hand over her cheek when she felt it start to heat.

'Yes, but I suppose I could ask you the same questions I meant to ask him. You do seem to be up on all the city codes.'

Coding. Great. She could deal with that. She clapped her hands together. 'Fire away.'

'I've got a line on one of those automated roadway signs. You know, the ones that tell you to slow down or buckle your seat belt.'

She frowned. 'I don't understand.'

He caught his bony arms by the elbows. 'I was thinking we could use it down at that despicable Satin Club. Some of those cars drive by so fast, I don't think they can hear what we're saying or read our handmade signs. If we had one of those big electric boards, though, we could type any message we wanted to send.'

Alicia frowned. She didn't like that idea at all. That was industrial-grade equipment he was talking about, and she cringed to think what he might put on such a thing. It would certainly be a roadway hazard.

'Paul, don't you think we're going at this the wrong

way? We've been going at the club for weeks now, and we haven't made any progress. There should be some method of compromise we could use with Bas.'

'Bas?' he said, his voice going hard.

'Sebastian. Mr Crowe.' She cleared her throat. The man who'd had her nipples under his tongue. 'It's not smart to poke a rattlesnake with a stick. I don't think the electronic sign would help.'

Paul scowled, his grey eyes going hard and his jaw jutting out. 'Well, maybe I should talk to your father after all.'

'Fine,' she sighed. This guy and his technology. His speakers were what had got them in trouble in the first place – with both Bas and the city police. They still had to pay off that fine, but her father and his strident follower refused to do away with their toy. They kept the volume below the legal limits now but, in their opinion, the more attention they drew to themselves, the more they thought they were winning.

She tried not to roll her eyes at the idea of an electronic roadside sign.

That would get the news stations and other media all over this. The idea made her pause. She couldn't afford that now, not with her side job. Someone might recognise her.

And then, all hell *would* break loose.

Doubts began to drift back in, and uneasiness filled

her chest. 'Dad went to get a cup of coffee down the street. If you want to wait in his office, he'll be back soon.'

Paul started to follow her down the aisle. 'I could just keep you company.'

She pivoted and help up a hand to stop him. She didn't want this man in her office. He made her uncomfortable enough, standing in the open sanctuary. She couldn't be closed in her tiny office with him. 'I need to get back to work,' she said firmly. 'I have calls to make.'

She needed to call Chanteuse to schedule some pole dancing lessons, but he didn't need to know that. She just wanted him out of her space. She wanted his leering gaze off of her body.

Men had to pay for that right.

Frustration rolled inside her. Darn it, how had things gotten so out of hand? Why was her church so intent on starting a fight? The Satin Club had been minding its own business when they'd come upon the scene. Of the two, the church had been the more aggressive and the less forgiving. It had certainly opened her eyes to her prejudices.

'We need to end this.' She walked away, shoulders held back, but she couldn't help tossing over her shoulder. 'Remember, Paul, let he who is without sin cast the first stone.'

Chapter Eight

'He's your master, and he will spank your ass.' Chanteuse gave the pole a firm slap and wrapped her fingers around it. 'Treat him with respect, and you'll get along fine.'

Alicia's eyes went round and she looked anxiously at the audience. A few of the regulars had heard, including the baby-faced businessman who was swiftly becoming one of her biggest fans. He grinned at her and gave her a small salute.

She gave a little wave in return and lowered her voice. 'Are you sure Bas is OK with us practising out here?'

'Where else are you going to learn?' the redhead asked. 'It's not like we have a pole back in the dressing room, and I'd bet good money that you haven't had one installed in your bedroom.'

She seemed to think that was funny and gave a hearty laugh.

'It's fine,' she said when she caught her breath. 'It's early and we're not on the main stage.'

No, but more and more people were coming over to watch.

Alicia rubbed her hands together nervously. If the pole was a master, then Chanteuse was its mistress. She could do stunts and acrobatics on the thing like she was weightless. Alicia wanted to learn how to do that, but there was more to the contraption than just strength and flexibility.

She eyed the pole, her gaze following it from floor to ceiling. Something about the thing just transfixed her. It looked slick, long, immovable and dangerous. She let out a puff of air that stirred a strand of hair around her face. 'I'm a bit afraid of it,' she confessed.

'That's because you're fighting it. If you want this hard rod to work with you, you have to show it a bit of affection.' With a slow twirl, Chanteuse not only circled the pole, she somehow managed to climb up it. The gleaming brass stood firm between her tightly clenched thighs and she arched back, letting her hair swing gracefully. She grinned. 'And a little bit of sass.'

Using her momentum, she swung around and did a wide split with the pole pressed hard against her crotch.

Another twirl, and she dismounted gracefully onto her

five-inch heels. She gave a smooth grind of her hips that made the fans hoot. With a wink, the redhead tossed her hair back and stroked her hands down her taut stomach. 'But most of all, you have to give in to it. You've got to submit.'

Alicia eyed the pole dubiously. She didn't like to give up control, especially on the dance floor. But wasn't that what she'd done last night? Turned off her internal dance critic and simply felt the music?

Of course, her brain hadn't been functioning very well. She'd just been seriously shagged.

She rubbed her thighs together. She hadn't seen either of her lovers since she'd stepped into the club. 'Is Remy here?'

'No, he's on some kind of assignment.' Chanteuse grinned. 'But he'll be pissed that he missed this.'

Leesha gave a quick shake of her head. She'd be having an even more difficult time if he was watching. 'I'm glad he's not here.'

No, she knew what could happen now if Remy watched her for long enough. As eye-opening as their lovemaking had been, it had also been intense and vigorous.

She wasn't quite ready for another go-round.

She patted her hands together again. They felt so odd. Chanteuse had recommended a drying agent to help her keep a better grip. It was also on her thighs and she couldn't help her uncomfortable gyrations. Her legs were clinging to her shorts and to each other. She couldn't stand it anymore. She wanted to spread them apart to ease the tickling sensation.

'Let me try again.' She approached the pole, took a deep breath and caught it with one hand. It might have been her imagination, but in that instant, the brass winked at her. A play of light? Or a challenge?

Determination gelled inside her chest. She could do this.

Bracing her other hand lower on the pole, she jumped and wrapped herself around it.

And promptly began to slide down, skin squeaking with every inch. 'Ow!' She hopped off and pressed her palms against her inner thighs. 'That hurts.'

'Well, of course it does. You have too many clothes on,' Chanteuse said.

'What?'

'It's physics, Angel.'

Alicia spun her head to the audience. Bas had showed up, appearing silently and stealthily. He had a drink and was relaxing in one of the semi-circular booths that faced the pole. He looked sophisticated surrounded by all that red velvet, like a mob boss out of the 60s intent on looking high-class and respectable.

He gestured towards the pole with his tumbler of Scotch. 'You need more friction,' he said in that low voice that sent shivers down her spine. 'Skin can provide that.'

She looked down at herself. Her shorts were skimpier than anything she wore out in public.

'Strip them off. More skin, less pinching.'

She eyed him sceptically through her waterfall of dark hair.

He leaned back in his seat with his eyes glinting. 'Off.'

She looked around hesitantly. She'd stripped in his club for several nights now, but it had always been part of an act. Taking off her shorts like this would essentially be dropping her drawers. There was a difference, and it made her awkward.

He cleared his throat. Sharply. She understood he wasn't asking.

She hooked her thumbs in her waistband. Before she could let her inhibitions grab hold, she pushed her boy shorts down and stepped out of them.

Someone gave a sharp whistle.

Her boyish admirer was gesturing at her. She bit her lower lip, but dipped her toe into the material and flicked it at him. She was astonished when he caught it and promptly lifted the garment to his nose. He inhaled deeply, his pleasure clear.

More customers gathered round, and she stroked her thighs self-consciously. She was down to the purple thong that was part of her new matching set.

'Pretty,' Chanteuse commented. 'Now hitch back on up here.'

That shimmering feeling was back on Alicia's skin, sparking from nerve ending to nerve ending. She felt exposed in her own clothes – lingerie that had been meant to be private. Her bottom was bare, and the thong had no give. It wasn't the spandex she was slowly adjusting to wearing while she danced.

Only this wasn't dancing.

She approached the pole timidly. Submit to it. Trust it.

She clapped one hand around the stiff brass and then the other. It felt sturdy. Thick. With a surge of adrenalin, she jumped, the muscles in her thighs firing. She swung them up and around the pole, clenching them tight. Her ankles crossed, her patent-leather heels knocked and she stuck. Her skin clung to the pole. She clenched her thighs tight, holding the metal for all it was worth, and her body was suspended feet above the unforgiving ground.

Bas let one eyebrow lift.

Alicia felt the tension in her legs move up into her core as she fought to hold the position. See what happens when you follow orders? She could hear the words he wasn't saying out loud.

Heat built up inside her. It took strength and determination to hold the position, but she wanted more. She wanted to push herself. Following the instructions

167

Chanteuse had given her, she arched back. She found her centre of gravity and let go with her hands, trusting that her legs and the drying agent would hold her secure.

'Damn,' somebody in the crowd muttered.

'Can you imagine having those gams wrapped around your hips?' someone responded.

She closed her eyes and felt the power and confidence inside her surge. Tightening her abs, she sat back up. The friction between her legs was beginning to burn, so she dropped her feet gracefully to the ground. The desire to spread her legs was still there. It was as if the powder was puckering her skin and making her itch.

Twisting, she put the pole behind her. Holding it firmly, she bent over and reached for the opposite wall. She might not know a lot of aerial moves, but she knew dance positions. With her balance found, she lifted one leg behind her until it was pointed at the ceiling and resting comfortably against the pole. It was a not-so-classic arabesque *penchée*, but the crowd got off on it, all the same.

'Da-yum,' Chanteuse echoed. Actual applause rang from the audience. 'Girl, you are flexible.'

Alicia finally dropped both feet to the floor and rested. Her body felt challenged, but capable. She could do this. She had the grace and the flexibility. She just needed to work on her strength and sexuality.

She peeked at Bas. He was helping her with both.

She reached back to pull at her panties, but realised there was nothing to adjust. She glanced at the young businessman. He wasn't going to give up her shorts any time soon.

Bas crooked his finger at her and her pulse jumped.

She held up a finger in reply, asking for a moment to find a robe.

He frowned and snapped his fingers. He pointed abruptly at the seat beside him.

'Uh oh.' Chanteuse turned and whispered, 'When he wants something, you need to jump.'

Alicia was beginning to understand that, but she was clad in a tank top and barely-there underwear. The glower on his face darkened and she moved quickly to the steps. Charlie was there to give her a helping hand. She slipped into the half-moon seat and felt the velvet brush against her reddened thighs. It was soft, but she was touchy after her acrobatic session.

Bas cocked his head.

Sucking in a tiny breath, she scooted around the table. The velvet stroked her bottom and the backs of her thighs in the most disturbing way. By the time she was seated next to him, she was all tingly. It felt odd to be sitting in the audience this way. Most of their clients were in suits, or at least shirts and ties. She was glad the table hid most of her bareness from view.

Until Bas spread his hand over her leg.

It was heavy and personal. He kept it high on her hip with his pinky finger dangerously close to the line of her underwear.

'You're here early today,' he said. 'Couldn't stay away?'

It was early for her. She'd done her stint protesting, but once everyone else had left, she'd driven across the street and parked behind the diner. She'd wanted to see Chanteuse – or so she told herself. 'I wanted some instruction on the pole.'

'You're a fast learner. In a lot of things.'

The soft invisible hairs on the side of her neck rose as his breaths brushed over her skin.

'How are you feeling today?' he asked.

His voice was hushed. Low and rumbly.

Alicia didn't know what to do with her hands. She saw the glass of water on the table and caught it. 'Fine.'

She took a quick drink, not stopping to think if it might be his.

His nose brushed against her temple as he leaned closer. 'Don't give me platitudes, sweetheart. Remy's big and he rode you hard.'

That pinky took a slow, circular trip under the line of her panties. So close, yet still so far. 'How are you? The truth.'

Her mouth went dry and she took another sip. Her hands shook, though, and she dribbled. The droplets of water fell on her chest, sliding under her tank top and between her breasts.

'Aware,' she said softly.

She didn't know where the word came from, but it fit. It was as if all her nerve endings had been dialled to a different setting, inside and out.

'Not tender?' His gaze was on the splash of water on her chest. Reaching out with his free hand, he swiped up the moisture with his finger. Watching her with heavy-lidded eyes, he stuck the tip into his mouth.

Her nipples hardened, and he squeezed her leg. It made her jump in her seat. When she settled back down, she was aware that that insidious pinky was now firmly under the line of her panties. Right in that seam where her leg started. If he followed it downward at all –

She squirmed.

'Not swollen or achy?' he murmured.

She couldn't answer, so she shook her head.

'Good girl.' He eased back in the seat beside her and took another casual drink of his Scotch. 'I might have something new for you to try then, if you're interested.'

She shot him a quick look.

'Dancing,' he said innocently. He slid his hand down her thigh, away from where she really wanted it. When it slid back up, his fingers delved deeper between her legs.

She gasped when they trailed fire over the spots where the pole had left friction burns.

'Hm.' He flicked his fingers at a waitress who rushed over. 'Be a dear and find us some ointment.'

Alicia's hair brushed against her shoulders as she looked around nervously. Nobody was watching. Everyone was studiously concentrating on the main stage now.

She swallowed hard. His fingers were just lying against her skin, but in such a sensitive place. 'What ... what kind of dancing?' she asked.

'Did you have a costume picked out for tonight?'

'No.' She'd only begun to get brave enough to look through the various schoolgirl, nurse and dominatrix selections.

'Would you have time to make up a routine if I gave you some direction?'

Direction. Her pussy pulsed. She nodded around the knot in her throat.

'Excellent, because you've had a special request.' His gaze stroked over her face. 'Ever played a cowgirl?'

'As in ten-gallon hat?'

'As in chaps.'

The waitress arrived with a tube of ointment on a tray.

'Thank you, Christine. This should help.' Instead of letting go of her leg, he passed the tube along. 'Open that.'

Alicia's fingers felt clumsy as she unscrewed the cap. 'Chanteuse told you to use Dry Hand, didn't she.'

'Yes.'

'I thought so,' he murmured as he finally moved his hand away from that hot spot on her inner thigh. He didn't move it far, simply rolled it over to accept a squirt from the tube.

Alicia felt another droplet of water slide down the back of her neck, only this time it was sweat. When had it got so hot in the place?

She peeked around again, sure they were going to get caught. He really hadn't done anything improper, but her body was lighting up like it was on fire. Was anyone watching what he was doing to her?

She found his gaze steady on her. 'Don't be stingy.'

She squeezed more ointment onto his fingertips and waited, tension riding her whole body. She knew it was coming, but her jaw unhinged and her eyes fluttered closed when he rolled his hand again and began soothing the salve over her tender thigh.

He was thorough and not all that gentle. His fingertips stroked round and round, moistening her tender flesh. It was in such an intimate spot and she was wearing so very little down there.

'Open wider.'

She pressed her tongue against the roof of her mouth as she followed instructions. The strictness in his voice unfurled something tight inside her. He didn't use that tone very often, but when he did –

'Oooo.' He'd switched to her other leg and his hand was thrust firmly between her thighs under the table.

He was soothing skin and stroking taut muscles. The hesitancy in her snapped and her knees dropped open wider. On the floor, her heels toppled until they were pointing at each other. Her belly was tight, but her lungs were shrinking and expanding with deep, slow breaths. Her eyes got heavy, but then she caught the boyish businessman sneaking a peak at her.

Lust and curiosity were clear in his eyes.

Instead of bringing out her hang-ups, the shy glance excited her. She melted into the booth, her spine curling along the shape of the velvet cushions. Her neck relaxed back and her hair slithered around her shoulders.

'That's my Angel,' Bas said with approval.

He lathered her up good until her legs were sticky and her muscles were mush. At last, he curled his hand around her mound. The hold was hot and firm. His fingers pressed harder, pushing the thin material of her thong into the crevices of her pussy.

Alicia groaned long and low.

More than just the young businessman were watching her openly now.

She turned her head towards Bas. His mouth was only centimetres away, and his green eyes were hot. Mysterious.

She licked her lips. 'Bas?'

'Yes?'

'Last night. Why didn't you ...'

'Fuck you?'

'Yes,' she sighed. She wanted to know. The questions were starting to consume her. Had she not performed well enough with Remy? She knew she was inexperienced, but the big operations man had seemed to enjoy her body ... her responses ... her taste ...

Was she just not attractive to him? Other than her breasts?

They were aching now, remembering the tug of his mouth and the rasp of his teeth.

That green gaze was hard as jade as it stroked over her flushed face and her aroused body. His thumb brushed over her pubic bone. 'You are a temptation.'

His hand squeezed tighter, almost harshly and her hips rose right off the seat.

He caught her yelp with a fast, explosive kiss, but then he was tugging her along the seat. 'I believe it's time to find those leathers.'

***

He found the chaps, but not much more.

For once, Alicia fought him. She put her foot down and said no, but in the end, that foot had been in a cowboy boot. The chaps were made of soft leather. They belted low on her hips and had ties going down her legs. Bas allowed her a cowboy hat and a gun belt, complete with silver toy guns. Underneath it all was a tiny brown bikini, but that was about to come off.

All of it.

The bottoms had Velcro that detached at her hips. It allowed her to strip them off and go completely bare while still wearing the leather. Alicia didn't want to dance that way, but Bas had a way of cajoling her, rationalising and flat-out dominating her. She'd never dreamed she'd be required to dance completely naked. She hadn't even known such things were allowed. It crossed yet another line she hadn't known had been in the sand. Her body would be on display and the way the chaps outlined her crotch ...

It was so wanton, she could hardly stand it.

When the lights went up, tension simmered in the air. The lights were hot and the music was grinding. Her legs were still sticky from the ointment Bas had applied.

But she loved the hat.

She pulled it down low over her eyes as her hair billowed down her back. She knew the role she was supposed to play and, this time, the music had her.

She strutted across the stage, twirling her six-shooters as she went. When she aimed them at the crowd and pulled the triggers, more than one fan dropped dramatically into his chair. She gave them all a saucy grin.

The gun belt was something she could take off and she started there. Her breasts came out to play next, but when she got to her thong, the entire place started to buzz. The noise was humming and surging as she played with the crowd. She started to rip apart the Velcro and then put it back together.

Inside, her heart was racing. Even she was looking down, watching herself. Her nipples felt tight and her pussy was shy. Eventually, there was no going back. She flicked one Velcro tab apart and felt the material sag between her legs. Her palms got sweaty and she realised the only way she could do it was to treat it like a Band-aid. She'd yanked on the piece of Velcro at her other hip and fisted the brown spandex in her hand.

Before she could turn from the crowd and frantically put everything back in place, she flung the thong at them. This time old Henry was awake and ready. He caught her panties and let out a holler.

In that moment, Alicia became Angel, a sexual being. There were no secrets here, and she was tired of being tied up with rules and mores.

Because she liked the eyes on her. She liked the nakedness. The freedom. The audacity of it all. The chaps added a special spark, emphasising what was showing rather than hiding what was covered. She did her solo that way and stayed on the stage for a second song.

They simply wouldn't let her go.

She spent the entire hour under the lights, in the get-up. The leather became heavy and she felt perspiration coating her body. Every way she turned, men were staring at her and practically drooling. She danced, unafraid of what might show.

And then there was the pole.

She'd been afraid that the chaps might hinder her, but she gave it the old cowgirl try. The crowd went nuts when she clamped her thighs around that stiff brass pole and lay out flat, hanging suspended. The ointment had nearly been soaked up by her skin, but there was still too much to let her stay where she was. She slid slowly down the pole, the burn bearable until she was lying on her back on the floor, her hips twitching.

That nearly brought the place down.

Charlie the bouncer was certainly smiling as he held the curtain back for her when she left the stage. 'Hot act.'

His gaze tried to slide down her body, but it got stuck on her breasts and then her naked pussy.

Alicia felt a bit of shyness return and she cupped her hands over herself. Bas had told her not to shave down there and her hair was starting to grow back in. She would have been more comfortable completely bare – or natural, with dark curls. This halfway stage was no-man's-land and, somehow, even more personal.

'Thanks,' she said, trying to catch her breath. People

didn't realise what a workout exotic dancing was, especially with that pole. 'I need something to drink.'

'I'll get it for you. Bas is waiting for you that way.'

Alicia blinked in surprise. The bouncer was pointing towards the hallway to the back rooms rather than towards the dressing room. She'd learned her lesson, though. She went to find Bas promptly.

He was waiting in the hallway, checking his smartphone. He tucked it away when he heard the swishing of her leather chaps. The costume was attention-grabbing for all the senses. Sight, touch, sound and smell.

She just wasn't willing to taste it.

'Complete nudity suits you,' he murmured. 'We might make it standard for you.'

'No.'

He let one eyebrow lift and those lines around his mouth deepened. 'No?'

She folded her arms under her naked breasts. She got the distinct impression that he didn't hear the word often. 'Too much of anything and it loses its appeal. I'll call the costumes. I'll decide when I dance naked.'

His lips actually curled upward in a smile. 'When. OK, now you're making sense.'

She lifted her chin. 'I do have a degree in business.'

He nodded. 'Supply and pent-up demand. I like it.'

There was approval in his eyes, something she hadn't seen before. It made her breathe deeply as pride expanded inside her chest. Confidence. She was becoming addicted to the feeling.

Charlie appeared with a bottle of water. To take it, she had to uncover either her breasts or her crotch. She let him look at her nipples as she took a long, satisfying drink. She smiled at him in thanks and he nodded before turning and going into a room.

Alicia was tempted to pour the rest of the water over her head. She was warm from her session, but she knew she'd just get hot and sticky all over again. It was time to put her bikini back on so she could do her routine in the second set. She just hadn't got much of a break.

'You wanted to talk to me about something?'

Bas turned towards her, leaning his shoulder into the wall. 'I did.'

He had that contemplative look about him again, and she instinctively moved closer. He was such an enigma to her. She never knew what he was thinking or what he wanted.

He stroked a finger down her arm and little shivers ran up to her shoulder and down to her wrist. 'Remember that special request I mentioned?'

She pushed back the brim of her cowboy hat and nodded back towards the stage. 'That wasn't it?'

He chuckled. 'No, but if I'd known you were going to do that, I wouldn't have added this.'

A tingling started at the base of her throat. 'This?'

He tilted his head towards the door on the other side of the hall. 'A client requested a private dance from you.'

'Oh. I didn't realise … Now?'

'Right now. Are you up for it?'

She looked up and down the hallway. It differed from the stage door entrance like they came from two different lands. The hallway where Remy had caught her was stark and utilitarian. This passageway looked like something you'd find in a swanky Victorian hotel. The plush burgundy carpeting continued from the main show room down this corridor. She was sinking to practically her ankles as she stood where she was. The lighting was set for mood and a vase of flowers decorated the skinny but expensive console table along the wall. The scene was elegant and top dollar. 'I … don't know.'

'That's honest. I can accept that.'

'No.' She set her water bottle on the table and rubbed her hands together. She felt embarrassed for the first time in hours. 'I mean, I don't know.'

She was standing in this beautiful hallway looking scandalously underdressed. She'd been in the cage on her first visit, and she was beginning to master pole dancing. But she literally didn't know. 'What goes on in a private dance?'

That got another small smile out of Bas, her second in one night.

'In this case, the client has requested a lap dance.'

'Oh. OK ...'

He reached out and stroked his hand through her hair, draping it over her shoulder. 'It's a dance where he'll be seated in a chair. You'll be dancing for him alone, and you can be more ... let's say *personal*.'

Her mouth went dry and she caught her water again. She took another long drink, downing nearly half of the bottle.

Bas watched the way her throat worked. 'You can touch him, and he can touch you. It's a close contact dance. Think of it as a tango.'

He flicked the brim of her cowboy hat. 'Maybe an Argentine one.'

Alicia worked her thumb over the opening of her plastic bottle of water. 'How much touching? And where?'

She'd learned that details were important.

'You control that. If you want penetration, I'll allow it.'

She blanched. Even with everything she'd heard, seen and done, it still pushed her a little more outside her comfort zone. Her voice was raspy when she finally managed to speak. 'I don't think I can ... Who is it?'

He caught her hand. 'Come.'

He directed her to the door where Charlie had disappeared. He opened it and allowed her to step inside first. Charlie snapped to attention, getting up from the deep, over-stuffed chair where he'd been seated. His suit jacket was draped over the chair next to him and his tie was loosened. Alicia quickly set her water bottle aside and covered herself with her hands. Charlie had paid for a lap dance?

She didn't know if she could work with him if she – No. It wasn't Charlie.

She turned to face the floor-to-ceiling window to her right. It opened onto the room next door, a room that was just a bit bigger with a larger, plush settee and pillows galore. A man was sitting with his back to her, apparently unaware that the three of them were watching him.

'Two-way mirror,' Bas said from close behind her. His hands were on her hips again, touching both skin and leather. It reminded her vividly of the first time she'd seen the Petting Zoo cage, and how he'd described it to her.

She pressed her knees together and the chaps creaked. She'd taken a lot of pleasure out of that experiment.

She tried to see the man's face. He had brown hair and strong shoulders. They were bare. Was he going to be naked too?

She let out a yip when he suddenly stood up. He raked a hand through his hair and then began to pace around the small room. He wasn't naked. He still had pants on and was only bare from the waist up. He looked young and nervous.

When he turned to go in the other direction, Alicia's eyes rounded in surprise. And a bit of delight.

183

The young gun. The boyish businessman.

She melted a bit inside. For some reason, his crush on her just touched her as sweet. He was obviously as new to this as she was. She watched as he puffed out a breath of air and interlaced his fingers behind his head. It turned her attention to his chest.

And his rippled abs.

And muscled arms.

Oh, my. She hadn't realised that a body like that was hiding underneath those business shirts and ties.

'Yes.'

Bas's hands tightened on her hips. 'Yes, you'll dance?'

She looked through the window and bit her lip. 'Charlie will be watching?'

'For your protection. There will also be cameras running.' He stroked her with his thumbs. 'Non-negotiable. They're both for your protection – and our customers' future enjoyment. If you get in trouble, you just signal to Charlie and he'll stop it.'

Leesha reached out to touch the glass. She understood. Besides, she was finding she liked it when people watched – but that was a secret she wasn't about to tell anyone.

'Yes, I'll give him a private dance.'

Bas pressed his face into her hair. 'Then saddle up.'

He nodded to Charlie and caught her hand. They exited back into the hallway, which was hushed and empty. He led her to the door of the room where her client waited, but smiled as he looked over her. 'Maybe you should have me hold onto that for you.'

She frowned, but then blushed. She still had tips stuck into her chaps. Walking around with dollar bills tucked into nooks and crannies had become normal for her. Together, they gathered her cache.

'One more,' Bas said, carefully working a five out from inside her knee. He rose up slowly before her, letting the paper money brush tantalisingly against her skin. He ordered it into a tidy pile and tucked it into a pocket inside his suit jacket. Finally, he leaned forward and brushed a kiss against her temple. 'Have fun.'

'Wait,' she said as he started to leave. 'What's his name?'

'You'll have to ask him.' His gaze was steady. 'If you want to talk at all.'

With that, he turned his back and left her. The carpet soaked up the sound of his footsteps and, the way he walked, he was like a bored panther looking for trouble.

Alicia faced the closed door and took a deep breath. It seemed like she'd just found it.

Catching the knob, she gave it a twist. The sturdy wooden door swung open on silent hinges. Her groupie didn't hear her until it clicked shut. When he did, he spun on a dime.

She wasn't sure if she should cover herself or how this was supposed to work. Bas hadn't let her put any more clothes on, so she cocked a hip and gave a sexy pose.

Her breasts were bare and her crotch was framed. Her client saw it all in a long, slow sweep.

She felt her nipples stiffening. She wasn't as nervous about this as she should be. This young man was so into her and he wasn't afraid to show it. Unlike Remy's rattling concentration, she found his undisguised interest refreshing.

'Hi,' she said, tucking her cowboy hat back down. 'I'm Angel.'

'Ben.'

She smiled slowly. She liked that name. It sounded gentle. 'Hi, Ben. You wanted a private dance?'

He dove for the settee and draped himself over it. His legs were spread like only a man could do and he rested his arms over the back. It was a macho pose, but with that muscled body he could pull it off.

Leesha wandered deeper into the room, wondering what she was supposed to do. Was she just supposed to start? Should they talk a bit first? No, Bas had indicated that wasn't necessary, but music was. How was she supposed to –

The beat started then, and she recognised the song immediately.

Pistol Pete's gaze stroked over her, hot and excited, and a wide grin spread across his face. Reaching out, he grabbed a cowboy hat from a table she hadn't noticed. 'Save a horse,' he said as he plopped it on his head. 'Ride a cowboy.'

Chapter Nine

Bas sat in his office with the door closed and all his concentration on the security feed coming from Private Room Two. He took a swift drink of a fresh Scotch, grabbed the stress ball from his top drawer and leaned back in his chair. This should be ... enlightening.

Bracing his elbow against his desk, he rubbed his temple. The shooting headache had come on fast, right about the time he'd walked down that hallway leaving Alicia behind. Could it be scruples finally rising up, demanding to be heard?

Maybe, but he wasn't about to let them get in his way.

It was an intricate game of chess he was playing with Reverend Wheeler, and he had no intention of losing, even if he had to play a little dirty. So the preacher didn't know who was on the board as pawns? He should watch his people more closely.

Especially his sweet-looking daughter.

The headache sharpened as Bas watched Alicia in the room with her client. The video was black and white, but crisp. It gave the picture show an old-time feel, a spaghetti western for the adult crowd. He watched the young buck carefully. The kid looked anxious and needy. Harmless.

Looks could be so deceiving.

Bas began moving the stress ball through his fingers, just getting the feel of it. How far would she go? She'd nearly had a hissy fit when he'd ordered her to dance naked. However many hang-ups and morals he chipped away at, he always seemed to find more with her. In the end, it had been the costume that had actually turned the tide. She'd thought that having some clothes on was better than having none at all.

Ah, the naivety.

After her performance on the main stage, they were going to have to turn away people at the door. He looked lazily at the pile of money on his desktop. She was racking up the tips right along with the fans.

Just how well would she perform in a more intimate environment?

He watched as she strutted around in her raunchy little cowgirl outfit. All her erogenous zones were bared and framed by the chaps. The leather was soft and supple, but it was tough. Even the clunky boots seemed geared towards sex, cutting off right where her calves got plump and bitable.

Her customer sat on the velvet settee. His eyes bugged out as he watched her, but he'd gamely plopped a cowboy hat on his head. The grin on his face was contagious, because Alicia smiled back. She was having fun with this, uncertain but intrigued. Her hips began to sway, a sure sign that the music had started. Bas flipped through the buttons on his remote and enabled the audio.

Music threw some kind of switch with her.

She started dancing in that indescribable way, only she was a good three feet away from her spectator. The man put an end to that fast, leaning forward and latching his arm around her waist. She let out a squeak and her hands landed on his shoulders. Instead of pushing him away, though, her fingers curled into flesh and muscle. Soon she was on the couch with the man, straddling his lap.

Bas watched the young gun bury his face between Alicia's full breasts. He knew how those tits felt, how firm and warm and lush. His grip tightened on the stress ball, compressing it before releasing it slowly.

Her hips were working to the beat of the music as the client's hands wandered over her bare ass and up the insides of her thighs. Things were getting hot fast, and she was already making those soft moans of pleasure that had filled his office the other night.

189

Right here on this very desk.

The stress ball bounced off the dark mahogany. Damn it, but he wanted her. He wanted to be the one standing between her legs, the one holding her in his lap, but he knew it was all lust. He wouldn't go there, no matter the cost. He could fantasise, though, and he could watch.

But was what he was doing wrong? Was he punishing her because he couldn't have her? Even if she enjoyed it? He was pushing her hard, he knew. The innocent was being led astray, but damn, she made it so easy.

She let out one of those surprised peeps followed by a low groan when the client turned her around so her bottom was rubbing against his crotch. With a nifty move, the kid spread her legs wide giving the camera a straight-on view of prime pussy. Her breasts bounced as the music continued, and the guy's hands were all over them. Holding them, squeezing them and playing with her big nipples.

A knock sounded on the office door, breaking Bas's concentration. 'Come in,' he said abruptly.

Remy stalked in, six feet of impatience. The door slammed shut behind him. 'Turn on Channel Thirteen.'

'I'm watching something.'

'You'll want to see this.'

'No, you'll want to see *this*.' Bas pointed the remote at the screen and turned up the volume. A sexual sigh filled the air.

Remy's head whipped around, and his eyes narrowed. 'What the hell? You assigned Angel a private dance?'

'I got a special request, and she didn't turn it down.'

'Probably because she didn't know what you were asking, asshole.'

Bas shrugged. 'I'm still waiting for her to say no.'

Remy's gaze locked onto the monitor. The edginess that always seemed to hover around him sharpened, but what was going on was hot. He rolled his shoulders. 'What's up with the outfit?'

'Cowgirl night. On-stage, too.'

'Like that? Damn.'

'I got it all on tape.' Bas twirled his remote. 'I'm thinking pay-per-view.'

'I'm not paying for it. Shit. Pull up Thirteen, too.'

Bas grumbled, but switched over from a security feed to an open channel on another monitor. The news was on, and the expression on the reporter's face was serious. In the background, blue and red lights alternated atop a police car. A familiar figure was visible, dressed in uniform. 'Is that Doyle?'

Remy nodded. He was leaning back against the other side of the desk now, with his arms folded. His gaze was alternating between the sex show on one screen and the late-breaking news story on the other. He didn't look happy about either.

'Doyle and Paul Simonsen.'

The microphone-lover. In cuffs.

Bas leaned forward, his attention won. 'You got him.'

'We got him. Illegal videotaping. He was stalking one of the Sunlight Epiphany's other parishioners, a lovely Ms Jeanne Young. I doubt she'll be playing the organ at their church services much longer. You wouldn't believe the number of cameras they took from her house.'

Bas scowled. He'd wanted dirt, but he hadn't expected anything like that. 'He was watching her without her knowing?'

Remy cracked his knuckles. 'I enjoyed taking him down.'

'That's good work, Remy. Honestly.'

His operations man lifted one eyebrow. 'What work? We had nothing to do with it.'

No, that was right. They hadn't. Bas slowly leaned back in his seat and kicked his heels up onto his desk. He tossed the stress ball back and forth between his hands as he watched angular Paul Simonsen dip his head to try to stay away from the media's cameras. Funny how it was, when the tables were turned.

He glanced at the other screen. Alicia's head was on her client's shoulder, her hat knocked askew as the fella stroked her belly and thighs.

Back to the news. 'What didn't we find?'

'We didn't find video of Jeanne bathing, dressing and sleeping.'

'Sick creep,' Bas muttered.

A sharp, surprised cry rang from the speakers and their heads swivelled in unison. Alicia had gone still atop her client, and her eyes were wide as saucers.

'Is that a nipple clip?' Remy asked, his voice low.

They watched, the strain in the room rising as the cowboy reached into the drawer of the table beside him and grabbed something. He wrapped his arm around a trembling Alicia, one hand cupping her other breast and holding it still. He pinched the small device he held in front of her, opening it up.

Her chest moved up and down as she gulped in air. Bas and Remy breathed right along with her. She seemed frozen on her client's lap, too stunned to move or too shocked to realise she could. She watched, her mouth open as that nipple clip came at her. It spread wide and closed slowly.

They all knew exactly when it began to pinch, because she let out an identical cry. One filled with pain, astonishment and need.

'I do believe it is,' Bas murmured. He took a long drink of his Scotch. His mouth was suddenly dry.

Remy tilted his head, watching as Alicia began to move. Her hands clawed at her breasts, but the client caught her wrists and held them away. That made Remy jerk. He pushed away from the desk.

'Dance,' the man said gruffly.

193

The order had enough silk and bite in it to make her spine stiffen. And then melt.

A weak mew left her lips, but with her hands caught and her nipples imprisoned, she began to sway.

Remy hesitated, halfway to the door. He seemed torn. 'She doesn't know that's the guy who was so interested in her back door that first day in the cage, does she?'

Bas swirled his golden-coloured drink in his glass. 'From the way she reacted to him, no.'

The muscles in Remy's arms bulged. 'Reacted?'

'Like he was a cuddly puppy.' Bas tossed back a drink. 'She trusted him. The girl needs to learn.'

'Not like this.'

'What? Did you want to be her teacher?'

Remy's jaw hardened. 'Did you give him permission to use toys on her?'

'I did.'

'Back there?'

The news report thrust itself back into the foreground. 'Authorities say that Simonsen met Young at Sunlight Epiphany Church where they both attend services.'

'Niiiice,' Bas murmured.

'Reverend Harold Wheeler had this to say,' the serious-looking reporter intoned.

With the lights flashing behind him and his gray hair sticking out at odd angles, the head of the Sunny

Epiphanies looked rattled. 'The devil is insidious,' he said. 'We must pray for both their souls.'

'Must we?' Remy glanced over his shoulder. 'Ms Jeanne wasn't in a very forgiving mood when I saw her, and I don't blame her.'

'I do believe we've scored a point.' Bas lifted his glass in salute. 'Satin Club one, Sunny Epiphanies zero.'

They looked at the screens, alternating between the two. It looked as if it would be Satin Club two before the night was through.

The music was still playing, but Alicia's harsh pants were audible. Her boyish-looking client had turned her over his knees. Her bare ass was thrust into the air, and the plump globes were outlined perfectly by the chaps. Her breasts hung heavily, their tips still pinched, but she was making no move now to free them.

No, her concern was on what was going to happen next.

And rightfully so.

The baby-faced man was playing some very adult games with her. Her face was white as he reached into the drawer of the small table again, but still she didn't say no or try to get away.

'You had first touch the other night, didn't you?' Bas asked. He could still call this off or change its direction.

The big man rolled his shoulders. 'I did.'

195

'I didn't think it would hurt if she got some play back there. It will stretch her a bit more.'

To ready her.

'He knows the rules,' Bas assured. 'Fingers and plugs are fine, but no cocks.'

Remy let out a long, decompressing breath and spotted the glass of Scotch on the desk. 'You got any more of that?'

Bas nodded towards the chair in front of his desk. 'Have a seat.'

Opening the deep lower drawer, he pulled out a bottle and another snifter. He plucked a few cubes of ice out of the stainless steel bucket on his desk – the same one that Alicia had knocked to the floor the other day. He poured the single malt and passed it along. 'Enjoy.'

'If you want to call it that.' Remy stretched out his long body, his legs spreading loosely. He rubbed the back of his neck as he watched the free show.

From that point on, neither of them was interested in talking. They watched the black and white screen with laser-like focus, the colourful newscast muted and forgotten. They listened as Alicia peeped, protested, cried out and groaned as her customer explored her body in all new ways. He petted her bottom and coated her tight little rose-shaped opening with lubricant.

Bas went back to his stress ball. That lubricant was slicker than the ointment he'd used on her reddened thighs, but he knew how taut and warm her dancer's body felt.

Her hips shifted and rolled.

That earned her a sharp rap on her right cheek.

She jerked in surprise and her cowboy hat fell to the floor. She moaned when a rigid finger stroked down her crack. She had to be used to material sitting there now, but not the touch of warm, firm flesh. Her shiver was visible and so was the clench in her butt cheeks when that inquisitive finger found something it wasn't supposed to.

'Oh!' she gasped. Her hips rocked again, but her legs spread open a few more inches.

The cowboy took the advantage, working his wrist deeper into her butt cleavage. He was purposeful as he stroked his finger round and round, lubing her opening up good. The guy watched her as he began to press more firmly. Alicia's hair flew around her shoulders as she twisted and caught his wrist. But then their gazes caught.

Bas could feel the tension from where he sat; both onscreen and from the man seated across his desk.

Leesha's body was stiff and trembling, and so were her soft lips.

'She's thinking of you,' he murmured.

Remy took a long drink, his head still resting back against the crook of his arm. The casual pose was deceptive. He could be out of that chair and in that room in under fifteen seconds. 'She likes it back there, but she thinks she shouldn't.'

Bas squeezed and released the stress ball now like it was a blood-pressure kit. 'She's going to let him.'

'Fuck,' Remy swore. 'She's too sweet and curious for her own good.'

Her sharp cry disintegrated into a series of pants as her customer pushed his finger deep into her. The lubricant made the passage easier, and he pumped inside her, then pulled his finger out to coat it again.

Alicia had stopped struggling. Music played all around them. The original song was long gone, but the tunes set the mood and comforted her. If the room was silent, Bas had no doubt she would have been out the door. He was somewhat surprised that she hadn't bolted for it yet.

But the choice of a partner had been perfect for her.

She was stretched out over the young guy's lap in a sexy pose on the velvet sofa. Behind her, she didn't see the anal plug that was about to go into her. Bas did and he leaned forward in his chair. Her cowboy was coating it up good, but it wasn't a small one. It wasn't the biggest in their collection either, but for an innocent like her, she'd certainly feel it.

And fight it.

She flinched when her partner pressed the screw top of the lubricant right against her pursed flesh, shoving it a bit inside. He squeezed the clear thick goo right into her and then tossed it on the floor. She watched as the tube tumbled across the carpet, completely oblivious until the penetration started.

When it did, her eyes flew open.

He didn't take it slow. The cowboy pushed the thick knobbish end of the anal plug into her, and the sucking *pop* was audible all the way through the security mike. Leesha gave a sharp cry and writhed like a snake.

It was too late to fight. The customer already had her under his control. Spreading her ass wide, he settled his palm against the base of the intrusive device and pushed steadily. It crept into her ass with determined slowness.

Remy's legs moved from their casual pose at Alicia's sounds of distress, pulling towards him until his feet were planted flat on the floor. The plug wasn't all that thick, but it was bigger than any fingers she'd had there. It was also harder and less merciful.

'You can take it,' her dance partner crooned. His boyish voice was gone, replaced by that of a dominant master. He looked the part, too, the smooth planes of his face creased into austere lines of determination. And pleasure. 'Bear down, Angel.'

She was whimpering, her legs twitching, but the look on her face was a combination of panic and ecstasy. A burst of energy went through her and she surged upright, pushing herself onto her knees.

And effectively impaling herself on the butt plug.

The thick black stub of rubber disappeared into her, probing deeply. The cry that erupted from her lips was a sob.

But the cowboy took advantage of her surprise. He caught her by the waist and turned her upright again, spreading her legs so she was straddling his lap. He locked his knees inside hers, spreading her legs wide.

Alicia was wriggling on his lap, but it wasn't pain written all over her face.

'She's going to come,' Remy murmured.

The businessman unzipped his pants. He wasn't wearing anything underneath them, and his cock settled in her notch. He was broad and worked up, but kind of stubby. His dick was nearly purple as he rubbed it back and forth along her pussy.

She was wet. Bas's gaze honed in on that prime spot. And she was panting.

The cowboy twirled his finger in the air and the volume of the music rose. That was when he really went to work.

Holding her firmly by the hips he began to thrust against her plump pussy lips. Forward and back he went along the groove. The head of his cock poked out between her legs with every pump. She let out a moan that echoed throughout the small room.

'Dance, cowgirl,' the guy said into her ear. 'Ride me.'

Her eyes fluttered closed, but her hips began to roll. Of her own volition, she lifted her arms overhead as the music and arousal coursed through her. They rocked that way for a while, and the man's cock got bigger and redder. Finally, he took advantage of her inattention and plucked the nipple clips off of her. They tinkled against the table as he tossed them aside, and the sound was drowned out by Alicia's pained, thrilled cry.

'That's almost worse,' Bas murmured. His stress ball was now one solid, cramped knot in his fist. Sex toys were funny that way. One would think putting them on and wearing them would be the difficult part, but when they were removed, the circulation returned. Hot blood gushed to starved flesh.

Leesha's nipples looked like they were on fire, and her client finally let her touch them. Her hands clapped over her breasts and her fingers worked urgently, trying to ease the sting. The young buck helped her, and it was enough to send her reeling. The orgasm swept through her, and her long moan drowned out the music.

Bas's Scotch sloshed around in its snifter.

'God, look at her,' Remy groaned.

'Don't say God or she'll snap out of it and run towards the door.' Bas was now working the stress ball in time with the thrusts of the lovers' hips. 'But she is something.'

Above all else, her arousal was clear. Whatever doubts or hesitations she had about what was happening to her – what she was doing – it was bringing her pleasure. Her

201

eyes were clamped closed and her mouth was open as she panted and groaned. She might have come, but her client had more stamina.

He was still stroking along her slick groove, his stubby cock bumping up against her clit with every thrust.

'Isn't he going to put it inside her?' Remy growled.

Bas gave a bark of laughter. 'He might be taking my "no cocks" rule a bit too far.'

Remy threw back a gulp of Scotch, not savouring it at all. 'Fine by me.'

'Hell, you're probably the one he's afraid of running into if he does.'

Alicia was caught up in the music and the sex again. She was playing with herself. She stroked her hands down low on her stomach to where her chaps were buckled.

Her fingertips swept along her thighs, tickled the leather ties and followed the worked leather up to where her hips were left bare. Her touch lingered there as her backside was alternately squished and released. The cowboy might not be fucking her properly, but he was riding her hard. One of her hands caught his hip, and her grip turned his flesh white. Reaching back, she caught him by the nape of the neck too.

Remy's fingers flexed and clenched at the base of his own skull.

Bas worked the stress ball and tried to remember to breathe. The two of them were voyeurs watching from the privacy of his office as the two lovers rutted in a room on the other side of the building. Despite its name, Private Room Two wasn't all that private. They had good seats, and Charlie had a prime spot as security in the next room. Plus, everything was going on tape.

Everything right up to the big climax.

For, as dominant as her client was, and as well as he was instructing her, the young businessman went off first this time. His muscled body jerked and Alicia rocked atop him. The kid cursed and caught her in a tight hug from behind. His last harsh thrust must have kicked at the anal plug, because she reared up and let out a sharp, satisfied cry.

Her body arched, her full breasts lifting as she found her second crest. She bumped against her partner's hat, knocking it onto the sofa beside them. When it was over, she sagged back against him. The kid had a satisfied grin on his face and he looped his thumbs in the belt of her chaps. He whispered something into her ear that made her face go red.

'They look like they've both been ridden hard and put out wet,' Remy muttered.

They did, but Bas was noticing something else. Sweet Leesha wasn't removing the butt plug. Remy was right. As much as she might protest, she liked it there – or maybe she didn't like it, but it made her so horny she accepted it anyway. Either way, he was intrigued.

He shifted in his chair uncomfortably. The boner he had was going to have to be patient.

Maybe he'd make her leave it there. She did have another hour left before her shift was over. Could she dance with that thing?

Dance dance. Not the bump and grind she'd just performed.

He considered it, but the regulars in the crowd hadn't paid for that. It was nice to know what perks money could buy, though. Especially with a dancer who was quickly becoming the most popular performer in his club.

'Looks like we've accomplished a few things tonight.' He picked up his remote and turned off the television. The news report was over and some late-night comedian was interviewing an aging movie star. 'The Sunlight Epiphany Church should be rocking back on its heels after tonight.'

Remy drained his drink and pushed himself up to his full height. Slashes of colour were high on his cheekbones. He shifted in discomfort and adjusted his jeans. 'They're resilient.'

Bas glanced over his friend's shoulder at the black and white screen. Alicia's customer had left her with a long kiss, and she was trying, somewhat unsuccessfully, to remove the sex toy that had been inserted into her rectum. 'Yes, they are.'

There was a wad of bills sitting on the table next to the nipple clips. Would she take it?

Remy rubbed his hand over his head. 'I was thinking ... The reverend has another disciple who followed him all the way up from Birmingham.'

Bas didn't need any more. 'Do it.'

The big operations man turned on his heel, and his gaze went like a magnet to the screen. Charlie was in the room now, helping Alicia. The bouncer had made her bend over so her elbows were braced on the table. Her lips pressed together hard as he slowly disengaged the anal plug from its snug home. He wrapped it discreetly in a handkerchief and patted her cheek.

'Think Charlie's getting enough eye candy now?' Bas murmured.

'You can be a Grade A bastard sometimes. You know that?'

Their Angel was more comfortable now, but questions and distress were now clear on her face. The signals of regret made Bas impatient, but Remy raked a hand through his hair. She was covering her private parts again, and she threw a nervous look at the two-way mirror. Had she only now remembered that she'd an audience?

The duality struck Bas. Paul Simonsen was probably headed to jail for his Peeping Tom fetish. Cameras in a private home were taboo if people knew about them, and flat-out illegal if they didn't. Yet here in the Satin Club people expected them.

Charlie finished up and opened the door. He held it for her, but Alicia didn't seem ready to face the world yet. After being so free and uninhibited, she was trying to hide her body again. She grabbed her hat from the floor and used it to cover her crotch. She held an arm over her breasts and stared at the tip her customer had left her. She hovered over it for a solid minute before picking it up. She left quickly and the click of the door was loud against the microphone.

'She's going to want to go home,' Remy said.

'Tough.' Bas sat up straight, put the stress ball away and finished his drink. 'She's here until closing time. That was the deal.'

'Tomorrow's Sunday. She'll want to get up early to go to worship service.'

Would she? 'I know.'

She was going to have to make a decision eventually. Just how much more would it take to tip her over to their side? From the way she was meeting every challenge they threw at her, it wouldn't be much longer. What had started as a threat to the Satin Club's very survival was turning into an opportunity.

He wanted her in his club permanently. Thirty days wasn't close to being enough.

'I don't want to risk her seeing the news. I want her to be surprised about Paul when she gets to church in the morning,' he said. 'Besides, that cowgirl outfit is pure gold. Another hour of her dancing in it and we'll be fighting them off at the door for the rest of the week.'

Chapter Ten

Alicia didn't want to go into the church.

She sat in her car in the parking lot, just staring at the building. It was early and worshippers were probably still having their Sunday breakfast. The morning was warm, but the real heat of mid-summer had yet to build up for the day. All was peaceful and quiet.

Except inside her head.

She'd sinned. Last night at the Satin Club, she'd gone down a very wicked path. Her actions had been greedy and lustful, and she had no justification for them other than she'd been seduced. She'd been so curious and tempted; she'd followed temptation to the dark side. She knew it. There were no excuses for it. She should be inside that church on her knees begging for forgiveness.

Yet did she really have to apologise?

She was shocked by what she'd done – and, more so, what had been done to her. She hadn't expected any of it. Dancing naked for the whole club had been scandalous enough, but what had happened inside that private room had been unspeakable. And thrilling and naughty and mind-blowing and debauched. Her customer looked so youthful and ingenuous, yet that baby face hid a virile and dominating man.

'Not so Gentle Ben,' she murmured. She shifted in her seat. The interior of her car was quickly warming.

The toys he'd used on her had been unfamiliar and a bit frightening. She'd never associated pain with pleasure before, but she'd learned very quickly that a nip or a sting could push her arousal to an even higher level. This morning, her nipples were still tender to the touch and her backside … She felt her cheeks flush. Her backside ached. Sitting wasn't helping her put the experience out of her head, but standing wasn't much better.

What was she supposed to do?

The awareness that had started when she'd set foot inside the Satin Club was growing by leaps and bounds. She was a sexual person. She revelled in the delights of the flesh. She was just beginning to understand that. Yet, the church frowned upon it.

'But why?' She didn't feel any different on the inside. She was the same nice, responsible person. Why was it bad to do things that felt good? When it was consensual? Why was sex so castigated when it brought pleasure to others?

The driver's seat was quickly becoming a hot seat.

She popped open the door and felt a breeze ruffle her hair and soft dress. Putting on her sunglasses, she lowered her head and made a beeline to the church's back door.

Her father was right. She was starting to have doubts. Not about her faith, but about all the rules that she'd been following for so long. The rules her father preached about with such fire and gusto … The rules Bas liked to chide …

She found herself at the door with her hand on the knob. The scene was so reminiscent of the day she'd stood in front of the Satin Club that she had a weird sense of déjà vu. Was this another mark in time?

A car drove by on the street and it spurred her into action.

She opened the door and moved quickly through the hallway. As a remodelled theatre, Sunlight Epiphany Church still carried some of the building's basic characteristics. The former dressing rooms had been converted into office space, while the stage and seating area were now the sanctuary. Normally she would have checked that area first to make sure that everything was ready, but today she avoided it.

For the first time ever, she felt uncomfortable here.

Nobody was around, but it felt like a thousand eyes were upon her. Pointing at her and judging.

Her hand trembled as she unlocked her office door. 'Breathe. Just relax. Nobody knows. Nobody needs to know.'

But she knew.

And there was proof.

She pushed the door shut with her heel and hurried around her desk. She opened her purse and pulled out the wad of bills that was weighing it down like a bowling ball. It was the tip money that her lap-dance recipient had left for her.

If that was what she wanted to call it.

She pulled her hand back from the money like it was poison. The dollars that men stuck in her G-string were one thing. This was another. She didn't want to be paid for what she'd done last night. That wasn't why she'd let it happen.

Flipping through her keychain, she found a smaller key and used it to open the top left drawer of her desk. She unzipped the bank pouch that would eventually hold the day's offerings and stared into its depths.

Was this worse? Was it sacrilegious?

She swallowed uneasily. She'd been back and forth over this all night. She grabbed the money and stuffed it inside. Before she could reconsider, she zipped it up tight and locked it away.

It was only then that she took a full breath. Her shoulders relaxed and her ribcage loosened.

She was about to sink into her chair when a loud thud made her head whip around. Had that come from her father's office?

'Dad?' She jumped from her desk and flew to the hallway. The door to his corner office stood wide open. Catching the doorjamb, she swung inside. She scanned the room quickly, praying that his knee hadn't given out on him again.

She was surprised when, instead, she found him stalking about the room. He hadn't fallen, but that heavy wooden chair that normally sat in front of his desk was overturned and he was in a state. He looked ornery and confused. Agitated.

She took a hesitant step inside. 'Is everything OK?'

'OK?' He whirled towards her and his heavy eyebrows lifted like the McDonald's arches. 'No, it's not OK. People are talking. They're going to associate what's happened with the church.'

Leesha's heart literally froze inside her chest.

'Reporters have already been making insinuations. Questioning *me*. How am I supposed to explain this to our parishioners?'

She felt her limbs go numb and her air choke off. Reporters? Oh, no. Somebody had made it into the club. They'd seen her, in those chaps and nothing else. They'd seen her dancing with that pole.

'People were calling me all night, taking sides.' He raked a hand through his shock-white hair. It was already standing on end. His tie was askew and he was wearing two different shoes.

Taking sides? The words rattled inside her head. Was someone actually defending her?

She couldn't think straight. How was she going to explain this to him? To the people who would be showing up in less than an hour? It was her life, her body. But still. 'I went there in the beginning to –'

'The devil has infiltrated our midst,' he said, beginning to pace again. He didn't have an established path. He just wandered around until something got in his way. 'He snatched away one of our most stalwart soldiers in this fight.'

'I'm not gone, Dad. I'm just ... experimenting.'

'And now Jeanne is walking away from us, too. A good woman, with strong morals. She doesn't want to be associated with us. I tried to talk to her last night, but she didn't want to listen.'

Jeanne? Jeanne was the one who'd come to the Satin Club? Alicia blinked. Well, she supposed the bouncers would be more apt to allow a woman who wasn't a member to enter than a man, but Jeanne had always seemed so quiet and demure. She couldn't picture the organist in the role of spy – especially at a strip club.

Unless one of the more strident picketers had put her up to it – like Paul or Steve, the self-righteous bullies.

'Those cameras. Technology.' Her father was muttering now. 'They're a sure sign of Beelzebub. Prying into places they shouldn't. Invading a woman's privacy.'

Leesha's knees went weak. The video had got out? Please not of the private room, she begged. Please not that.

'It's that vipers' pit, I tell you!' Her father came to an abrupt stop, his fists lifting from his sides. 'That depraved Satin Club got into Paul's head. That has to be what started all of this.'

Paul?

Alicia shook her head. Which was it – Paul or Jeanne?

'Yes. That's what must have happened.' The light in her father's eyes sharpened and he hurried back to his desk. 'Paul fought it, but standing across the street from that immoral place day after day put ideas into his head. We didn't pray enough. Evil found a weakness.'

He found a stubby pencil and began writing in jerky motions on his legal pad. 'People will understand that. We'll have to band together and fight harder.'

He seemed to be making sense of things, but Alicia was getting more confused by the moment. The one thing she did understand was that he wasn't raving about her. If he was, she'd have his full, undivided attention. Testing her knees, she walked closer to his desk.

'Dad, what's going on?'

'The dispute between Jeanne and Paul.' He looked up

briefly from his writings when she said nothing. 'You didn't see the news?'

She swallowed hard. She hoped he didn't ask for an alibi. 'I missed it.'

His brow furrowed. 'And the paper? It's all over the front page.'

She righted the chair and sat down primly. Her fingers were white as she clenched them in her lap. 'I came in early to get some things done. I didn't look at the paper.'

'But I left you a message last night.' He frowned and then waved it off. 'Darn phone anyway. It's Paul. He's fallen.'

She leaned closer, trying to see what he was writing. His scribble was so large and frantic, she couldn't make it out. 'And Jeanne?' she pressed.

'Wronged.' His fingers curled into a fist on the desktop. 'Shamed.'

Reaching out, Alicia wrapped her hand around his. She made him stop writing and look at her. 'What happened?'

The air left his lungs with a rasp. His chin quivered once before settling firmly into place. Whatever it was, it had affected him deeply. 'The police found video cameras in Jeanne's house, and they traced them back to Paul. She didn't know they were there. They say that he's been *watching* her.'

A shiver of abhorrence ran down Alicia's spine. She'd

always got a slimy vibe off of that man, but she hadn't expected anything like this. He was so staunch and devout, almost fanatical. What a hypocrite! He demonstrated against the Satin Club, while he was doing precisely the same thing. They watched women, too, but at least they were open and honest about it.

'Was he arrested?' she asked.

Her father flung himself back in his old stenographer's chair. It squeaked as he rocked back and forth. 'With red and blue lights flashing and television reporters everywhere I turned.'

'You were there?'

'He called me. He wanted my support.'

'Oh, Dad. I don't think we want to get involved in something like that.'

His watery eyes narrowed and his lips pursed in anger. He pointed at the picture behind him. 'He is one of our flock, a lost sheep that we must bring back to the fold. We will not leave him in his time of need.'

Alicia sat back on the hard wooden chair, feeling just as rigid. 'What about Jeanne? How will she feel about that?'

The question brought confusion back to those blue eyes.

She sighed. What a disaster. How were they going to work through this? And how had she missed it? The signs had all been there. Paul loved technology. He'd been responsible for the speaker system and that mobile electronic sign idea. He also liked to sidle up to the women of the church, looking for attention. She doubted she was the only one the man made uneasy.

Cameras.

She shuddered. Poor Jeanne. A woman should be secure in her own home. What had Paul seen? Even more sickening, what had he been doing as he'd watched?

She fought not to gag. 'How did they catch him?'

Her father waved his hand airily. 'I don't know. Something about someone picking up the feed. One of those teenage hackers, I think.'

She scrubbed her face with both hands. This was a nightmare. The church was already infamous for its face-off with the Satin Club, and their attendance numbers had been dropping steadily. She didn't know how they'd survive this disgrace.

They were a small church, non-denominational and independent. After the fiasco in Birmingham, none of the major churches had been interested in supporting her father. They'd turned their backs on him but, instead of giving up on his mission, his determination had only grown. He'd built Sunlight Epiphany from the ground up. He and his followers had renovated this theatre by hand. She'd supplied the funding with the inheritance she'd received from her mother, but she was becoming more frugal with that.

She just wasn't sure her mother would want the Bradford family money going towards some of the issues the church was pursuing.

She patted her father's hand and left him free to write. 'You're right. You need to work on your sermon. Your followers will be looking to you for an explanation as to how this could happen to one of their own. Two, actually.'

Poor Jeanne. She should call her to talk. She couldn't imagine the horror over such an invasion of privacy. How long had those cameras been sitting there, watching and taping? How had Paul got into her house in the first place?

A gasp left Alicia's lips and she clapped a hand over her mouth.

Her father looked up sharply. 'What is it?'

She shook her head abruptly. 'I – I just remembered that we purchased video cameras last Christmas to tape the children's play.'

Her father paled. 'Go. Go check that they're still here.'

She jumped to her feet. As fast as her feet were moving, though, her brain was heading in a totally different direction. The cameras were a concern, yes, but they weren't what had her feeling sick to her stomach.

Paul Simonsen had been one of several worshippers who'd helped her move new furniture into her apartment a few months back. They'd rearranged her living room, and she'd paid them in pizza.

The sick freak had been in her apartment for hours.

* * *

It wasn't until her second break that night that Alicia had time to go find Bas. It had been an exhausting, dreadful day. As her father had predicted, the media had been all over Sunlight Epiphany Church. She'd handled calls well into the evening, and that had only been between visits from concerned church members. The morning service hadn't gone well at all.

Neither had her search of her apartment once she'd managed to get home.

She'd scoured the place from floor to ceiling. If there were cameras there, she hadn't found them. Unfortunately, that didn't settle the queasiness in her gut. Were they not there? Or was she not looking in the right places? The uncertainty was driving her nuts.

Trying not to disturb Marguerite's act, she made her way to Bas's office. Charlie was standing guard, but she couldn't meet the man's gaze – not after the service he'd performed for her last night.

She cleared her throat. 'Is he in?'

The bouncer's gaze raked down her body. She was clad in a skimpy nurse's uniform tonight. It was low-cut and short-skirted. The boys in the crowd had appreciated the view of her garter belt and stockings. Apparently, so did he. Nodding, he stepped aside. 'For you? Always.'

Leesha pondered that for a moment, but then knocked. 'Come in.'

She opened the door and poked her head inside. 'Bas, do you have a minute?'

'I have two.' He waved her in and Charlie shut the door behind her.

Bas moved aside some paperwork, clearing his desk. His gaze was shrewd as he watched her cross the room. Between them, the dark mahogany gleamed. The air got a bit heavier when Alicia finally stood in front of it. Neither of them mentioned it, but they were both aware of what had happened on that desk the last time she'd been in this room. 'You had a good first set,' he said.

'Thank you.' She smiled feebly and touched her nurse's cap. She didn't think real nurses wore them anymore, but it played into the fantasy. Right along with the stethoscope. 'I need to talk to you about something.'

'Regarding last night?'

'Yes,' she sighed. She sat in the chair and wiggled, trying to get the skirt to cover at least her panties. She was still distracted by the mahogany desk, but her head snapped up when she realised they were on two different wavelengths. 'No! I don't want to talk about ... I mean I don't need to talk about *that*.'

'So you enjoyed yourself?'

'I –' Her day had been so horrid that she'd forgotten

219

about how she'd spent her evening. When the vivid memories resurfaced, she knew that 'enjoyed' really wasn't the right word, but that wasn't why she was here. 'This is something else. Did you see the news about the man who was arrested for spying on that woman in her home?'

'The video voyeur? It caught my eye.'

It would. Nothing got past this man, but a person would have to be living in a cave not to have heard the story. It had been the lead on every broadcast she'd seen. The news stations had hammered on the connection between Paul and Jeanne, but she knew he wanted her to say it out loud. 'Paul Simonsen is a member of our congregation.'

He relaxed back into his luxurious leather chair. 'Well, now. Isn't that an interesting turn of events?'

'Don't gloat. Please.'

Bracing his elbows on the armrests, he steepled his fingers together. He watched her from atop them, his mood unreadable. 'OK, I might have recognised him from across the street. I can't say it broke my heart to hear he won't be there anymore.'

'Yes, well ...' She was hoping that after all the unwanted attention the church had received, none of them would be putting themselves out on display anymore. 'Be that what it may, it's not why I'm here. I need your expertise.'

A corner of his mouth twitched. 'What expertise would that be? As you might know, I have many.'

Again, she looked at the mahogany desk and felt her breasts get heavy. Yes, the man had talents. The one she needed just wasn't so physical. Twisting in her chair, she pointed at the wall of monitors. 'That. You know a lot about cameras and videotaping.'

He tilted his head. 'The club is well-equipped.'

'So was Paul Simonsen. I need your help sweeping my apartment. He's been there, and I'm afraid that what happened to Jeanne might be happening to me, too. I just don't know what to look for.'

His expression turned serious. 'Ah, that is disturbing.'

Picking up his remote, he gave it a twirl. He ran his thumb over a series of buttons. 'I'm sorry, but I can't help you.'

She frowned. 'Can't or won't?'

'I'm not being pissy, Angel. I think the guy is despicable. I always tell my girls when they're being taped. I told you.'

She felt her face flare. When was she going to get used to all this frank talk? 'So what's the problem?'

'You've got the wrong guy.'

She looked pointedly at the monitors.

He gave her a wry smile. 'I might be an expert channel changer, and I can watch five things at once, but you're looking for a technology expert. You need someone who understands electronics and security and surveillance techniques. In a word, you need Remy.'

221

* * *

Remy followed Alicia up the front walk to her apartment, feeling somewhat bemused and somewhat pissed off. It was ironic that she'd turned to him for help when he'd been the one to discover Paul's secret obsession in the first place. She didn't know that, though, which was by design. Nobody was supposed to trace the police's actions back to him, and they wouldn't.

He just hadn't thought things through.

He should have considered that she might be another victim of the pervert. It was a logical jump, but one he hadn't taken. If the sicko would tape plain Jeanne, he sure as hell was going to try to get a camera on hot little Angel. Remy could kick himself. He should have checked her place first.

Without her knowing, of course.

He watched her as she walked at his side. She was tapping her fingers against her thigh and the cadence was getting faster as they neared the front door. 'You OK?' he asked.

'Nervous,' she admitted.

She was afraid of what they might find. So was he.

He didn't like the idea of anyone messing with her. Had Simonsen cozied up to her on Sunday mornings? Acted all protective and outraged as he'd protested the Satin Club with her from across the street?

Hell, at least they put all their cards on the table.

She glanced at him as they neared her place. Her eyes were wide and innocent. 'Are you sensing anything?'

Oh yeah. He was sensing all kinds of things, but she meant on his smartphone. He held it up so he could see it under the security light that lit the path. It was late on a Sunday, and the apartment complex was pretty much shut down for the night. 'No, but it depends on what type of camera set-up he used. If he's transmitting to a central network video recorder, I might be able to hack the feed. If he's using a decentralised IP camera, then there won't be a transmission to pick up.'

Her eyes turned glazed. 'What?'

'It depends on if the camera has built-in recording capability.'

'Oh.' She paled under the moonlight, and her keys jingled as her hand shook. 'I could be wrong about this. There could be nothing here at all. Maybe he was just watching Jeanne?'

They paused together on the landing in front of her door.

'Sure,' he lied.

She pushed her soft hair over her shoulder and took a steadying breath. She looked so sweet and beautiful, Remy felt his gut clench. This was another side to her that he'd seen only on a few rare occasions. Too often, she was bound up in her prudish schoolmarm outfits.

Just a short time ago, she'd been at the other end of the spectrum. That saucy little nurse's outfit had nearly sent several of their customers to the doctor with heart palpitations. But this?

His gaze stroked over her. She had on a fitted T-shirt and snug jeans. Her feet were free and easy in a pair of sandals. She looked like the girl next door.

The one everyone wanted to fuck.

Including him.

He reached back to rub the tension in his neck. He was here to protect her. She'd asked for his help, but being here, in her space, was playing all kinds of games with his head.

It was the boyfriend fantasy. This way, she was his wet dream. The unobtainable nice girl, and she was about to invite him into her apartment.

The monitor in his hand spiked, the needle jumping. He knew how it felt and shifted uncomfortably, trying to be discreet as he adjusted himself inside his jeans. He needed to get it together. This wasn't a date, much as he liked that particular daydream.

She unlocked the door and pushed it open. Her breasts lifted as she took a deep breath. 'Please, come in.'

He looked around with curiosity when she turned on the light. The apartment was feminine without being frilly. The colours were light, and the feel of the place was warm and welcoming. The kitchen opened into a small dining area, which flowed into a living room. His gaze landed on the comfy furniture there. It was over-stuffed and stylish and had served as Simonsen's ticket into the place. 'Is that what he helped move?'

She dropped her purse onto the kitchen table with a plop. 'Yes.'

'May I?'

'Please.'

Remy swept the room, looking for any sign of a closed-circuit television signal. If Simonsen had spent any time in this room, there might be cameras hidden here. Some weirdoes liked to watch people go about their daily lives, watching television or paying bills. There was something about the intimacy of it. It made them feel like they were a part of their victim's lives.

He found nothing, but kept moving towards the door off the end of the living area. If there were any cameras at all, the bedroom was the most likely place they'd be.

He was impressed when Alicia followed. She wasn't cowering from this. She was trusting him to help her.

'How does your phone work?' she asked.

'Unless Paul had regular access to your place, he most likely used wireless cameras. That way he wouldn't have to enter the premises and physically download tapes or flash drives.' He saw the way she grimaced. 'Could he have got a key?'

'I want to say no, but I'd also like to tell you there

was no way he could have installed cameras in the first place.'

Remy watched the readings and swore softly. It wasn't a program anyone could download from an app store. He stuck the phone in his pocket and flicked on the overhead light. He looked around her bedroom with an astute eye. He was looking for the best place to hide a camera, but that didn't mean he didn't see the bed.

Her bed.

This was the closest he'd got to the real woman, and it made him feel like a bull in a china shop. Big, antsy and out-of-place. This wasn't the world he was used to. This was 'normal'. He suddenly realised how much of a fish out of water she was when she came down to the club every night, yet she adjusted well. Hell, she put on her Angel persona like it was a tight-fitting glove.

Could he do the same? Could he ever fit into her world?

His jaw hardened. 'What about the air vent?' he asked. 'The cold-air return?'

She looked around in confusion, following his gaze up the wall opposite her bed. The vent was unobtrusive, painted to blend into the background. It made it the perfect place to hide something. It was also the place an amateur would use if they watched enough bad television movies. He pulled a screwdriver out of his pocket and moved the dainty-looking chair that was tucked under a vanity. He climbed atop it and unscrewed the vent. Dust puffed into the air as he took it off and began searching the ductwork.

She let out a sound of distress when he pulled out a tiny camera.

He brushed it off and handed it to her. The red light on the thing was glowing.

'So small?' she asked. 'Does it really work?'

'There are some out there that are even smaller.'

She turned the thing this way and that before finally poking the off switch. The red button faded. 'That son-of-a-bitch,' she whispered.

It was the first time Remy had ever heard her curse, and it pissed him off. She was hurt. Her trust had been broken.

He took the camera from her and flipped open a compartment. He took out the storage device and hooked it up to his phone. 'Let's see what he got.'

She raked a hand through her hair.

The video came on the tiny two-inch screen, and he played a bit. He could see her in her bed, her hair spread over the pillows. The quality was clear, but the video was jerky and segmented. It soon became clear the camera had a motion detector. He hit the rewind button. Maybe all the bastard had got were clips of her turning over in her sleep.

Or maybe, having sex.

Remy's jaw locked down when the vivid black-and-white video started playing a very different scene. There was no audio associated with it, but it wasn't needed. He recognised the gawky nerd riding atop her. 'Boyfriend?' he asked anyway.

She whipped around, her eyes going wild. She looked over his shoulder at the intimate scene playing out on the little screen. 'Oh, my God!'

She grasped for the device. 'Stop it. Turn it off.'

Oh, hell no. If this was what she got off on, he wanted to know. He held the phone up and out of her reach.

She jumped for it, and he realised one thing pretty damn quickly. She *wasn't* getting off.

Her boyfriend's body was thin, but she kept clutching at his back, trying to pull his weight down upon her. All those luscious curves, and it looked like the guy didn't know what to do with them. He kissed her breast politely when she pulled his head down to her hard nipple. She was tilting her hips this way and that, while he was jerking his like he was trying to do the funky chicken.

What the hell? If sex was a dance, she'd chosen a partner who didn't know the steps. 'Frustrated much?' he asked.

She clawed at his arm, using her weight to try to drag it down. 'That's none of your business.'

He suddenly noticed the date stamp in the bottom right corner of the screen. 'The hell it isn't.'

He turned on her. 'This was the night you told me no.'

Her hair swung around her shoulders as her attention turned back to him. There was a look of horror on her face.

He watched the video stone-faced as the dweeb jerked out of her and came all over her stomach. It was messy and gross, but the guy obviously didn't know that she hadn't come, too. He was cleaning her up as she squirmed and begged for more. When she didn't get it, she pushed the idiot away and ran to the bathroom. That was where the bizarre scene ended.

Or did it?

Ah, hell. Paul's first arrest. He'd been caught in a women's restroom.

Remy's strides were long and determined as he headed to the bathroom.

'What are you –' Colour was high in Alicia's cheeks, and she looked miserable. When the light dawned, though, she clutched at her stomach as if sick. 'Oh, no!'

She literally bumped into the back of him as she rushed into the bathroom. 'No, there can't be another in here. Don't look at it.'

This one took a bit more skill, but Remy finally spotted the black wire against the pipe behind her toilet. Crouching down, he traced it until he found the whole set-up. Tricky. The thing was tucked away under the water reservoir and tilted a bit upwards. It was pointed at the shower, and he had no doubt Paul Simonsen had a standing date to watch as she stepped out from her bath, wet and dripping.

Tape squelched as he pulled the camera away from the porcelain.

'Please don't,' she said hoarsely. She was clutching the sink, but looked as if she might need to use the toilet soon. Her face was that green.

Remy ignored her. This was about them. That was supposed to have been their night, but she'd cut him off and had gone home to that ignoramus?

He attached the new camera's storage card to his phone and began rewinding fast. He was so surprised by what he found, he nearly ran right past it.

There it was. The date and time stamps were clear. She'd told them that she'd played with herself and had found her own satisfaction that night, but she hadn't mentioned *this*.

The tip of his cock batted against his belt buckle.

Holy hell.

He couldn't remember the last time he'd seen anything so erotic – and that was saying a lot. But this was Leesha, alone, and she wasn't just masturbating. She was fucking herself with something that obviously wasn't a dildo. He looked quickly around the room. Her hand clamped over the toothbrush holder that sat beside the sink, but it was too late to hide it. He looked at her face.

Her eyes were wild and her hair sat in tangles around her shoulders.

'Vixen.' He caught her and pulled her to him. Standing behind her, he locked her against him with one arm while holding the phone in front of them both. She moaned softly and he nipped at her ear.

'Boyfriend didn't do it for you?'

She turned her head away. 'He's not my boyfriend anymore.'

'I can see why.'

She shifted against him, but Remy just rubbed his erection against her soft ass. Her actions on the video screen were getting more desperate. She was plunging that hard plastic into her as her fingers toyed with her swollen clit. She looked so hedonistic with her shoulders pressed against the wall and her legs spread wide.

The look on her face, though. Need and pleasure were written all over her. Her eyes were closed and her mouth was open as she panted for air. He could have satisfied that need if she hadn't stopped him. He could have given her the pleasure of a real man's cock.

'Were you thinking about me when you did this?' He thrust the phone in front of her face when she turned away.

'Did Paul see that?' she moaned.

'I'm seeing it.' He dropped the phone onto the countertop, where it stared up at them, continuing with its

231

X-rated story. He turned her around so they were belly to belly. Catching her by the chin, he made her look up at him. 'Couldn't church boy give you what you needed? Were you still hungry for me?'

She squeezed her eyes shut. 'Yes,' she hissed.

He could feel her body against him, her nipples stiffening and her hips softening. 'Was that plastic toy enough?'

'No.'

He watched over her shoulder as she shook with her orgasm, finally dropping to her knees. It was good, but he could do better.

'Ask me to fuck you, Alicia. Say yes and get it out of the way.'

Her eyes popped open in shock. Was she really still so tender?

He cupped her ass. 'Say it. We both know you want to.'

Her lips trembled and there was an unbearable moment where he thought she was going to turn him away again.

'Yes,' she finally said, giving in.

Thrill jumped inside him, but he scowled in disapproval. 'Not that.'

Those sweet dots of colour appeared on her cheeks. Didn't she know how irresistible all that innocence was when wrapped in such a sexy package? He leaned down until their noses nearly brushed. 'Ask me for it so we both know you want it.'

Her lashes fluttered down, hiding her big brown eyes. 'Make love to me, Remy.'

He spanked her hard and she jerked, squishing all those delicious curves against him.

'Ah!' Her eyes flew open again, and this time she held his stare.

He gave her another, softer, love tap, and this time she melted.

'Fuck me, Remy.' She relaxed against him, her fingers biting into his waist. 'Fuck me all night long.'

Chapter Eleven

That was what he'd wanted to hear.

Sealing his mouth over hers, Remy picked her up and carried her into the bedroom. The apartment was quiet. There was nobody else around. They could indulge in each other all they wanted without anyone watching or barging in. He knew she liked to be watched and he didn't mind it, but just once he wanted her alone.

He set her on her feet by the bed and caught her T-shirt in both fists. She already had his rucked up to his chin.

'I want to touch,' she said. 'Nobody ever lets me see.'

Oh, yeah? He stripped off her T-shirt and then grabbed the back of his. He yanked it over his head. She wanted to see? She could touch him anywhere she wanted. 'Put your hands on me, baby.'

She wasn't timid as she laid both hands flat on his chest. She traced the lines of his muscles, and Remy couldn't help it when his six-pack squeezed. The sensation of those delicate hands stroking him was a turn-on, but so was the look of concentration on her face. It was as if she'd never spent time with the male body.

'I'm hard where you're soft.' He nearly ate his words when she flicked his nipple.

'Not everywhere.' There was a devilish look in her eyes as she smiled up at him.

She wanted to play? Oh, they were going to play.

He picked her up and tossed her on the bed. She gasped, but bent one leg instinctively. She laid on the lily-white bedspread where she'd landed, looking up at him with wide eyes. He toed off his shoes and unbuckled his belt. She looked so fresh and natural, with her dark hair falling around her shoulders.

Did that idiot boyfriend not know what he'd had? Remy's gaze raked over her in her bra and jeans. Even a nice girl needed a good roll in the sack. That's what kept her nice. He pushed down his jeans and yanked off his socks. Finally, he stood over her, naked and hungry.

He stood a little straighter when her dark gaze went straight to his cock. After seeing that video of her, he was hard and at attention. She'd fucked herself with a plastic tube because of him. He cupped his balls and pointed his dick at her. She wasn't going to need anything artificial after he was done with her.

'That won't fit into my ass,' she blurted, her eyes big and round.

Blood rushed down to his boner. Damn, just those words coming from her lips were about to send him off. 'We'll have to see about that.'

He caught her ankle and pulled off her sandal. He did the same with the other and pressed his thumb firmly into her arch. She moaned softly. She'd been on her feet in stiletto heels for hours. He rubbed in circles, watching as her eyelids drooped in pleasure. Just when she was sinking into the feeling, he lifted her foot to his mouth. Opening wide, he sucked her big toe deep.

She jerked upright, her stomach clenching. Her toes curled, but he wrapped his tongue around the one he had. She shuddered and fell back on the bed, lifting her arms over her head. The way she squirmed, he knew he had her.

He'd bet his last nickel that skinny boyfriend had never done this for her. Or fucked her breasts, or her mouth, much less that tight backside of hers. Hell, he hadn't even known what to do with her sweet pussy.

Remy finally gave up her toes and settled her leg back on the bed. Leaning over her, he began working on the tab of her jeans and the zipper. She shimmied her hips when he tugged on the denim and helped him with her skimpy panties. No more cotton, he noted. The thong was lacy and black. He dropped it on the floor. All the lights were on in the room, and he looked his fill.

She was gorgeous lying there in her bra and nothing else.

The hair on her pussy was starting to grow back. It was a dark shadow between her legs. He stroked his hand over it and her legs dropped open. The prickliness of the new growth was just starting to turn soft. 'From the front or behind?'

There it was, just a hint of the pink he loved to see in her cheeks.

'Don't worry, Angel. You'll get it both ways before the night is through.'

Along with a few other surprises.

She lifted her arms towards him. 'This way.'

That was right, she wanted to touch him. He could oblige. He knew the feeling.

Placing one knee between her legs, Remy crawled onto the bed with her. He hovered over her, the muscles in his arms bunching as she stroked him hungrily. Curiously. Her hands played over his shoulders and down his chest. She measured the span of his biceps and shivered.

He was twice her weight and probably ten times as strong. She wanted to know what a man felt like? He was better than most, and he knew it. He worked at it, and this was the prize he got for keeping his body honed and his mind sharp.

He fingered the front closure of her lacy black bra. It was centred between her breasts. All he had to do was pop it and they'd spring out, all soft and cushion-like. She was already naked from the waist down.

'Think you can take this off for me?'

That impish look returned to her eyes. 'I've become a pro at that.'

Watching him closely, she traced the edges of her bra over her generous curves. Finally, they made it to that centre tab. She turned it loose, but kept her motions slow as she pulled back the cups to expose herself.

He caught one heavy globe and plumped it high. 'Yes, you have.'

He worked her nipple with his thumb as he leaned down to kiss her again. He liked her mouth, all wet and sweet. She gave a murmur of pleasure and her hands glided down his back. She was just as curious about the muscles she found there and he let her explore all the way down to his butt.

Remy blew out a breath. Much more of that, and he'd be in a puddle at her feet.

Stretching out atop of her, he looked down into her eyes. The missionary position suddenly seemed fitting. He lowered himself onto her, letting her take more of his weight. His hips found the cradle of hers and they sunk in deep.

'Mmm,' she sighed. 'You're heavy.'

'Don't forget big.' He nuzzled against her neck. 'Men like hearing how big they are.'

She stretched underneath him and he rubbed deliberately against her breasts. Her nipples stiffened at the contact and her fingers bit into his bottom.

'You frighten me sometimes,' she whispered.

'Because I want you so bad?'

She nodded.

He cupped the top of her head and looked directly into her eyes. 'I won't hurt you,' he promised. 'But that doesn't mean there won't be some pain.'

She licked her lips. 'I want to learn.'

'You will.' He shifted his hips, and she opened her legs wider to accept him. He lined himself up at her opening. 'I'll teach you good.'

He thrust into her and they both groaned. She was still tight as a fist, but slick. He worked a hand underneath her and lifted her. Finding traction with his toes, he pushed harder. Her legs worked around his waist and her hands clamped onto his shoulders. Her internal muscles weren't fighting him, just taking their time in surrendering.

She tried to catch her breath. 'It's so much.'

'And you love it.' Bracing himself on his elbows he bore down steadily, working his cock in until she had all of him. His own breaths went ragged. 'So do I.'

God, he loved the way she felt, grabbing at him like she never wanted to let him go.

'Get ready,' he growled.

He began fucking her in heavy, steady thrusts. Those sexy little sounds she made when she got excited filled the room, and she clutched at his shoulders and then his waist.

Remy nearly went off. He was fucking the pastor's daughter in her room on a pristine white bedspread. 'We're going to stain this thing,' he warned her.

Her head rolled against the mattress. 'I don't care.'

He kept at her as long as his control could take, pumping into her warm pussy and sliding back out. He felt each thrust right down to his balls, and she was shaking and moaning. When he felt himself coming undone, he caught one of her legs and lifted it until it was draped over his shoulder. The position opened her up and allowed him to swing his hips freely.

Her eyes popped open at that and she looked at him in astonishment.

'One of the benefits of being flexible, Angel.'

He stopped holding back and rammed his aching cock into her. He hit a spot deep inside her and she jerked. She was coming before he could work her other leg up, too. Her internal muscles milked at him, and Remy bowed his head in surrender.

'Fuck,' he groaned as he started to spurt.

It was over much too fast, but that didn't mean it wasn't fantastic.

Wrapping his arms around her, he rolled onto his back. She draped herself over him like a cozy blanket, snuggling up tight. Her breaths were short and rapid as she waited for the thrill to subside.

'That was a nice start,' he murmured.

'Mmmm.'

'You want to lead for round two?'

'Two?' she squeaked.

He patted her bottom softly. He was still inside her and he had no doubt he'd be ready again soon – especially if he let her do her thing. Her inquisitiveness and her willingness drove him wild. 'Angel, baby, I'm just getting started with you.'

She slowly sat back onto her haunches, straddling him. Her pretty face had an indescribable expression as she looked down between her legs to where they were still connected. He might have blown his wad, but he was still more than she'd got from her long-gone boyfriend. The twerp. She finally found a comfortable position. When he put his hands on her thighs, her gaze lifted lazily.

She was in control – or so she thought – and growing more confident in her sexuality. When they'd first started this mating dance, she hadn't been able to look him in the eye. Now she was not only looking at him, she was on top.

She glanced around the room. The lights were blazing

and the window shades were wide open. Anyone looking in could see, but she made no attempt to climb off him and close them. She looked over her shoulder at the wall. The vent grate was on her vanity, next to the dead camera, and the open duct was gaping.

She shivered, and it went all the way through him. 'Do you think there are any more?'

'It depends on how much time and access he had. I need to check the living room more closely and the kitchen.' He nearly added, 'if it's at all like the set-up he had in Jeanne's house,' but he stopped himself just in time.

'Are the police going to find pictures of me?'

'Probably.' He wasn't going to sugarcoat it. He hadn't been in Simonsen's place, but Doyle had said the man had quite the collection. The authorities would be looking through everything to see if more charges were warranted.

'You know Bas has videos of you, too.'

Her chin dipped. 'That's different.'

She took a long breath and turned her attention to his chest. 'How could Paul do that? He was in church every weekend. He claimed to be so devout.'

'People aren't always what they seem, Leesha. Sometime black isn't black and white isn't white. Everyone's multi-faceted and we're all good at putting up fronts.'

'Some better than others,' she whispered. She began exploring again, her fingers light and deft. They stroked

242

over his five o'clock shadow and he could have sworn her nipples stiffened. 'How do you know so much about cameras and technology, Remy?'

For a second, he worried that her sharp little mind had somehow tied him into the stalker case, but when he saw the simple curiosity on her face, he relaxed. She was asking about him. She was interested beyond the sex and animal attraction.

And that made his cock start to swell inside her.

'Surprised I'm more than muscle?'

'Everyone has their facets,' she repeated. Her eyes had turned dark and dewy.

Yes, they did. Just look at her. She was turning into the most complicated woman he'd ever met.

'It was my job,' he confessed. And was a bit surprised when he did. He rarely talked about that time in his life. Then again, few had ever asked. Most people felt too threatened by him, but he was glad she was getting past that stage.

She tilted her head and her dark hair fell over her shoulder.

'Military,' he said simply.

'How did you end up at the Satin Club?'

'You know I'm not much for structure and rules.' Unable to resist, he ran his fingers through her soft hair. He hadn't spent this much time talking to a woman in bed before, but it was nice. Intimate. 'I was skilled at what I did, but when my time was up, I left. Bas and I had grown up together and, when I got back to the States, he'd just opened the club. He needed help with security and background checks, so we partnered and grew the place together.'

'You knew each other as kids?'

'There were three of us that hung out: Bas, me and Sam. We were tight. Still are.'

'You know him well.'

'Better than most.'

She braced her hands against his shoulders. Slowly, determinedly, she lifted herself and sank back down. Remy grunted. He wasn't quite hard yet, but if she did that one more time, he'd be stiff as a pipe. He ground her breasts in the palms of his hands and she let out a soft mew.

'Why hasn't he …? He's touched me, but …' She dropped down onto his cock again, and arched her neck back when he thrust up to meet her.

'Why hasn't Bas fucked you?'

'Ooooh,' she moaned as she began to ride him faster.

'Find the rhythm,' he instructed, shagging her from below.

'I can't read him,' she panted. 'I knew what you wanted from the very beginning.'

'This?' He pinched her nipples between his thumbs and forefingers.

'*That*,' she squeaked.

The natural-born dancer found the beat and Remy's toes curled. God, she was good at this. Quick-learning and eager. Athletic and responsive. Once they got rid of her remaining hang-ups, she was going to be unbelievable. He watched her body sway as she rode him, her curves moving sinuously.

'Is he gay?' she asked.

That brought a bark of laughter from him. 'Bas? Hardly.'

'Then what?'

He looked at her speculatively. Most of the girls at the club had an edge, but he didn't think she'd ever develop one. She was too sweet. Too naturally innocent and beautiful. She wasn't dancing because she had to; she performed for the sheer joy of it – and that was more enticing than she knew. 'You're a difficult one for him.'

She lifted her hair off her neck as her body rocked. 'I don't understand.'

'It's not what you think.' He curled upwards and gave her nipple a lick. 'Do you want him?'

She followed him as he lay back. She wanted more of his mouth. He gave it to her, and her hair fell forward, forming a curtain around him. 'Yessss.'

Remy tamped down the feeling of jealousy that surged inside his chest. 'Then ask him.'

Her hips were working wildly now. Catching her by

the waist, he rolled so they were both on their sides. Their hips slammed together hard, and the bed rocked noisily. He kissed her hungrily as their hands moved over each other's bodies. Stroking here, scratching there, interlocking everywhere …

'Leesha,' Remy groaned. He rolled her underneath him.

He didn't want to talk about other men. He finally had her all to himself, and he wasn't going to waste a second of it.

* * *

When Alicia awoke, the lights in the room were off and the bed was mussed. She lifted her heavy eyelids to see moonlight streaming through the window. It was so bright, the moon had to be full. She heard a rustle to her right. Was Remy awake again?

The man was insatiable.

Exhausted, she lay limply where she was. She felt like she'd been dancing for hours – with a very enthusiastic partner. Her body was heavy and replete. She couldn't have moved a muscle if she'd tried, but she did shiver a bit. It was chilly lying naked in the air-conditioning. Remy had covered her most of the night, but other than the sheet wrinkling beneath her belly and the mound of pillows lifting her hips, the rest of the bedding seemed to be missing.

She stretched and looked for the clock on her bedside table. It wasn't there. At some point, it must have been knocked to the floor.

'Remy?' she murmured.

The mattress dipped as he climbed onto it again. 'Don't worry, Angel. I'm right here.'

She relaxed. That hot body of his would warm her up.

She let her eyes drift shut. The heaviness of sleep was tugging her back under when she felt fingers stroking up her inner thigh. 'Mmm,' she grunted.

She'd had enough. She didn't even know if she could physically take him again. She felt swollen and tender. He'd been right about the nip of pain.

'Mmm,' he agreed, but with a much different tone.

Her eyes popped open when a hard finger suddenly slid up inside her, pushing firmly against her butt hole and gaining entrance. He hadn't warned her at all, hadn't touched or played first. His finger was slick, though, and it burrowed deep.

She popped up onto her elbows, her fatigue forgotten. 'Remy!'

He caught her butt cheek and spread her open. That finger of his was already pumping in and out, relearning the touch and feel of her anus. 'It's time,' he said in a low voice.

Time for –

Alicia's breath caught as she came startlingly awake.

'Relax,' he ordered. His spread his hand wide between her shoulder blades and pushed her back down to the mattress. 'I planned on having it inside you before you woke up.'

He thought she'd sleep through this?

Alicia moaned as that one finger became two. She lay prone with her hips tilted up on a mound of pillows, ready to accept his penetration. He'd positioned her for this. He even had lubricant.

'Where'd you get that?' she asked when she heard the tube squirt. She knew it hadn't come from her bathroom.

'I've been carrying it on me for a while – ever since the first time I touched you there and you nearly came.'

She cried out when he added another finger, stretching her entrance wide. The sting was biting and the sensation of fullness a bit distressing. She'd seen his cock. She'd been up close and personal with it all night, and she knew it was a lot bigger than those fingers.

Her leg bent at the knee and her toes pointed up into the air.

She let out a yelp when she felt a nip on her big toe.

'Remy,' she said worriedly as the mattress rocked again.

His knees were inside hers and he spread them further apart. She tried to push herself up onto all fours. 'We'll get to that,' he breathed into her ear, 'after I get inside you. Now lie down and take it.'

Leesha felt herself cream. Stickiness coated her pussy and her thighs. Her bottom was slick with lubricant and his fingers were twisting inside her now, trying to loosen her up.

Her breaths went short. She just couldn't unwind. She knew what was coming after those fingers. Everything inside her was tightening and quivering in denial. She'd never done this before. She wasn't sure she wanted to.

A stinging swat landed on her backside. She let out a yelp and jumped in surprise.

'Stop that,' he growled. 'I could accidentally hurt you if you fight it.'

'I don't know if I want to,' she said, her voice tiny.

He hesitated above her. 'Do you trust me, Alicia?'

She curled her fingers into the sheet beneath her. He'd always intimidated her, but he was also the one who swooped in when she needed rescuing. She trusted him to protect her, and she'd experienced nothing but pleasure under his care.

A dark, consuming, addicting pleasure.

'Yes,' she whispered.

'Then let me give you what you need.' There was the sound of more rustling and he leaned over her. He set the lubricant on the nightstand and looked into her face. 'I watched you the other night, you know.'

He traced his finger down the bridge of her nose. 'You

liked that cowboy, didn't you? You liked what he did to you.'

He ran that finger along her bottom lip. 'It's OK if you did.'

'I did,' she confessed.

He pulled back to position himself and Leesha stared at that tube on the table. It was dark, but the moonlight outlined its shape clearly. Nothing like that had ever been in her apartment.

He didn't have any of the cowboy's toys with him, did he?

Her breaths went a little ragged, but then Remy's fingers left her. She whimpered when she felt the head of his hard cock take their place. 'You liked that rubber dong inside you, baby, but that was like riding with training wheels.'

He rubbed back and forth, pressing and then retreating. 'You're about to get the real thing.'

Leesha squirmed beneath him, and she let out a cry when his hold on her hips locked down tight, spreading her cheeks wide. She knew she should relax, but she was strung tight as a piano wire as that thick tip glided down her butt crack to her secret entrance.

When the pressure started, she cried out again, the sound trailing off to a gasp. 'Oh, God!'

Remy stopped with just the head of his cock spreading her opening.

He waited, but for what she didn't know.

'I'll take that as a yes,' he finally said.

The pressure intensified and she ground her forehead into the mattress. It was hot and biting and so more real than that toy. That was Remy's cock she felt back there. He'd been warning her for a long time that he was going to do this to her.

And she wanted to give it to him.

Her fingernails clawed at the fitted sheet as he worked in short, rapid thrusts, trying to penetrate deeper. 'Did you watch the video of me with him?' she moaned.

She had to know.

'I saw it live. It was hot, and it made me jealous.'

He kissed her spine and adjusted the pillows underneath her, plumping them higher.

He was jealous?

She melted a bit and the feeling of fullness intensified. It hurt, taking him somewhere she shouldn't, but an almost unspeakable pleasure was starting to come with it. Dark and lush. Dangerous and slick.

'I could tell how much you loved it,' he growled behind her. 'It shocked you and repelled you, but you took it.' Sweat dropped from his brow and splattered against her back. 'That was the only thing that stopped me from walking into the room and grabbing him by the throat.'

Leesha's backside felt like it was on fire. 'Re ... Remm ... Remy!'

Her muscles lost the battle. The moment she gave in, his thick cock bulldozed all the way into her. Without her fighting him, he pushed in straight and true, all the way until his balls bumped against her pussy.

'Oohh,' he groaned. 'That's fucking incredible.'

Alicia was past words. The heaviness made it hard to breathe, and she realised he'd been holding his weight off her. Not now. He was using it to pin her down. She felt so full, spread so wide. Heat burst inside her and she caught at the hands that were clamped on her hips. 'It hurts,' she gasped. 'You're too big.'

'It will get better,' he promised.

Reaching underneath her, he gently tripped her clit.

The sensation was like lightning as it went through her, jolting from her clit to her pussy to her thoroughly invaded bottom. She flinched and their groans blended in the air.

He stroked his hands up her sides and leaned over her. He locked his fingers with hers and pressed his face into her hair. 'The good part starts now, tiny dancer.'

Alicia's air went choppy as he slowly dragged out of her. The relief was intense as the fullness gave way to nothing, but then the tide changed and he was pushing back in again.

He'd begun fucking her ass.

'Ooooo,' she moaned. The physicality was one thing, but she hadn't expected the emotions that came with it.

They bubbled up, hot and true. The act was so intimate, it left no room for secrets. The confessions tumbled out of her. 'Oh, God. I can't take it. It's so good. I don't – but I *do*.'

'Oh, yeah, you do, baby.' He ground into her and her buttocks shuddered. 'That's it. Just let me.'

'I want it,' she cried. 'I shouldn't … It's awful. Perfect. Please. *Please*.'

'Christ, you are something.' He began thrusting faster. The slurping sounds intensified, and she moaned as he dragged his fingers through the wetness of her pussy. She felt those fingers bump against her bottom as he coated himself with her natural lubricant, but she wasn't trying to push him out anymore. She liked him just where he was – filling her ass and making her his.

The dark pleasure was consuming. It wrapped her up, stealing her air and heating her from the inside out. Alicia gave herself over to the feeling. This time when she pressed back against him, he drew her up onto all fours. The position freed both their hips and she began to dance the carnal dance with him.

He plunged deep and she squealed.

She tried to follow his lead, but she was shaking and sweating. Her core was so tight, she thought she'd explode.

'Oh, Remy. I can't stand it!'

He was using her roughly now, riding her ass. Alicia's

head dropped forward and her hair spilled all around her. The pain, the wicked delight and the astonishment were overwhelming. She rocked back into him, accepting his thrusts and participating in her own degradation.

'Fuck, Leesha.' He caught her breasts as they dangled and swung. One hand slid down her belly, fingers spread wide. She was ready to beg when he finally touched her clit.

That one little pluck. That last little tickle.

And she blew.

She cried out when the orgasm ripped through her, tightening all her muscles and lifting her feet off the mattress. Her toes pointed at the back wall and her fingers bunched into fists. The elastic of the fitted sheet popped over the corner of the mattress and she pulled it to nearly the centre of the bed.

The ecstasy was so complete, so multi-dimensional with shadows and light. Shame and pride. Fear and daring. For the first time in her life, she felt like her own person. A confident soul who could stand on her own.

Only when she got her strength back.

She slid onto the mattress, feeling like jelly. The pillows propped her up again, cushioning her and welcoming her.

Remy was still tense and erect inside her, but not for long. With no resistance from her, he plunged and retreated until his hips were twitching in near spasms.

Her bottom felt hot and raw, but when he came, the gush of heat and wetness was delicious. Alicia hummed in delight.

She loved this.

She loved being with him this way.

He finally pulled out of her and collapsed on the bed at her side. He looked at her in amazement before pulling her closer. She snuggled like a weak kitten. She wouldn't have been ready for that the first night. He still unnerved her, but she was a stronger woman now. More understanding of her needs and desires.

'I told you your ass was mine.'

'Mmm.' She wasn't going to argue with that.

He cupped her bottom possessively. 'The cowboy can play with his toys, but nobody else takes you there. Do you understand?'

She nodded quickly, but then stared at him. He was assuming there'd be more private dances with the young businessman. Would there be?

They stared at each other in the moonlight, something heavy and important hovering just out of reach. For once, she held that dark gaze of his. Her heart was slowly picking up its pace. What was he saying?

He swallowed hard, the ligaments in his neck showing in stark relief. 'That's what you want, isn't it? To dance for your fans?'

'Yes.' Dance.

'What about that silver-haired fox? Would you give him a private dance, too?'

She felt an after-tremor go through her. The strict boss? Her heart began to pound for real. 'Maybe,' she whispered.

'And the buff black guy?' His voice had gone tight.

What were they talking about here? Lap dances or more?

Alicia didn't know how to answer. She didn't know what he expected out of her. She'd never had a steady lover before, much less multiple partners. And she hadn't meant to do more than dance for that businessman in the first place. Things had just got out of control.

His dark gaze bore into hers, but it looked shuttered. 'I can get Bas to make it happen – but you'll have to work on him yourself.'

Alicia felt a pang inside her chest. She'd thought that tonight had been about the two of them. Their chemistry. They'd been dancing around each other ever since they'd first seen one another. This night together had been inevitable.

But anything more than that?

She didn't want to disappoint him. Her fans had already proved they could do wondrous things to her body, but they couldn't compare to what he'd shown her tonight.

She closed her eyes and rested against his muscled

chest. She'd thought it had been more than just sex, but now she was confused. And so very, very tired. She couldn't think about this right now. It was too much.

She just knew one thing. Alicia Wheeler, good girl, had left the building.

Chapter Twelve

It was much too early when Alicia was awakened by a noise. It pulled her out of a deep sleep and, for a moment, she was disoriented. Her body felt heavy and a headache gripped the back of her skull. Beside her, Remy grumbled. Rolling away from him, she swatted at her alarm clock.

She hit the nightstand instead.

'Ow!' The sting in her fingers made her pull back sharply. It also woke her up.

Remy pulled a pillow over his head. 'It's not your alarm. Someone's at your door.'

He was backed up by the sound of knocking.

Leesha found the clock on the floor and turned it over so she could read it. It was 6:15 in the morning. She winced. 'Who's here so early?'

She'd barely got any sleep at all.

Her feet were clumsy when they hit the floor, and she nearly tripped on the tangle of sheets. The knocking intensified and she hurried to her closet to find her robe. Remy's gaze followed her every step of the way. She'd been naked the entire night, but still he watched. The sun was low on the horizon, and it felt warm as it hit her body. They'd never got around to closing the curtains.

The doorbell started alternating with the knocking. 'Alicia?'

She whipped her head towards Remy as she knotted the belt at her waist. 'It's my father!'

He rolled onto his back and stretched. 'Son-of-a-bitch.'

What was she supposed to do? Her dad couldn't find them together like this. He'd think she was sleeping with the enemy. That was bad enough, but in his world she didn't even have sex. Her tired brain kicked into damage-control mode. 'I'll take care of him. Please be quiet?'

Her lover's gaze was hot and lazy as he watched her. He was sprawled across her bed, naked and insanely gorgeous. He'd do exactly as he wanted, and she knew it.

He was not a man who could be handled.

She tried anyway. 'Shhh.'

For her sake, she hoped he wouldn't cause a scene.

She closed the bedroom door behind her, but heard a key scratching in the lock to her front door. Her stomach turned queasy when the handle started to turn. Was that how Paul had got in? Had he somehow managed to get hold of her backup key? She yanked the door open and planted herself in the way. 'Dad?'

He took a step back in surprise. 'Oh, you are here. I was starting to get worried. Why didn't you answer the door?'

'I was sleeping.' She pulled the robe closer together at her neck and threw an anxious look at her bedroom. She didn't trust that Remy wouldn't follow her out, naked and grumpy. She pushed her hair out of her face. It was best not to tempt fate. 'Why are you here? Is something wrong?'

He lifted a white bag and a cardboard carrier with two coffees. 'I wanted to talk to you, and it's been so long since we had breakfast together.'

Her heart softened a bit. One whiff and she knew he'd stopped for apple tarts at the bakery near the church. When her mother had been alive, apple tarts had been one of her specialties.

'That's sweet of you.' She shot another peek at her bedroom door. 'Let me get dressed, and we can eat them outside on the picnic table.'

He pushed right past her. 'It's already muggy out there. This is fine.'

Leesha bounced on her toes, uncertain what to do. She closed the front door and hurried along after him.

It was all one big open area, but at least the kitchen table would be further away from any sounds Remy might make. Although the man could move like a ghost when he wanted.

She chose the seat on the opposite side of the table so she could watch the door. With nervous hands she tugged at her clothes. The summer robe she'd grabbed was short and slippery. Satin, she noted.

Bad choice.

She tucked it around her legs and wished she'd taken the time to put on underwear, at least. She was naked underneath and much too tender down there.

She took a gulp of coffee to try to hurry things along, but paused when she looked more closely at her father. He looked haggard. Old. At his age, it wasn't healthy to be standing outside in the heat and sun all day long. He got so wound up when he was on one of his missions that he tended to forget to take care of himself, but this thing with Paul had struck him hard. 'How are you feeling, Dad? You look tired.'

'Tired and tried,' he admitted. 'It's times like these that test men's faith.'

'Did you get many calls last night?'

'Some.' He'd been taking as many calls regarding the Paul situation as she had – enough that he was even learning how to use that cellphone she'd purchased for him months ago.

'Are people looking for guidance or are they blaming the church?'

'Both.' He wiped his mouth with a napkin and took a sip of his coffee before planting his elbows on the table. 'Actually, that's what I want to talk to you about.'

'Really?' He looked to her for management of the day-to-day activities of the church, but rarely spoke to her about the spiritual side. She took her counselling in the pews with everyone else on Sunday mornings.

'I know we have differing opinions on what happened with Paul.'

Her eyes narrowed. That was safe to say. She thought the man was scum.

'But I still feel we need to open our hearts to him. I spoke with him again last night, and he's full of regret. There are extenuating circumstances, much as I expected. He's in need, Leesha.'

The apple tart suddenly tasted sour. She set it aside and wiped her hands. 'I don't care what excuse he's using. We should have nothing to do with him.'

'He needs our support and understanding. He could use our help with his defence.'

She lifted her eyebrows. She understood about love and forgiving, but it was much too soon for her. 'You want me to defend that man? After what he did to Jeanne?'

'You don't need to speak for him, although it concerns

me that your heart is so hard. If the church could just assist with bail money and his legal fees –'

Alicia's spine went rigid so fast, her robe fluttered around her arms. 'Absolutely not!'

Her father folded his hands together and his countenance was one of patience. 'It is better to forgive than to let hate overtake you, child. You know that.'

Hate had nothing to do with it. Not yet, at least. She hadn't got past the anger. 'I will not let Mom's money go towards that despicable man.'

Something flickered in her father's watery blue eyes. He'd loved her mother very much and had been crushed when cancer had taken her from them. Alicia had often got the sense that it irked him, though, that the inheritance from the Bradford family had been passed on to her rather than him. 'Your mother was a kind-hearted, understanding woman.'

Yes, but she hadn't been a pushover. 'She wouldn't have condoned what that man did in any shape or form. Neither should you.'

'He made some mistakes, and he's sorry for them.' Her father shook his head in disbelief. 'Why are you so vengeful? It frightens me.'

'Vengeful?' This from the man who had been picketing an establishment for weeks? One that had done nothing to him? The double standard finally got to her and she slapped both hands onto the table. 'I'll show you why I'm vengeful.'

She launched herself from the kitchen chair and was halfway to her bedroom before she realised what she was doing. Remy! She stopped in her tracks, but her father had already risen from his seat. 'Leesha?'

'Wait right there,' she said sharply.

She'd just slip in, grab the camera and slip out. Using her body to block his view, she opened the door a few inches. She was surprised to find the bed empty. Worriedly, she looked around the room. She blinked when she saw the window open and the curtains fluttering in the morning breeze. Had he jumped out the window so they wouldn't get caught? Relief swept through her. She could kiss the man.

Although kisses with Remy usually led to much more.

She grabbed the camera off her vanity, but came up short when she turned.

Her father hadn't listened. He was standing in the doorway, looking at her demolished room. Her head snapped back around, looking for any tell-tale signs that might remain. To her, the story was clear. The bedding was twisted and pillows were under the nightstand. Her clock wasn't the only thing that had landed on the floor, and a lampshade was knocked awry. She felt all the blood drain from her face, though, when her gaze locked on something else on the nightstand.

The tube of anal lubricant sat there, naughty but proud. Its label was bold and black.

Her backside throbbed, and she stood frozen in horror. There was no way she could hide it. She was all the way across the room.

She thrust the camera into her father's hands. 'I found this.'

Confusion pulled at his face. He wasn't good with technology, and the implications flew right over his head.

'It's one of Paul's cameras.'

'What?' He stared at the device for a long moment before glancing around the room again. His gaze automatically went to the bed, precisely where she didn't want his attention.

'It was up there.' She pointed at the opposite wall. The grate was still off and the hole to the vent looked dark and suspicious.

It was clear when the clues clicked together in her father's brain. Shock, disgust and nausea followed one another in succession on his face. 'That rotten cur.'

He juggled the camera as if not wanting to touch it. Finally, he thrust it at her and hurried out of the room. 'I'm sorry, Alicia. I didn't know.'

She felt a pang of regret. She wished she hadn't had to show him like that, but she'd felt so disrespected. So taken for granted. She wasn't about to endorse or enable Paul Simonsen's behaviour by bailing him out of jail.

She was one of his victims.

She dropped the camera, suddenly unable to touch it

too. Pulling her robe tighter, she followed after her father and lingered near the living-room wall, feeling uncomfortable. They never spoke about things like this. Feelings and relationships were almost too much for him, but sex, perversions and obsessions ...

Paul had betrayed his very belief system, but she prayed to God nobody ever showed him the tapes.

'The immorality went further in him than I expected. Satan burrowed deep.' Her father's agitation was back. He dragged his knotted hands through his hair as he stalked about the room. 'He begged me for forgiveness. He told me he'd been weak – that that filthy club had got into his head and put the idea there.'

The club? She stood a little straighter. He was turning this around on the Satin Club?

He spun on his heel. 'Did you know they have a new dancer there? They're calling her the Angel. The perversion of it!'

Alicia flattened her hand against the wall. How did he know about that? What had he been told? Had anyone described her?

'Ahhh!' He gave the paper bag on the kitchen table a swat. 'That man. The dirty Crowe. This is his fault.'

'You're blaming this on Bas?' she blurted. And quickly backtracked. 'I mean, Sebastian Crowe?'

'He's the root of the evil. Just look at his past ... the drinking, the gambling, the strippers, and then there was that car accident that hurt that girl … The sickness is spreading,' her father railed. 'We have to stop it! More men are being tempted. They're drawing them in with promises of angels and heaven, but then they trap them in their depravity.'

Alicia felt her patience shredding, and she pointed at her bedroom door. 'That camera was not the Satin Club's fault. That was Paul and Paul alone. He *taped* me.'

'Ah, but they're insidious,' her father argued, eyes brightening. 'The signs are everywhere. Just look at you.'

'Me?' She sucked in a breath. Had he seen her and Remy through the window?

He waved up and down her. 'You in your short, slinky robe. Where did you find such a thing?'

She tugged at the robe, trying to make it longer. She was unbearably conscious that she was still naked underneath. 'I've had this for years.'

He spun away again and headed back towards the kitchen. 'We need to rise up. We've been weakened, but we'll not let them win.'

'No, this has to stop.' For once in her life, Alicia was adamant. 'There's no battle here. No more fighting. I won't be authorising any funds for Paul, and I refuse to stand on that hot sidewalk one more day.'

He turned on his heel. 'You must!'

'I mustn't anything. We need to take a long look at ourselves first.' Her hands clenched into fists, but then all her energy left her. It just drained out her feet and into the floor. 'Dad, we need to concentrate on getting people back into the church. We need to think about the message we're giving them. We should be concentrating on peace and love.'

Her father stopped in his tracks, his face twisting angrily – but then his eyes glazed over and his mouth rounded. The finger he'd pointed at her slowly dropped towards the floor. It was as if he'd had an epiphany. 'You're right,' he murmured. 'We've been going about this all wrong. We've been communicating with bystanders. Innocents. We haven't dealt with the devil himself.'

'Yes.' Finally. It was what she'd been saying all along. If they had an issue, they needed to work it out with Bas one-on-one. He was a hard man, but he was reasonable. If not somewhat calculating.

Her father tapped his fingertips against his thumb, deep in concentration. 'We need to change tactics. Retreat and reassess.'

'Yes, we need to think about the direction ...'

Her words trailed off when he turned towards the door. He left, without so much as another look her way. The door just clicked and she was suddenly alone without any goodbyes. From her lover or her father.

'... of the church,' she finished. She ran her hands unsteadily over her satin robe, more shaken than she expected. Had she got through to him? 'People in glass houses shouldn't throw –'

She let out a shriek when Remy suddenly appeared in the doorway of her bedroom.

'Well, that was interesting.'

'Remy!' She clutched a hand to her heart. She had to have jumped five feet. 'What are you doing here?'

He frowned at her. 'You told me to be quiet.'

She hadn't meant black-panther stealth mode. She looked over him swiftly. He'd put on his jeans, but not much more. 'I thought you'd gone out the window.'

He let one eyebrow lift. 'Like a sixteen-year-old boy running from his girlfriend's daddy?'

No. Definitely not that. She patted her chest, waiting for her air to return. 'Why was the window open?'

'Because the room smelled like sex.'

Oh, God. She hadn't even thought of that. She must have his scent all over her. She tugged at the sleeves of her robe, but then gave up. It was hard to be embarrassed around him after what they'd done together. 'How much did you hear?' she asked.

'Enough.'

'He knows about Angel.'

He pushed away from the doorframe and stood in front of her. 'He doesn't know it's you.'

'But he thinks she's the source of all evil.' She bit her lip. 'That I'm evil.'

Reaching out, he caught her by the nape of the neck. 'You're not evil, baby.'

'No?' She let out a shuddering breath and stepped closer to him. Wearily, she leaned her forehead against his chest. 'I don't know what I am anymore, Remy. Good girl or bad. I just want all of this to stop.'

His thumb stilled where it had been stroking against her jaw. 'All of it?'

He felt big, warm and protective. Dangerous, but not evil either. Her father liked to talk of soldiers. Remy had been one. 'Not all,' she said softly.

He kissed the top of her head and caught her hand. He began walking backwards towards the bedroom. 'Come.'

'Oh,' she groaned. 'I can't.'

'Let me take care of you.' With sneaky hands, he untied her robe and pushed it off her shoulders. 'We're going to take a shower, and then I'm making you breakfast.'

She followed meekly, her steps shuffling. 'I don't think I can eat.'

He tugged her into the bathroom and closed out the world. 'Believe me. You'll work up an appetite.'

* * *

Several days later, Bas sat in his office watching the security monitors. There was an array of views to choose from. One camera was focused on the stage, there was one for each private room, and various external ones guarded the premises. The one that had his attention was directed at the park across the street.

'Something's wrong,' he said into the phone. 'It's empty.'

In recent weeks, the park had become the home for the protesters.

'Maybe they just haven't shown up yet?' Sam suggested.

No, that wasn't it. The Sunny Epiphanies showed up like clockwork. Bas could feel the wariness prickling at the back of his neck. It was a warning sign he never ignored. 'I don't like it.'

A heavy sigh came over the line. 'Isn't that what you wanted? For them to go away?'

'Yes, but only if they stayed away.' He plucked up his stress ball. There was something off about this. The Sunny Epiphanies were a hardy bunch. Crazy, but hardy. They wouldn't just not show. 'There wasn't any compromise, no last hurrah.'

'Maybe they figured out that daylight isn't prime time for a gentleman's club?'

He scowled. The last thing he needed was for those loonies to start riding his high-rollers when they came in. Business had finally turned for the Satin Club. They needed to protect their clients' privacy and keep them happy.

A knock came at the door and he waved Remy in.

'They're not anywhere around the neighbourhood,' his operations man said.

Bas shook his head. 'I've got to go, Sam.'

'Don't get too worked up about this. Things might finally be going right.'

He didn't think so. One thing he'd never had in his life was good luck. He said his goodbyes and hung up.

Remy stood over the desk with his arms folded over his chest. 'Maybe Alicia got to them.'

'Alicia?' Bas said. 'Not Angel?'

He leaned back in his leather chair and stared at his friend. The tension that usually hovered like a cloak around the guy was gone. He hadn't built any toothpick bridges or ripped off any waiter's heads for days. He seemed relaxed, easy-going and, hell … almost content. What the fuck?

'Are you going soft on her, Rem?'

The question earned him a glare, but Bas wasn't impressed. He tossed the squishy ball back and forth in his hands. He might not catch every little detail of what went on in the place, but he got people. He was a student of human behaviour. 'I knew you wanted to fuck her, but what's going on between you two?'

Remy shrugged. 'Maybe I'm just the one who remembers the rules of your bet. You told her to convince the protesters to stop.' He glanced over his shoulder to the screen. 'It looks like they've stopped.'

Bas looked again at the empty park. As parks went, it had always been a lonely place, but this seemed too good to be true. 'You really think she got through?'

'She laid down the law with Wheeler the other day.'

Bas grinned and pointed at him with the ball. 'You mean the day he almost caught you with your pants down?'

The big guy scowled. There it was – the old bad attitude. 'She cut off his money. I'd say that's something.'

'His money?'

'Her inheritance. Her rules.'

Bas pursed his lips. Well, now. That was something. He considered the screen again. Maybe she was making progress.

But then another knock came at his door, and his wariness returned. 'Come in.'

Charlie poked his head inside. 'Boss, it's Chanteuse. She wants to –'

The redhead blew right by the bouncer, strutting into the room. Only she wasn't strutting, Bas realised. He sat up straighter. She was stomping. He looked her up and down. For someone who was usually a happy spirit, smoke was pouring from her ears and fire was sparking in her eyes. She was late, considering what time she was supposed to go on the stage, but she hadn't even dressed yet.

'They were at my house,' she said through clenched teeth. 'With their signs and their bullhorns.'

Bas's head snapped hard towards the empty park and Remy reached for his phone. His eyes had gone thunderstorm black. Oh yeah, that bad attitude was back with a vengeance.

'The protesters?'

'Who else wants to save my soul? Or tell me about my misdeeds and how I'm infecting the neighbourhood?' She planted her hands on her hips and tapped her toe fast. 'I live with my boyfriend, Bas. He's a schoolteacher!'

'Fuck,' Remy snarled.

'I had to walk through their picket line to get to my car. They were on his sidewalk.'

Bas slammed the stress ball down on his desk and let it fly. It bounced and hit the back wall. He was already out of his seat and moving to the window. The view wasn't any different out of it. There wasn't one Sunny Epiphany in sight.

Because they'd been at Chanteuse's place instead. How many others were finding them on their doorstep?

The dancer raked a hand through all that glorious red hair. It was wild and flowing tonight, just like her mood. 'How did they find me, Bas? I'm not in the book. I don't give out my real name.'

He looked to Remy. 'Has anyone new been in the club?'

'No. We've been holding tight to the membership requirements ever since this standoff began.'

He looked at Charlie, who was still standing in the doorway.

'It's like Remy says, boss. We've even been watching over the deliverymen. They've all been the old stand-bys.'

'Then what the hell is happening?' he snapped.

Chanteuse flinched, but cocked her hip and flipped back her hair. It was clear that she wanted an answer, too.

She wasn't going to get one. Bas signalled to Charlie. The fewer ears that heard, the better. He kept his employees happy with plump salaries, but gossip could poison the best of work environments. If he had to take care of this, it wasn't something he wanted getting round. 'Call all the girls scheduled to work tonight and see if anyone needs a bodyguard or a ride. Chanteuse, you might be holding down that stage tonight.'

Charlie shuffled his feet. 'Ivy called in a few moments ago, saying she was sick. I didn't know, boss.'

'Call her back. Get the truth.' Bas spun in a circle with his arms lifted. 'Hell, all of you, get the fucking truth. I won't have my girls being intimidated or harassed.'

Remy nodded at Charlie, and the bouncer accompanied the dancer from the room. Bas braced a hand against the wall and hung his head, trying to rein in his temper. Without asking, Remy took the chair behind the desk. He'd put away the phone, but he'd pulled a flash drive out of his pocket. He plugged it into the computer's USB port and began clicking and typing fast.

Bas moved around the desk so he could see. 'What is that?'

'My notes on the picketers. I compiled them in a database.'

Of course he had. The guy was systematic. 'What are you looking for?'

'I don't know, but something's ringing a bell.' The operations man tapped his thumb against the desktop as he flipped from parishioner to parishioner. It wasn't a simple database. He had pictures and bios popping up on the screen with every click. '*That.*'

Bas found himself looking at a pug-faced man. He read the name underneath. 'Steve Anders?'

Remy pointed at the man's bio. 'Owns a towing company.'

Anger was fogging Bas's brain, but the gears began to turn. 'So he knows a lot about cars. Makes, models, plate numbers ...'

'And he probably has friends either in the police department or the DMV.'

Bas slapped the desk and spun away. So the bastards had watched his employees. Son-of-a-bitch. He kicked the stress ball and it bounced across the floor. They'd either caught them as they'd arrived for work or waited until their shifts had ended. Either way, these parasites had connected the cars to his staff. His people trusted him to keep them safe.

He hung his head and rubbed the back of his neck. Pain was suddenly shooting through his head like metal spikes. 'Remy, take care of this Steve guy.'

'It's an assumption, Bas. I should confirm.'

'I don't care. I've got women being taunted and trapped in their homes.' His vision was blurring. He closed his eyes and said very softly, 'Find Steve.'

* * *

Alicia was late to church that Sunday morning. It had been a long, troublesome week. She should have known her father wouldn't back down. She didn't know why she was surprised at the way he'd twisted her words, but she was.

He'd targeted the Satin Club's employees.

Her friends. Her co-workers. She was still embarrassed and apologetic to everyone. They'd been called sinners and harlots and worse.

He'd been so proud of the way his people had traced the licence-plate numbers. She still got woozy thinking about what could have happened if she hadn't got into the habit of parking next door at the diner.

The capper, though, had to be the added joy of bailing her father out of jail. Clearly, he hadn't listened to her when she'd explained the zoning code and the rules for lawful assembly. She couldn't remember the last time she'd been so angry and disappointed in him.

The irony didn't slip past her. This was twice that the 'good guys', members of her church, had been arrested.

She took a deep breath before she entered the place of worship. She used to find such peace here, especially on Sunday mornings. She missed that side of the church, that side of her faith. It had been so long since she'd felt her spirit uplifted.

Raised voices caught her attention when she passed by the sanctuary, and her shoulders slumped. All this fighting, all the turmoil. What was it today?

She braced herself and followed the commotion. The vaulted ceiling of the sanctuary made sound carry. There was a group gathered around the front pew. Talk was rapid, a few people pointed and one woman had her hand over her mouth.

Alicia steadied herself. She didn't like the looks of this.

She hurried down the main aisle. Was someone hurt? Was it her father? Had he collapsed?

She wove her way through the crowd and came to a sudden stop.

Oh, my.

Someone was down, all right. The reek of alcohol was strong. She waved her hand in front of her face, trying to find clean air. She couldn't help but stare. Steve Anders was stretched across the front pew, snoring like a motor boat.

And wearing a lovely pink dress.

Leesha really couldn't find words. The big, mustachioed tow-truck driver was using a purse for a pillow. His dress had cap sleeves and a full skirt, and it matched his pink pumps perfectly. From the look and fit of the ensemble, it was tailor-made.

Oh, the poor man.

She looked around worriedly at her fellow worshippers and saw judgment already forming harsh lines on their faces. Apparently, gruff conservative Steve, the man who stood at the front of the picket line every day, was a cross-dresser.

Chapter Thirteen

'We've had an interesting time of it lately, haven't we, Angel?'

Alicia looked up with surprise when Bas came backstage later that week. It had been a while since they'd talked. Things between them hadn't exactly been strained, but they were different. He seemed more tense these days. The cool collectedness he usually exuded was gone. She knew she wasn't responsible for other's actions, but she felt as if she'd disappointed him somehow.

'Bas, I wanted to tell you again how sorry I am.' She wished she could have stopped her father and his crowd.

He held up his hand. 'You've apologised enough.'

She wasn't sure about that but, thankfully, the picketing had tapered off. It turned out that most people of

the church weren't willing to go to jail for their cause.
The more strident were dwindling in numbers. Steve
Anders would likely still have been at the front of the
protest lines, but, after the incident with the pink taffeta,
he'd essentially been cast out of the church.

It wasn't fair, but she wasn't sorry to see him go.

'Did you need something?' she asked.

He leaned back against Marguerite's table and let his
gaze sweep over her. She was wearing a black-cat
ensemble tonight, complete with a saucy little tail. She
was covered in a tight-fitting black long-sleeved shirt and
long stockings, but she felt like a stray kitten in front of
this black panther. He'd always made her just a bit
nervous, but that sizzle had a little something extra lately.

She watched as he reached up and rubbed his temple.
Stress lined his forehead and his jaw was stiff. She knew
she turned him on. She'd learned all the signs, including
the one giveaway he couldn't hide. For as large as the
bulge in his slacks was, though, there always seemed to
be an iron fist of control that held him back.

Tonight, that control seemed to be slipping a bit. It
made her edgy. She'd met out-and-out lust in Remy. Bas
was something else entirely.

He looked at her bikini bottoms and she squirmed.
They were more than she usually wore on-stage, but it
was hard to attach a tail to a thong.

'Let me see.'

She looked at him blankly.

'Pull them down.'

Her nipples tightened, but she slipped her thumbs under the stretchy fabric at her hips. She'd learned not to hesitate or ask questions. Still, her hands shook a bit as she worked the fabric down over her curves.

'That's good,' he said when her panties were around her thighs.

She stood uncertainly as he walked closer. With the rest of her covered, the exposure felt indecent, especially when the tail hanging off the backside of her underwear tickled against the back of her calf.

She flinched when he reached out and petted her. His fingers slid down her mound and between her legs. Biting her lip, she widened her stance. The touch was so light, so teasing. Her hips swivelled towards him, wanting more contact, but he wouldn't allow it. He pulled his hand back, trailing his fingers along sensitive skin before circling in the soft hair covering her pubic bone.

'I think you're ready for that appointment with Ricky.'

Heat collected in her face. She'd hoped he'd forgotten about that.

'Go to Private Room Four after your last set.'

Oh, God. 'Do I ... do I need to do anything?'

He smiled that enigmatic smile, only it was tighter than normal. 'You know the answer to that. Just enjoy yourself.'

He slid his hand between her legs for one last feel. She went up onto her tiptoes when he gave her clit a firm rub, but then he was turning and heading to the door. It was only when he glanced over his shoulder that she realised her panties were still down around her thighs. She worked them back up, feeling her tail swish.

'By the way, you'll have an audience.'

Her head snapped up. 'That's not dancing.'

'Consider it a way to make things up to me.' His eyes had turned dark forest-green. 'Or a way to be honest with yourself.'

Her lips parted. What did he mean by that? It was too late to ask, because he was gone.

Alicia pressed a hand to her stomach. An audience? People were going to be watching as she was waxed?

Who? Him?

Adrenalin started pumping through her veins, a mixture of fear and intrepidness. Was he punishing her? Or challenging her? He'd seemed angry, though he'd held it in, but she was just learning the extent of dark pleasure that was out there.

She ran the tips of her fingers over the placket of material between her legs. Did she dare? How was it done? She knew nothing about the process itself. Would she be able to cover up at all? How did they ... position themselves? Nobody had been so up close and personal with her most private area, except Remy.

Would he be there?

She cupped herself more tightly as dread and excitement twirled inside her. She had until after her last set to decide, but she already knew what her decision was. It was going to hurt – it had to – but the pain of embarrassment just might kill her.

Just who was this Ricky?

***

By the time she made it to the long hallway that led to Private Room Four, Leesha was a bundle of nerves. She'd worked herself up into a state and nothing, including more than one glass of white wine, had settled her down. The memory of what had happened during her last private session was vivid in her head. In Technicolor, accompanied by sounds and sensations.

What was waiting in that room for her?

Her tail swished back and forth as she slowly walked to her fate. The crowd had gone crazy for her kitty routine, but all she'd been able to think of the entire night was this. Another pussy …

She squeezed her hands into fists as she stared at the door. She still hadn't decided if this was payback. Chanteuse seemed to think it was a treat.

Movement caught her attention, and her head snapped around. She took an instinctive step back. Remy was stalking towards her, a carbon copy of the day they'd first met. He was dressed in an impeccable black suit, and he looked dark, predatory and irritated.

His footsteps were muffled as he strode down the hallway, but he covered ground fast. 'I was just told.'

She felt her stomach dip in disappointment. She'd been hoping he'd be her audience. If he wasn't in there, who was? Bas alone?

'You don't have to do this.' His eyelids got heavy. 'We could do it in private. At your place ... or mine ... Or you could let it grow back in. Won't make no difference to me.'

Alicia trembled. When he said things like that, the tiny hairs on her skin rose. He was so virile, so openly sexual. She could picture the two of them in her bathroom, with him kneeling before her. Or did they wax from the back?

She swallowed hard and glanced at the closed door. She could say no. She always seemed to forget about that in the heat of the moment.

But she didn't want to disappoint Bas. Something was under that man's skin. 'Bas asked me to,' she said softly.

A muscle flexed in Remy's jaw and he paused for a long, tense moment. Finally, he stepped back and opened the door to the accompanying room. He jerked his thumb at Charlie. 'Take a break.'

'Sure, boss.' The bouncer hurried away without complaint.

Remy planted himself in the doorway, one hand braced against the doorjamb. His gaze was direct and blistering.

Anticipation simmered along Leesha's nerve endings. He was going to do the security himself. He'd be right next door in case anything got out of hand. She trusted him to protect her. One crook of her finger and he'd be in the room to help her.

But he'd also be watching. And she knew he'd like that.

He took a deep breath and stepped into the room. The door clicked behind him.

Her hands loosened, and she stroked them down her body. She'd been on the verge of backing out, but now she was curious – and more than a little excited. Her thirty-day window was rapidly narrowing. Bas hadn't asked her to stay and she knew she couldn't offer. This wasn't her real life. She was walking on the wild side, and she knew it. She'd have to go back to her staid, boring world soon.

She didn't want to miss out on anything because she was scared.

She grabbed the door handle before she could think about it any longer. The lighting was dim when she stepped inside. It took a moment for her eyes to adjust, but she could feel that this room was larger than the last one she'd been in, yet just as sumptuous.

As her vision cleared, her gaze went straight to the padded table in front of her. It looked like a massage table, but there were no sheets she could crawl under. A table of implements stood at its side. She stared hard at those things, unable to look away.

'Welcome, darling.'

The voice came from behind her as the door was shut, and she whirled around. The person who'd spoken stood patiently, hands folded. Ricky was wearing a white aesthetician's jacket. His hair was short, his face was plump and his body was stout.

Anyway she thought it was a man. The husky voice made it hard to tell.

The aesthetician's touch was soft as he reached out to cup her elbow. 'Angel, isn't it?'

She nodded.

A kind grey gaze slid over her. 'My, isn't that a saucy little costume you're wearing?'

She suddenly felt silly with her black ears and swishing tail. She pulled the hair band off and held it uncertainly in front of her.

'Bas says this is your first treatment?'

She cleared her throat. 'Yes.'

'Well, I'll be as gentle as possible, but I'll warn you that I'm thorough. Now, why don't you just relax and get comfortable.'

Alicia knew she was staring, but she couldn't

distinguish any facial hair. Diamond earrings glittered from Ricky's ears, but his short neck hid what could have been an Adam's apple.

Could it be Ricki instead of Ricky?

A big hand settled between her shoulder blades. 'Do you know our guests?'

Alicia jolted. She'd got so distracted, she'd forgotten there would be others here. How had she forgotten?

'She knows me,' one of the men drawled.

Her heart jumped, hoping it was Bas, but when she turned she found three men in the room. They were all very recognisable to her, but none of them was her boss. It was her entourage. The young businessman/cowboy, the studly black man and the strict boss were all lounging in plump, velvet-lined chairs. She smiled weakly at them.

The three of them. Had Remy told Bas?

Her thighs locked together, and she looked with dismay at the set-up. Their comfy chairs circled around the end of the table. For best viewing?

It was shameful, disturbing and thoroughly arousing.

She swallowed hard. Was she really going to allow this to be done to her?

Ricky was washing his hands in the sink. Her hands? 'Please, take off your clothes and climb onto the table, dear. I need to see what I'm dealing with.'

'Grade A prime pussy,' the black man said.

The aesthetician turned on him with a scowl on her

face. 'Enough of that. We agreed you'd be quiet throughout the procedure.'

Oh, please. Yes, she needed quiet. Alicia set her headband uncertainly on a side table. She couldn't take it if they provided raunchy commentary through the whole thing.

Ricky stirred the wax that was on the nearby cart. Glancing up, she patted on the table. 'Right here, dear.'

As always, removing her clothes in a private setting was more disturbing than stripping on-stage. Alicia glanced around for a partition or anything she could change behind. It was silly, she knew, given the striptease she'd just performed in front of a packed audience – these men included.

'Do I need to take off everything?'

Someone coughed and earned another harsh stare.

Ricky looked her over assessingly. 'I'm careful, but accidents happen. Remove anything you wouldn't want wax on. The panties definitely need to go – and the tail, of course.'

Butterflies settled in Leesha's stomach when the aesthetician smiled. Which would be worse? Stripping down to nothing or just taking off the most important article of clothing that covered her? She remembered the chaps.

Oh, dear. Maybe naked was better.

The long-sleeved shirt she wore was so modest. It made things even worse when she pulled it over her head, going from so much cover to so little. She was left in her black bra, black panties and black stockings. She bent over to work at the strap of her shoe and heard someone groan.

Blood rushed to her head and she felt dizzy. This was … inflaming … and in so many different ways …

No, she didn't want to be naked.

Changing her plans, she reached for her panties instead. She hesitated, but then caught them and pushed them down, tail included.

All the air left the room in a sudden whoosh.

Hiding behind the veil of her hair, Alicia hurried to the table, but her face flared when the tail of the kitty costume wrapped around her ankle. It refused to turn loose, even when she kicked, and she finally had to bend towards the floor. By the time she untangled herself, the tension in the room was heavy. Clinging.

She spread her hands uncertainly on the table. 'How do you want me?' she asked huskily.

'On your back is fine for now,' the aesthetician said.

Even his/her voice sounded breathless.

Alicia scooted onto the table and lay back nervously. She stared at the ceiling. Her nipples were unbearably tight and her knees were locked together. She'd never been more aware of the dusty covering on her pubis. Everyone in the room seemed to be staring at it.

A hand circled her ankle, and her muscles locked down.

'Relax.' Ricky lifted her right leg. 'Let me take the weight.'

Alicia tried to loosen up, but she couldn't as the aesthetician lifted her leg off the table. Up, up it went.

Again, Ricky gave her leg a wiggle. 'Trust me,' he/she said in that gruff, indistinguishable voice.

Alicia tried, but she was stunned when her leg was lifted high and wide until it rested on the aesthetician's far shoulder. The position opened her up for interested eyes – the person who would be waxing her, the three men who sat on the edge of their seats, and the one in the room behind that mirrored wall.

Remy. She squeezed her eyes shut, concentrating on him. It made her spine unlock just a bit.

Still, she flinched when Ricky reached between her legs to examine her.

'Fine hair, not too coarse and grown-in just enough.' The aesthetician spread her leg wider and opened her folds.

Alicia stared at the ceiling so hard, her eyes went dry. She felt hot down there, burning up.

'Yes, you'll do fine.' Ricky set her leg back on the table and turned away. 'Just let your knees drop open.'

There was the sound of chair legs moving against carpeting. Someone had shifted closer for a better look. Alicia began breathing through her mouth, trying to control lungs that were pumping too fast.

Ricky was at her side again too soon, ready to take his/her place between her legs. He'd rolled the table of implements closer, and she could see the pot of warm wax and pile of gauze strips.

The aesthetician patted her leg. 'Up.'

She was expected to lift it up there on her own? Exposing herself? Her leg was shaking as she followed orders, yet she froze when a light clicked on. A hot lamp was focused on her pussy, warming the area and making it clearly visible to anyone who wanted to see. Her pulse began to roar.

'We'll tidy up your bikini line along your leg here,' Ricky said, tracing the area. 'I'll clean the area first. Then you'll feel warmth as I apply the wax.'

The scent of something astringent filled the air and Leesha couldn't help but watch as the aesthetician stroked her leg with a damp cotton pad. The wax came next. It was warm as it was painted along her upper thigh and into the seam of her leg, only it wasn't at all soothing. She tensed as the gauze strip was pressed over the sticky area, but she wasn't ready when Ricky yanked it free.

'Aiyeee!' The sting was scorching. Alarming. She jerked, her chest lifting, but then Ricky's big hand closed over the area, applying a steady pressure.

'There, there. You're a sensitive one, aren't you?'

She slowly lay back on the table and her fingers curled

around its side. Of course she was sensitive down there. Her hair had just been ripped out at the roots!

Ricky pressed his/her fingers against the smooth patch of skin. 'Looks good. No allergic reaction. Just a nice nip you seemed to enjoy.'

Enjoy? Leesha wasn't given time to analyse that, because it was starting all over again. Ricky worked quickly, and she heard the breathing around the room become harsher as her leg was lifted and bent, exposing her to both sight and touch. Her denuded skin felt hot and vulnerable, especially when Ricky stroked her in a way that didn't feel at all clinical.

But then the more delicate waxing started.

And Alicia's heart began hammering against her ribcage.

The intimacy was stark as her vulva was prepared. Ricky's concentration was intent as she cleaned the area and then applied a powder. The warm wax came next and Leesha squirmed. One of the men in her audience coughed. Her pubic hair suddenly seemed protective. She'd feel even more naked and defenceless without it.

That hot sting. How would it feel there?

She didn't have to wait long to find out. Ricky yanked off the strip like an unwanted bandage and Alicia's hips flung themselves into the air.

'Oh! Oh, God!' The words were more air than tone. She twisted in hot discomfort and embarrassed arousal, but Ricky's hand was there, pressed firmly against her pussy, easing the sting.

And transforming it into something entirely different.

Someone swore and another stood.

Leesha rocked against that hand between her legs, trying to increase the pressure, but Ricky went back to her task. The aesthetician continued the waxing, baring more and more of her. Baring her soul. Instead of getting used to it, Alicia found herself tensing harder and harder. The crowd around her seemed to be closing in. They weren't talking, but she could feel their body heat. She didn't dare look at them.

They were getting excited.

Her nipples tightened into tiny buds that rubbed against her bra. So was she.

Ricky moved to her other side, and she didn't know if she could take it. She wriggled on the table, but the aesthetician stopped the involuntary movement by spreading her hand wide over her abdomen. His hand? She wished she could tell!

'Easy now.' The husky voice was one of a smoker.

Alicia focused on the ceiling. There was ornate tiling up there, something she hadn't noticed before.

'You don't want to run around half-waxed now, do you?'

Maybe! She could feel herself starting to lose it.

Would Remy mind if she stopped halfway? Could they do the rest themselves? She pressed her hand below her breasts and felt the fine coating of perspiration on her skin. Was he sitting on the edge of his seat next door? Was he pressed up against the window?

Music suddenly started. It piped into the room, low and sexy. Something bluesy. Seductive. She latched onto it, closing her eyes and sinking into the vibe. He was watching. He'd just reached out to her in the most intimate way possible.

She concentrated on that and settled her hips back against the table. She let her knees drop open, and low groans chorused from the peanut gallery in front of her. She swallowed hard. 'Please. Finish it.'

'That's a trooper,' Ricky said, cleansing her with that swab of stinky cotton. 'You'll like the results, I promise.'

Alicia found it hard to think about results when she was still fighting to get through the procedure.

'Tilt your hips up just a bit, dear. Show me what I need to see.'

Fire built in her abdomen as the waxing continued, getting more and more intimate. More sensitive. Harder to take. Her lower lips were even spread as Ricky became more detailed in her work.

Around her, her viewers forgot their promise as they started swearing in low voices and whispering comments to one another. They were getting more and more aroused. She could hear it in the tightness of their words. She could feel it sparking in the air.

'That's nice,' Ricky said, cleaning up the last bit of wax.

Her face was practically buried in Leesha's crotch as she used tweezers to get those last, stubborn hairs. Her breaths were hot and rapid against her skin and the heat from the lamp was growing.

His breaths? It didn't matter anymore.

Ricky patted her knee. 'Now turn over and get on all fours.'

'Fuck, yeah,' someone whispered. The black man?

Alicia's head snapped up from the table. 'What?'

Around her, she could see that everyone was now on their feet. They were so close she could have reached out and touched them.

'Bas pays me to be complete,' Ricky said efficiently from her work table. Yet her eyes were sparkling as she said the words.

Alicia covered herself as her gaze went from the young businessman to the big black man. The way they hovered over her made her claustrophobic.

'On all fours,' a low male voice growled.

It was the boss man. Alicia's thighs tensed at the order. The music coming from the invisible speakers turned sweaty and gritty. Her stomach squeezed and she felt herself get wet. She rolled over a bit uncertainly. The position felt safer as she lay pressed against the table, but that wasn't what she'd been ordered to do. Gathering herself, she lifted up onto her knees and braced her hands wide on the padded table.

She could imagine how she looked in her bra and stockings, with her butt bare as she lifted it into the air.

'Look at that,' the cowboy sighed. She recognised that drawl.

Hands suddenly caught her bottom, and Alicia's hips rolled. The grip intensified.

'Let me see,' Ricky cooed.

Leesha sucked in a breath so hard, her belly button nearly clamped against her spine, but she held the position. Shivering, sweating and creaming.

'Oh, look,' Ricky tsked, sweeping his finger through her dampness. 'I knew you'd like this.'

'Like' was such a tepid word, and Leesha still wasn't sure what all 'this' entailed. Her pussy felt like it was on fire, but goosebumps popped up on her skin when her buttocks were caught. They were gently spread apart and she could feel Ricky's breaths.

'Not bad, but it definitely needs attention. Do you mind if I have some assistance?'

Before she could answer, someone stepped up behind her. 'What do you need?'

'If you could just hold her open, like so?'

Four hard fingers settled close to her crack and a hot hand spread wide over her buttocks. Leesha couldn't stop the moan that left her lips. Looking over her shoulder, she saw the older businessman. The silver-haired fox.

'And you over here,' Ricky instructed.

The cowboy stepped up to her other side. Together, the men spread her cheeks, exposing all that lay hidden in between as Ricky stepped up with that dreaded, provoking pot of warm wax.

Leesha trembled so hard, her teeth started to clatter, but then the black man caught her attention. She watched him nervously as he rounded the table. It was hard to concentrate on anything other than what was happening down below. The bluesy music swelled, the beat strong and pulsing. She looked up at the man standing before her as the astringent was applied and then the powder.

She couldn't have been more surprised, when he leaned down and kissed her.

His lips were soft, but his tongue was firm as it licked the seam of her lips. The contrast was so sharp with what was happening between her legs, she wasn't ready when that strip of gauze was ripped off a very sensitive area.

'Ahhh!' she gasped.

His hard tongue filled her mouth and the kiss deepened. Reaching beneath her, he caught her breasts in his hands. Leesha whimpered when he began playing with her. He squeezed and tugged, and she felt her nipples pop out of the confines of her bra. She kissed him back as the care between her legs continued. Hot and spicy. Dark and intimate.

Her hips began to move, caught up in the rhythm of the music. The beat of the intimate dance.

'Hold her still, gentlemen,' Ricky instructed. His/her voice was higher but rougher, making it even more indistinguishable. 'Just a bit more.'

Leesha made out with the black man, loving the way he kissed and the way he handled her breasts. He was flicking her nipples with his thumbs now, bringing her some relief but arousing her even further.

Another sudden yank removed wax that was even more intimately placed and her back arched in distress and delight.

'Honey, you're getting too wet,' Ricky chastised. He cleaned up her dampness with a wipe and she heard the base of the hot lamp slide against the carpeting. The heat between her legs became nearly unbearable as he examined his work.

The boss man to her right adjusted his grip, making it more intimate as he spread her pussy lips. Alicia knew they were all looking into the pink heart of her. They could see how she was reacting.

'Mmm.' She was reacting like a volcano. She could feel the lava bubbling, deep inside her, working its way to the surface.

At long last, the sting of individual plucks stopped. Ricky pressed firmly, easing the irritation, but stirring up all kinds of other sensations. 'I think that's it,' he/she said breathlessly. 'Would anyone like to inspect?'

'I would,' the young man said eagerly.

Alicia tried to break the kiss to look over her shoulder at him, but the man she was kissing wouldn't let her. The cowboy made her nervous. She never knew what he was going to do, and she'd already experienced enough pain to take her right to the edge. She was so finely tuned and anxious, she didn't know how much more she could stand.

Yet his fingers were gentle as they stroked over her tender pussy. Curious as he spread her. 'So soft,' he murmured.

'And so plump,' the boss man said. His touch was stricter as he examined the area around her clit. 'Look how red she is.'

Leesha's hips rose, seeking the attention and trying to get away from it at the same time. She was so sensitive and aware. So amped up.

There was the sound of a zipper. 'I'll take her first.'

Her eyes snapped open. *First?*

Her head whipped around, and her hair smacked against the man who'd been kissing her. Her cowboy had his cock out and was rubbing it hard. He had one knee on the table before the boss man stepped up between her legs. 'Who says you get to go first?'

'I can't wait,' the young gun whined.

The silver fox tilted his head, but didn't seem put out. He merely stroked higher on her butt cheeks. 'You take her from below then. I've got this.'

Alicia jolted when his fingers swirled over her anus. 'No,' she said sharply.

All three men jerked to a stop. They stood, watching her in disbelief and some discomfort.

Her chest rose and fell, her breasts still held by the black man's big hands. She'd said no – and they'd stopped. The music pulsed all around them. She was wetter than she'd thought she could ever get with her pussy on fire like it was. She was lustful. Needy. Did she really mean no?

'Not there,' she said hoarsely. 'Only Remy does that.'

The cowboy's eyes brightened, and the lines of the boss man's cheekbones stood out in relief.

'Then turn her over, boys,' he instructed.

'Wh-what?' Leesha gasped as hands clutched her, taking control.

She was suddenly on her back with her black-clad legs spread wide. Her feet hung off the side of the table and she tried to sit up.

'Scoot her up higher.'

What were they doing? Her thoughts became disjointed as her bottom slid along the padded mattress. She couldn't keep track of who was where or what they were doing. Her head snapped straight when she felt the table shift. The silver fox was climbing onto it with her. His pants were unzipped and his cock jumped out as he pushed them to his knees.

301

She stared at him, stunned. He was fit for his age, and that cock of his didn't need any assistance. It was firm and long as it pointed straight at her.

Panic flared inside her chest.

It wasn't so long ago that she wasn't familiar with the male body. Now she had cocks in her face everywhere she turned. Were they all going to stick them in her? At the same time, or in turns?

Her chest hurt and her throat seized up. She wanted to please Bas. She wanted to do this for Remy.

But she couldn't.

'No!' she cried. It was too much. Too depraved.

She'd gone too far. She'd allowed temptation to pull her to someplace dark and twisted. She'd revelled in it, but it was only now that she realised how far she'd let temptation take her. She was about to have raunchy, sticky, nasty sex with three complete strangers.

What was happening to her?

She clenched her legs together and shielded herself with her hands. 'Remy!'

The door crashed open and the operations man loomed in the opening, backlit by soft light. He looked big and hulking and thoroughly pissed off. 'Gentlemen, thank you for your patronage, but the show's over now.'

'But I paid –'

'Get out.'

Fury pulsed in the room, ricocheting off the walls. The

men hovering around her wisely zipped up their pants. The cowboy took a nervous step towards the door, but an angry hulk stood in his way. Remy's eyes narrowed at the show of fear and respect. He entered the room and planted himself between the door and the padded table.

The clients scurried out like rats.

Only one person remained in the room, and he jabbed a finger in their direction. He swung that finger towards the door, and Ricky hurried away as fast as his stubby legs would take him. Her? Alicia had forgotten the hermaphrodite was still in the room.

The room fell still then, and the music became too loud. She could feel it raking over her skin. She laid curled on the table, watching Remy. She was thankful, but trepidation still had her nerves stretched thin.

He looked like a man on the edge.

With three steps, he closed the door. When he turned, she knew the look on his face. For the first time in a long time, fear simmered in her belly.

Instead of coming at her, he walked to the chairs at the foot of the table. Without a word, he began to undress.

'Remy,' she whispered as he swung his jacket around the back of a chair.

He didn't respond, and her nerves sang. He always talked to her during sex. He had plenty of sexy, naughty things to whisper into her ear.

His shirt and tie came off next. He was unbuckling the belt of his dress pants as he stepped up to the end of the table.

She sucked in a breath when he caught her and pulled her down right to the edge. Spreading her legs, he stepped between them and thrust into her. Hard and deep. She let out a cry and her back bowed.

'Oh, mercy!' she moaned.

The sensory overload nearly shut her down. The heavy pressure. The biting sting. Her pussy felt raw and hyper-sensitive. He began thrusting roughly and she twisted on the table. He didn't ease up. His hips slammed against hers repeatedly, his hips jerking like a jackhammer.

She came, her cry filling the room. 'Ahhhhh!'

His hold dug deeper into her hips, but he didn't break his jagged rhythm.

She felt herself spiralling up again, and she looked into his eyes. They were hot and excited. She pushed herself up onto her elbows and reached for his chest. His body was burning up and his heart was racing fast.

She sat up and wrapped her arms around his neck. Her legs locked around his hips and she bit his shoulder as she came again.

He bucked and she rocked on the table, her hair swinging wildly.

His breaths were ragged in her ear. He was pounding his big cock into her and all she could do was accept it.

Take comfort in it. Thrill to it. She kissed the hurt she'd caused and raked her nails down his back.

That was all it took to set him off.

When he came, his whole body jerked. Hot come spurted deep inside her womb, and Alicia hummed. The dampness was stark against her sensitive pussy. She felt everything so more clearly, and the way their bodies connected was astonishing. His balls were tucked up against her, hard and soft at the same time.

And he wasn't waxed. The rasp of his pubic hair against her naked flesh was perfect.

Another softer orgasm went through her, an after-tremor of the explosions she'd felt before. She held him possessively. His chest was hot against her nipples, and her heels dug dangerously into the back of his thighs.

'No more,' she whispered. 'Only with you … or Bas.'

He let out a long breath and dropped his forehead against hers. 'You got that right.'

She sighed and let herself drift away. Only with the men she cared about.

Chapter Fourteen

'Forgive me, Father, for I have sinned.'

Alicia sat in the back row of the sanctuary with her head bowed. Her hands were clenched in her lap and, try as she might, she couldn't look at the altar at the front of the church. She was still conflicted over what had happened in that private room at the Satin Club. Looking back, it had been so debauched. So over the line. She'd stopped it before she'd been completely lost, but she should have said no from the very beginning. She was supposed to be there to dance, but she'd allowed her curiosity to get the best of her.

Curiosity and temptation.

The dark side was pulling at her. Even now, she wondered how it might have been if she'd let those men have their way with her. How would they have touched her? Who would she have touched? How many times would she have felt a hard cock slide into her? She understood now why sex was so seductive. It felt good. It was freeing. It made her feel alive.

Was that really so wrong? Or was it just the conventions that society placed on things?

She wasn't sure, but she knew now that she couldn't do it again. As aroused as she'd got, the sick feeling in the pit of her stomach wasn't worth it. Never again with strangers.

She pressed her ankles together as she sat primly.

Remy no longer qualified as a stranger.

Emotions swirled inside her chest, and she lifted her gaze as far as the organ. The sanctuary was silent this morning, warm with colourful light streaming through the stained-glass windows. It didn't look judgmental. It looked beautiful and welcoming. She took a deep, cleansing breath.

She'd been enticed, but she'd fought off the temptation. In the end, she'd made love with someone she cared about. It had been rough, impatient and significant. Married or not, she couldn't consider it wrong. She might be a sinner in the eyes of the church, but she was at ease with her decisions and actions.

She wasn't a saint; she was a woman.

She pushed herself to her feet and made her way back

to her office. She was still deep in thought when she heard a sound that made her stop in her tracks. Was that laughter? Leaning back, she peeked through the window in the door to her father's office. It had been so long since she'd heard that sound.

She was surprised to see a visitor. They hadn't had anybody new drop in on the church in weeks, other than the media. Was this woman a reporter?

The young blonde was having an animated discussion with her father. Alicia couldn't see her face, but she could see his. For the first time in a long time, he didn't look dishevelled or distracted. Colour was in his cheeks and he was listening to whatever the woman had to say.

Alicia felt her heart open. Reporter or not, this woman could visit any time she wanted. She wished she knew what they were talking about, but she couldn't spy on them any longer. Not without getting caught, and she didn't want to interrupt such a magical moment. She made herself continue on to her own office. Whatever the woman's reason for visiting, she just wanted to hug her.

Her father needed to get back to talking with people. He was so wrapped up in ideologies, he'd lost contact. The church needed new blood and new ideas.

The sound of laughter tinkled down the hallway again, and it inspired her.

She looked at the work waiting on her desk and pushed

the bills aside. What they really needed to do was find a way to repair the church's image, both internally and externally. She had experience with marketing and promotion. There had to be a way they could change people's impressions back to the positive. They just needed to regain their focus.

Feeling reinvigorated, Alicia dove into the task. She was brainstorming ideas when she heard a knock on her door. She glanced up. 'Come in.'

The door swung open, but she didn't see anyone. Confused, she stood. It was only then that she saw the blonde woman who'd been speaking with her father.

'Oh,' she said in surprise. 'Let me help.'

She hadn't realised the woman was in a wheelchair.

She hurried around her desk and opened the door wider.

'Sorry, some of these older buildings have narrow doorways,' the visitor said. She adeptly manoeuvred until she could roll through.

Alicia stepped back to make room, and the woman held out her hand. 'Hi, I'm Samantha, a friend of Remy's.'

Leesha's hair flew around her shoulders as she looked down the hallway to her father's office. His door stood wide open. She quickly shut hers. 'Remy's?'

The woman smiled self-consciously. 'I just wanted to meet you. He's been so different these days. Now I understand why. You're beautiful.'

Alicia moved away from the door, uncertain and uncomfortable. Who was this woman? Where had she come from? She started to go back to her desk, but that seemed inappropriate. Instead, she chose a chair and sat. It didn't seem right to tower over her visitor.

'I've never seen him so hung up on someone,' the woman said candidly. Her eyes were bright blue and astute.

The questions on her face made Alicia squirm. Remy was hung up on her? The butterflies in her stomach did a little dance, but she was still thrown. Her two worlds were colliding. Nobody outside the club was supposed to know about the two of them. 'I ... How did you say you knew each other?'

'We grew up together.'

'Oh,' Alicia said, understanding dawning. *Sam*. 'He mentioned you. He said the three of you were inseparable.'

The woman giggled. 'That's true. Him, me and Bas. The terrible threesome. Some of us have settled down a bit more than others.'

Alicia looked at her inquisitively. She'd just assumed that Remy had been talking about a man, but this woman was anything but. If she was beautiful, then Sam was stunning. She had long blonde hair that curled halfway down her back. Her features were delicate and there was a glow about her. Despite her handicap, she seemed energetic and happy.

But if she'd wanted to meet her, why had she come here? Why not the club? 'I'm sorry, I still don't understand. Why were you talking to my father?'

The woman pushed her hair over her shoulder and sighed. 'Oh, it's this business between your church and the Satin Club. I wanted to see if there's any way we could end this stand-off. It's gone on long enough, don't you think?'

Alicia felt prickles at the back of her neck. This woman had talked to her father about the Satin Club? How much did she know?

'I … You and he spoke …' But the two of them had been laughing and so friendly when she'd peeked through the window. 'What did you say to him?'

'Well, I thought about waving a white flag, but I just told him the truth. I want to call a truce.' The woman frowned when Alicia said nothing, but then her eyes popped open in understanding. 'Oh! Don't worry. I didn't say anything about you. I know better than that.'

Alicia shifted in her chair. She hoped to God not. Still, she felt a bit nauseated. This woman knew that she and Remy were involved, but did she know about the dancing? And, dear heaven, the *private sessions*?

She crossed her legs and tried not to look as unnerved as she felt. She'd thought she'd been leading two separate lives. How had this woman learned so much? Were there more like her out there? 'How did he respond?'

'Very well. He's so sweet. I think we may have worked out a compromise.'

Sweet? Alicia was taken aback. Her father hadn't been sweet in years. He was studious and driven – although he had been more relaxed when her mother had been alive. Had this woman with her bright-blue eyes and shining smile managed to somehow charm him?

'What kind of compromise? I've been trying to get him to draw back for weeks.'

'Well, I just offered him something I know we're going to give him anyway.' The look on Samantha's face turned sly and impish.

The prickles at the back of Alicia's neck dug deeper. 'And what was that?'

'I told him that Angel would be gone in a few days.'

Her head went woozy. A million thoughts and emotions roiled inside her and she couldn't sort them out. She burst out of her chair, uncaring of how it might make her visitor feel. 'Angel? But you said you didn't tell him about me!'

Samantha held up her hands, palms out. 'Easy. I didn't. He just knows that Angel is our most popular dancer, the one who's drawing in all the crowds.' She winked. 'He doesn't know that you were on a limited-time engagement anyway.'

No, he didn't. Because he didn't know she was dancing at all!

Alicia wandered around in circles, unable to stand still. She really felt as if she might be sick. 'But I wasn't dancing there when this all started.'

Sam shrugged. 'You and I both know that, but I think he's forgotten.'

That could be true. His focus had honed in on Angel only recently. All his ranting and raving had made her distinctly uncomfortable. Her reverend father was offended by the name and appalled at the concept. If he ever found out that the dancer he reviled and she were one and the same –

It just might push him over the edge.

'He's very tired,' Sam said sympathetically. 'I offered him a way out of this mess, and I think he wants to take it.'

Leesha gripped the back of the chair. If that were true, the sooner the better.

'Although it would be a shame for you to stop dancing ...'

Leesha's head swivelled around again. 'What do you mean?'

'Bas showed me some of your tapes. You really are amazing.'

'He showed you the tapes?'

'Have you ever considered being a featured dancer? You're so creative with your routines, your choice of music and those costumes! And with that body, you could tour.'

Bas had showed this woman the tapes? How many other people had seen them?

'But as for the Satin Club, one month was the deal, right?'

Alicia folded her arms around her waist. She felt manipulated, blackmailed almost, but the look on Samantha's face was so pure and innocent. Could she really have negotiated such a simple deal? One she thought everybody wanted?

One everybody should want. Including her. Leesha swallowed hard. Her time was coming to an end and, surprising as it was, that made her sad. She loved dancing on that stage. She loved the freedom and the power it gave her. But she wasn't supposed to, not in the 'proper' world – the world that she came from.

She was only visiting at the Satin Club. She couldn't continue to live a dual life. It was too dangerous. The façade was already starting to crack.

Samantha frowned. 'You were planning on quitting soon, weren't you?'

'Yes.' Taking a breath that finally made it to the bottom of her lungs, Alicia pulled back her shoulders. She'd been living in a dreamland, testing temptations and experiencing new pleasures, but she needed to return to the real world. She looked around her office. This world. 'A month is a month. I'll be done at the end of the week.'

***

Bas stood at the bar surveying his club. Things were rocking tonight. The place was packed, with a line curling out the door. That wouldn't make the regulars very happy, but it did him. Not only had they recruited new membership, but some of their older clientele had returned. There was a buzz about the place, one he couldn't have engineered if he'd tried.

It all came down to talent.

He watched the crowd's response as Marguerite gave a sassy little wave and exited the stage. She'd upped her game. All the dancers had. Angel had inspired them to do more than bump and grind.

Only tonight that would all end.

He felt the tension simmering between his shoulder blades. It had been bugging him all night. He wasn't sure what was wrong or what might be coming. He just had that sense.

He gave the main performance area another sweep. The booze was flowing, as were the tips. He couldn't put a finger on what was making him edgy. Was it the anticipation that was singing in the air? Angel was up next.

He signalled to the bartender. 'Scotch on the rocks.'

How long would they be able to keep this up after his star dancer left?

He swirled his drink in his glass. He didn't want her to go, although she should. She was like a cigarette for a chain smoker to him – hard to resist. He couldn't ask her to stay, and she hadn't asked. They'd made a deal, one that he'd promised Samantha he'd uphold. Still, he'd been waiting for a knock on his door. It had just never come.

She liked dancing here. He knew she did. She also liked the perks that came along with it, although Remy had said those were going to end. He glanced at his operations man, who was handling something with the bouncers. Remy didn't want her to go either.

But she was, and it was making Bas itch.

He ran his finger along his collar. It felt too warm in here tonight. He walked over to the thermostat and turned it down. He felt overheated and agitated. Expectant.

Tonight was his Angel's last dance. She'd have something special planned, no doubt. She'd become a master of performance. Her outfits, the music and the choreography were chosen with the utmost care. After some initial missteps, he'd turned control over to her – and the results had been phenomenal. She knew instinctively what would get the crowd going. He couldn't fathom how an innocent thing like her knew what secret fantasies men held, but she tapped into that wet-dream world almost every time.

She certainly had him pegged.

He tossed back a healthy gulp of his Scotch. It was smooth as it went down, but provided a kick when it hit his gut. Maybe getting sloppy-on-his-ass drunk wasn't such a bad idea tonight. Maybe it would tamp down the impulses he was trying so hard to fight.

Another drink of Scotch followed another, but then the lights went down low and the music changed. 'Ladies and gentlemen, get ready for the Satin Club's own Aaaannnngelllll.'

Hoots and wolf-whistles filled the air, but the entire crowd went silent when the red curtains pulled back.

'Oh, shit.' Bas's glass hit the bar. He raked a hand through his hair and swallowed hard.

She was pulling out all the stops tonight. Holding nothing back. On-stage, she captured everyone's attention in an outfit nobody had expected, but should have. She was barefoot – which went against the mould right there – but that was only the beginning of the unconventional costume. She was wearing a short white robe, a halo and fluffy white wings.

She was an angel, in the flesh.

The crowd seemed to inhale as one when she began to move, and Bas knew immediately that this routine was different. This was a coming together of everything about her. Alicia and Angel woven as one – the good and the bad, the stripper and the classically trained dancer.

Everyone was entranced. Waiters stopped waiting. People stopped talking. He stopped breathing.

He sucked in air only when his lungs began to burn.

She was ethereal up there, floating and flying effortlessly across the stage. Clothes were falling, first being the robe, but this was no bump and grind. She was doing leaps and pirouettes. It was a thing of beauty. She was a thing of beauty.

She stripped off her bra and then her panties. She was holding nothing back tonight. She was dancing now in only her halo and wings.

'Holy Christ,' he whispered. She'd been shapely before, but weeks of dancing had honed and lengthened her muscles. Her breasts were high and full, and her hair was a dark cloud floating around her.

But then she went for the pole.

And the hardening of his cock made his spine seize up.

She was no longer scared of the thing. The front row craned their necks to watch as she flew round and round, twisting effortlessly and hanging suspended as if in the heavens. She was totally nude, and his gaze snapped to that hot place between her legs. She was white and smooth, pink and plump when she flared open her legs on a spin move.

She was everything holy and indecent in one. A gift and a dark temptation.

His fallen Angel.

'Leesha.' His hands fisted at his sides. The stress ball was in his office, but he knew if he had it, it wouldn't come close to easing the grinding tension inside him. No, only grinding into her would do the trick.

Need came over him in waves until he was nearly drowning in it.

He had to have her. He needed her underneath him, moving like that and making those surprised little sounds of pleasure. He'd denied himself when she'd been splayed out and needy on his desk. He remembered how soft her thighs felt, and how red they could get. That damn video of her being waxed; he'd watched it too many times.

He needed to fuck her until she did more than make little sounds. He wanted her to scream out his name.

When the piece finally ended, nobody was quite sure what to do. Some clapped. Others were already on their feet. More than one was rubbing his crotch.

Expectation was heavy in the air. They wanted more.

He was going to get it.

Bas was moving towards the stage before he gave it conscious thought. He was so hard. His balls were drawn up so tight, he didn't know if he'd make it to her before he burst. He took the steps two at a time.

She watched him, her eyes widening and her cheeks turning a pretty pink. 'Bas!'

He snagged her about the waist and pulled her to him

roughly. She lifted her hands instinctively to his chest. 'What are you –'

He cut off the words with a harsh kiss. Right there on the stage, in front of a packed house, he sealed his mouth over hers and pushed his tongue deep.

All hell broke loose.

Men started stomping and thunder carried through the flooring and up through the stage. Tremors ran up his feet and into his legs, stimulating him more. He was beyond hungry for her; he was voracious. He cupped her bare ass with both hands and nipped at her lips. He tilted his head to come at her from another angle, and she opened her mouth to accept him.

She kissed like she danced. Like an angel who'd been cast out of heaven.

He ground his aching cock against her, and he heard the catch in the back of her throat. 'Bas?' she said uncertainly.

'Do you want it?'

That tension between his shoulder blades was burning now.

Her gaze darted around the crowd at all the eager eyes.

'Forget about them. Do you want me?'

Her dark gaze connected with his, and he could feel the tension enter her body.

'Yes,' she finally whispered.

It was as if something broke free inside him. Catching

the backs of her thighs, he hitched her up to him. The shouts from the crowd were deafening. If there was music, the frenetic energy of the throng drowned it out.

That anticipation, that exhilaration, swirled inside him. He was like a thirsty man who'd just found water. He needed to be inside her. He needed to feel her tight, wet pussy clutching at him.

She wrapped her arms around his neck and her legs around his waist. Not caring who was watching, he slid his hand between her legs and cupped her pussy from behind. She was soft and plump, readying herself for him. He pushed a finger into her, and his vision narrowed. She was as tight as he'd expected, but wetter.

'Ah!' she gasped, her back arching.

It thrust her breasts into the air and the crowd went berserk. From the corner of his eye, Bas saw Remy tangling with someone. If he took her on-stage, they'd have a riot.

But he was going to take her.

He was going to fuck the hell out of her.

Turning with her wrapped around him like a vine, he carried her up the runway. Charlie was waiting with the curtains pulled aside at the back of the stage.

He'd started with one finger, but had worked his way up to three. The bouncer was watching those fingers intently as he accompanied them down the hallway to the private rooms. 'Room Two, boss?'

'The Satin Room,' he said through gritted teeth. The one with the queen-sized bed.

Charlie hurried ahead and opened the door at the end of the hall. Bas bumped it shut behind him, backed up and leaned against it. He kissed Alicia again, slowly and sultrily. When he pulled back to look at her, she was a vision. Dark hair wild around her face with her halo knocked askew – naked body writhing in his arms – white wings spread out behind her.

He ground his hips against her naked pussy. 'Dance with me, Angel.'

Chapter Fifteen

Alicia had always wondered what it would be like if Bas ever lost control.

She had a feeling she was about to find out.

His hands were all over her and his body was straining hard. She stroked her tongue against his and whimpered when he pushed deeper inside her. He was stretching her down there. She didn't know how many of his fingers she was taking, but she felt the pinch – and the associated pleasure.

His mouth was voracious as he carried her across the room and lowered her onto the bed. She stretched out upon it, arching up to meet him.

She'd dance with him any day. She'd wanted to dance with him from the first moment she'd seen him in those mysterious dark sunglasses.

'Was it the angel outfit?' she asked as he reared upright and began tearing at his clothes.

'It's you,' he hissed.

He stripped down fast, and it was only then that she saw his tattoos. They were dark and vivid, like warrior markings. They slashed across his chest and circled his arms. Two were low on his stomach, drawing her attention to something even more mysterious.

She sucked in a breath. No, he wasn't gay.

His cock was pointed straight at her, thick and rigid. He wasn't Remy's size, but he wanted her. Badly.

She reached out to touch him. The moment she cupped him in her palm, his head snapped back and the tendons in his neck went taut.

'Stroke it,' he said fiercely. 'Pump it, sweet angel.'

She did as instructed, exploring the feel of him from the tip of that hard cock down to its broad base. He was hot and smooth. She could feel the energy pulsing inside him. She gripped him tighter and rubbed her thumb over his sac.

'Fuck!' he bit out.

He jerked out of her hand so abruptly, she thought she'd done something wrong, but then he was climbing onto the bed and pushing her knees apart. She scooted higher on the bed, trying to make room for him, but she let out a cry when he leaned down and buried his face between her legs.

'Oh!' she cried. 'Bas!'

He worked his shoulders between her thighs, spreading her obscenely. His mouth felt hot against her pussy, the act more intimate now that she was bare. He rubbed his cheek against her and the sting of his five o'clock shadow brought her right up onto her elbows. She propped herself up, squirming and watching as he ate her.

Her toes curled as he held her open with his thumbs and licked her all the way from her perineum to her clit. He settled in for a good suck, and her head dropped back in astonishment. Oh, heavens. It was like he'd been starving for her.

She whimpered when his teeth brushed against her sensitive bud, but then the hot suctioning began again. Reaching down, she ran her fingers through his silky dark hair. He wasn't giving her up and she held him close as he investigated her crevices and thrust his tongue into her opening.

He finally pulled back and nipped at her inner thigh. 'My fallen angel.'

Alicia held out her arms, waiting for him to crawl up over her, but his hard grip settled on her waist. He flipped her onto her stomach and used his knee to spread her legs again. Her face was buried in a pillow, but her head snapped up when she felt the penetration.

'Ah! Oh, God!' she gasped.

She hadn't expected him like this – wasn't ready for

it, yet his cock bore into her from behind, going deep. He wasn't gentle about it, and she shuddered as unexpected nerve endings fired. He felt huge this way – a dominating conqueror. She spread her legs wider, trying to relax and not fight him.

He planted his hands on the mattress on each side of her and began thrusting heavily. Alicia fought to keep her panic and her excitement from overwhelming her. The position wasn't quite right for her. Digging her knees in, she tilted her hips back.

'Mmmmm,' she groaned.

That was what she needed. The sound of his hips smacking against her bottom seemed loud in the silence. No music was being piped in this time. Was anyone watching from the next room?

She ground her forehead into the pillow. His balls were bouncing against her pussy with every thrust, and she was more tender down there than she'd ever been. She latched onto the slats of the headboard. Her arm brushed against the glittery halo that was still perched on her head, but now tilted at a bizarre angle. She watched as it bobbed and weaved each time Bas lunged into her.

'God, you're still tight. I thought Remy had been using you.'

Her fingers turned white as she squeezed them tighter. 'He has.'

'Then you must have been like a fist when he first

started.' His weight came down more heavily upon her and he worked his hands underneath her, pushing the sheet aside. He cupped her breasts greedily and Alicia heard the wings on her back crinkle. 'What is it about you that ties men up in knots? You're so damn fascinating. Innocent, yet dirty. Shocked, but eager. How the fuck am I supposed to leave you alone?'

Her cries were getting louder and faster as he pumped into her. The position led him straight to the very heart of her and his balls were bouncing against her clit. Her body undulated beneath his solid weight. She couldn't take much more of this.

'You've been begging me for it,' he said harshly into her ear. 'Now take it.'

She did – and soon she was coming. The orgasm pulsed through her, hot and gushing. It swept along her veins and through her muscles. Her body convulsed in pleasure and she felt warmth spilling into her. His come was warm and sticky between her legs. She let out a breath she hadn't realised she'd been holding. 'Bas, I –'

She let out a surprised squeak when he rolled her over and penetrated her again, this time face-to-face, stomach-to-stomach.

'Ahhh,' she gasped. She caught his shoulders as she curved into him. Her wings poked into her back. The sight they must make – him in dark tattoos and her naked except for angel's wings. She wrapped a leg around his hip. She hadn't thought he'd be able to do this again so soon, but his cock still felt hard inside her.

She melted a bit. Why had he waited so long if he'd needed her so badly? She'd been willing ... waiting ... wanting ...

They both jerked when the door suddenly sprung open. Bas lurched up onto his elbows. She instinctively covered herself, but she recognised the figure filling the doorway. The light in the hallway emphasised his height and form. Muscled from head to toe and thoroughly disagreeable.

She shivered. 'Remy.'

Bas's hips stopped pumping momentarily, though his cock remained buried deep inside her. A look passed between the two men, and Leesha felt the tension in the room rise. She looked worriedly from one to the other. Remy looked angry, yet when his gaze turned on her, it turned excited and aroused. Bas, on the other hand, looked pained. Almost apologetic. Somewhat ashamed.

But then Remy reached for his belt buckle and stepped inside.

When that door clicked shut behind him, Alicia knew it was another mark in time, another passage she wouldn't forget. She watched him, anxious and buzzing, as he stripped down in front of them. Anticipation grew inside her, just like Bas's cock.

He began thrusting into her, more lazily now, as he

watched his friend get ready to join them. 'I couldn't hold back,' he bit out. 'She pushed me over the edge.'

Remy's heavy cock bobbed as he set one knee onto the mattress. 'She does that to a man. Don't you, Angel?'

She cupped his cheek as he leaned down to kiss her. His lips were soft against hers, always so soft.

He ran a hand down her side and covered her breast. 'Roll her onto her side.'

Alicia's nerves gave a jitter she hadn't felt since the first time he'd caught her in that hallway. A jitter of uncertainty and confusion. She rolled with Bas when his momentum pulled her along, but she watched Remy over her shoulder. What was he planning to do?

Bas caught her chin and pulled her around for another hot kiss. His edge was back, his tiredness gone. 'We did too good of a job with you. The good girl is tempting the bad boys.'

'You're not bad,' she said, looking into his green eyes. There were shadows there. She'd thought that making love with him would remove them, but they were gathering like a storm front.

'Yes, we are,' Remy whispered as he pressed up against her. His body felt like an oven against her back.

Alicia shuddered. She was naked in bed with two lusty men. They were both touching her now. She kissed Bas as Remy played with her breasts. He worked her nipples into hard knots and bit at her shoulder.

Her wing jutted out at an odd angle.

Oh, God.

His hot cock was stroking up and down the cleavage of her bottom, bumping into the base of her spine. She reached back and caught his hip. His muscles flexed, and her fingers clenched.

Bas was fucking her like a machine. Steady, pounding and unending. Remy held her breasts to his mouth, and his buddy latched on. He suckled at her strongly and Leesha twisted in near delirium.

She was sandwiched between the two, and they were both taking their share. A fervour had settled in the room, and she groaned at the charge sizzling through her.

But then Remy moved away.

She reached back for him, but tensed when she heard a drawer open. She knew what that sound meant now. It always accompanied something that excited and unnerved her.

Twisting her head around, she tried to see what he was doing, but her body seized up tight when a long finger pushed into her behind. Lubricating without warning. Without any discussion.

'Remy!' she cried.

'Oh, yeah,' Bas grunted. He pressed his face into her breasts. 'She loves that, Rem. Give her more.'

Alicia's legs worked in distress. It didn't hurt, but she

wasn't sure what it meant. She'd taken Remy anally. It had been an effort, but they'd worked up to it together. But she was already making love with Bas. He was stroking in and out of her pussy in smooth, confident glides, and he wasn't small.

Was Remy going to put that plug into her again? Her nipples stiffened against Bas's chest. It had hurt the first time with the cowboy, but that added fullness? That forbidden pressure in her backside? It had made her come harder than she'd ever come before.

'Easy, now,' Remy murmured as he scooted up close behind her.

Too close.

Her breath sucked in when she felt the tip of his slick cock replace his finger. It bumped up against her anus and she rolled her hips away in distress. The move pushed her right onto Bas's cock, and he groaned in pleasure.

'You can't,' Alicia gasped. She looked over her shoulder, wide-eyed and little panicked. He wasn't going to use a toy. He was going to push that huge penis inside her.

She was already filled. She couldn't take him back there, too.

Yet neither of the two men in the bed was backing off.

She was caught between the two of them, and they were so much stronger than her. Bas was lean and muscled, but Remy was a hot, looming blast of energy.

Her body was stiff as Bas looped her top leg over his hip and held her there.

Remy was rubbing against her, intensifying the pressure bit by bit. His gaze was steady on hers. 'We can,' he assured her.

'Remy,' she begged.

His hand was gentle on her hip. 'Are you telling me no?'

His voice was calm and deep, not angry or accusing. He would stop if she asked him to, but in all her time here the only thing she regretted was saying no to him. As much as this scared her, she didn't want to reject him. She didn't want him to think she preferred his friend.

Because she didn't.

'Maybe afterwards?' she said in a tiny voice.

His cock broached her protective barrier and slid a good three inches into her ass. 'Now.'

Her mouth fell open on a silent cry. Oh. Oh, God!

He cupped her breast and buried his face in her hair. 'Trust me.'

Alicia's body bowed, but trapped as she was, the move was erotic. All her senses went into overdrive. She could feel the hot brush of skin everywhere. She could smell the sex in the air and hear the soft curses and slippery sounds.

But down between her legs, she felt everything. Pressure and heat. Throbbing electricity. The fullness was too much. Overwhelming her.

Trust him. Could she? Her heart was racing and her breaths were raspy in her throat. It hadn't started out that way but, out of everyone, she trusted him the most. He'd never hurt her. He'd promised her that.

Although that didn't mean there wouldn't be pain.

She pressed her shoulders back against him as he went deeper into her. Her white wings were crumpled beyond repair. Bas was watching her with those intense green eyes. His strokes were steady and measured. Relentless.

Remy's words were tight. 'Just let me get it in. Then you'll know.'

She squeezed her eyes shut. She already knew. It hurt, but the pleasure was dark and sucking. It was more than ecstasy or hedonism.

It was a wicked rapture.

They were both big and, as much as she'd been experimenting, she still struggled to adjust to two cocks inside her. She felt full to the bursting point.

'Bear down,' Remy instructed, his voice gruff.

'Ahh! Not like that,' Bas said. 'I'll blow.'

Alicia squirmed between them, unthinking. She was beyond conscious thought. She'd been reduced to a mass of emotions. A purely physical being. With one last push, Remy worked himself in to the hilt.

His breaths were hot against her ear. 'Yes?'

'Yes!' she cried. Her need had become voracious.

The dance began then, a complicated rumba – the

dance of sex. She'd never dance it on-stage the same way again. The three of them moved in sensual rhythm, both men pulling back in tandem and penetrating again in unison. Alicia's head spun. Such relief to such sublime pleasure. The pain drifted away and became a companion.

She felt herself spinning upwards. Twirling and pirouetting. Leaping and reaching.

Her halo fell off and rolled onto the dip in the pillow between her and Bas.

And she came.

The orgasm was hard and grinding. Sudden and intense.

It left her fighting for air, but the dance hadn't ended. Her partners were intent on ravishing her. She began moving in time with them again. Their hips rolled in sinful unison, her pussy clasping Bas and her ass squeezing Remy.

It was on her third orgasm that the two of them joined her. Hands clutched at her. Legs tangled. Breaths intermingled. In that moment, they were one – and she found heaven.

They collapsed against the bed and Alicia sagged against the pillows. Her lovers' bodies warmed her from the front and the back, and a thin coating of sweat made their skin stick. She intertwined her fingers with Remy's at her hip.

'Dear God,' she whispered.

A muscle in Bas's cheek twitched. He watched her intently, the relaxation on his face turning into something else. Confusion? Uneasiness?

Instinctively, she reached out to cup his cheek. 'What is it? What's wrong?'

His groan was different this time. Low, rumbling and full of pain. Catching her by the waist, he pulled out of her. The slickness of their connection made the move easy, but Alicia still flinched.

It made her all the more aware of the cock still inside her.

'Bas?' she said with concern.

He'd rolled onto his back and was grinding the balls of his hands into his eye sockets. 'Fuck! Shit! God damn it, Remy. Why did you let me?'

Alicia felt Remy's arm wrap around her more tightly. 'I'm not your keeper, Bas.'

'Fuck!' With a burst of energy, Bas sat up and swung his legs off the side of the bed. He hung his head and clenched his hands into fists.

She reached out in concern. His lungs were pumping so hard, the dragon tattoo on his back looked as if it was breathing fire. She brushed her fingers over the markings, but he shied away.

She pulled back when he flew off the bed and spun around to face her. The look on his face was one she hadn't expected. It was full of anger and anguish. He

335

covered his crotch with his hands as if embarrassed to have her look at him – or as if she shouldn't.

'God forgive me,' he rasped. He yanked his gaze from her and bent down to grab his clothes from the floor. 'Because I'll never forgive myself.'

'What's wrong?' Alicia asked. She was so confused. It had been so good, for all of them – or so she'd thought. 'What did I do?'

'What did you do?' His hands were shaking as he zipped up his pants. 'You tempted me to do something I've never done before. Son of a bitch! I should have been able to resist, but you walk around with that body.'

He suddenly couldn't look at the bed.

He raked a hand through his hair and it stood out in tufts. 'And your dancing! You pulled me down until I couldn't hang on.'

His shirt hung open and he left his suit jacket and tie on the floor. He swept up his shoes as he stormed towards the door. 'Delilah.'

The door slammed shut and Alicia cringed. He was so angry, with himself and with her. She still didn't know what she'd done, but she knew the story of Delilah.

The temptress who'd brought down Samson.

'Aw, shit,' Remy hissed. Holding her hips, he gently pulled out of her. He rolled onto his back and rested his wrist against his forehead. His breaths were deep and raspy.

So much hurt filled the room. Such a sense of betrayal. Apprehension filled Alicia. 'Why's he so upset?'

'Because he's married.'

She jack-knifed up to her knees on the bed. '*Married*?'

Remy sighed. 'Yeah.'

'To whom?'

'Her name is Sam.'

Alicia's brain spun, but then she was caught with the vision of the beautiful blonde who'd visited the church – the one in the wheelchair. Guilt kicked her in her gut so badly, she nearly doubled over. 'Samantha?'

'They've always been an item. He's never cheated on her before.'

Alicia was horrified. She'd slept with a married man. She was an adulteress.

'But he –' He what? Ran a strip club? Was around naked women all day long? Provided 'private' entertainment for high-paying clients?

'You might not think it, given his line of work, but he takes his vows seriously. Or maybe I should say took ...'

Alicia clutched the pillow to her front, ashamed now of her nakedness. Her wings were still looped around her shoulders, but they were limp and broken. She looked around the room, trying to find clothes to cover herself, but she didn't have any. A ragged sob left her lips.

'Aw, babe.' Seeing the distress on her face, Remy leaned over the side of the bed and grabbed his T-shirt. 'It's not your fault.'

He handed it to her and she pulled it over her head with shaking hands. It wouldn't stretch over her wings. Her angel's wings. She ripped them off and threw them away. The halo glittered from the headboard. She dived forward, grabbed it and flung it to the floor too.

'Yes, it is.' She was the one who'd kept pushing at Bas, wondering why he wouldn't touch her. He wouldn't touch her, because he was upholding his marital vows. Lashing out, she shoved Remy's shoulder. 'Why didn't you tell me? Why didn't you stop him?'

'Me?' He hitched himself up onto his elbows. 'I tried. I didn't see him cart you off. I was dealing with a disturbance at the door. By the time I got here, you two were already getting busy.'

Alicia felt queasy. She'd never said it aloud, never given it conscious thought, but she'd always considered herself in the right in this whole situation. Holier than thou. On the 'good' side. Yet she'd seduced him. She was Bas's temptation to sin. She was the one who had pulled him down, a devoted husband.

She rolled out of bed, unable to look at it anymore.

Because what they'd done had felt so good. The three of them, dancing in carnal debauchery.

She rushed to the door and stumbled through it.

'Shit,' Remy cursed behind her. The mattress squeaked as he climbed off of it. 'Alicia!'

She moved blindly down the hallway. She hung her head low and hid behind her hair. She was mortified and crushed. The plush carpeting soaked up the sounds of the club, when all she wanted to do was howl.

Someone was suddenly in her way, and she jumped. She'd been so intent on staring at the floor she didn't see the other person until his shoes were in her line of sight.

'Sorry,' the man said, catching her by the arms before she crashed into him. 'Angel, isn't it?'

Marguerite was suddenly there, looping her arm through her customer's and cuddling up against him. 'You're mine tonight, Doyle.'

Doyle. The cop. The one who'd ticketed her father for the loudspeakers.

Alicia stared at him, eyes wide, even though she felt dampness pressing. She knew she'd seen him somewhere else. A blue light flashed from on the main stage, and she remembered the news video of Paul's arrest. He'd been on the scene there, too. She stumbled back, but watched the couple as they made their way into Private Room Two.

A hand wrapped around her arm. 'Let's find somewhere we can talk about this.'

She whirled on Remy like a dervish and pointed at the now closed door. 'What's he doing here?' she hissed.

'Who?'

'Sergeant Doyle.'

Remy shrugged. 'He's a regular.'

A regular customer who was also on the payroll? The man seemed to show up at the most convenient times for the Satin Club.

What was going on here?

Remy tried again to coax her away from the main stage. 'Let's go back to the room.'

He was bare-chested and barefooted. He'd literally given her the shirt off his back, but everything was clicking for her now. All the pieces were assembling in her head. He wasn't the man she lusted after, the one who was beginning to make her heart go soft. He was the ex-military man – the one who knew about computers and background checks and technologies. Bas was the one with the power, the money and the connections.

And the wife.

Leesha pressed her hand to her aching stomach. Had this all been part of a manipulative scheme? She'd always thought it honourable that they hadn't responded to her church's taunts – that they'd taken the higher road. But had they? Or had they taken out Sunny Epiphany's members one by one? Paul was obvious, now that she thought about it. And Steve? How had he ended up drunk at the church?

'Did you send Samantha to speak with my father?'

Remy's face darkened. 'She went to the church?'

OK, so she was innocent. Of everything. Just an interested party and an unintended victim.

But what about herself? They'd known she was a dancer. They'd talked to her about it the first time they'd met. Had this all been part of their game, too? A strategic move to bring down her father?

'Was this all planned?' she asked. They had the power and the know-how to carry it off. 'Did you come after my church intentionally? After me?'

His shoulders stiffened and a closed look settled on his face. 'You came after us first.'

The words slashed like a knife. Her father took her for granted. Bas had used her to make money, but for some reason Remy's betrayal cut deepest.

She yanked her arm out of his hold.

'Well, we're even then,' she said softly. 'Because none of us won.'

Chapter Sixteen

Remy was fifteen minutes behind Alicia. He'd stopped first to make sure Bas wasn't tearing up his office or, worse, driving anywhere. After assigning Charlie to look after him, he'd left. The guy might be his best friend, but he made his own decisions. Some were better than others, including this whole battle with the Sunny Epiphanies ... and his romp with Angel. Everyone was going to have to learn to deal with the outcomes – including Alicia.

He headed up the front walk to her door, feeling more on-edge than he'd felt since he'd been in the field. The apartment complex was the same as every other time he'd visited, quiet and dark. The streetlamps lit small patches of grass and concrete. Locked doors held out the bad and the scary. He was both, but he wanted in.

He wanted her.

His fingers curled in towards his palms. This wasn't over by a long shot. She'd had her say, but it was time he had his.

Moving into the light, he knocked at her front door. The raps were loud in the stillness that surrounded him. He knew she was in there. He'd seen her car in the lot and there were lights on behind her curtains.

'Alicia,' he called.

He could feel her on the other side of the door. Her tension and misery blasted all the way through the hard steel. He knocked again.

'Go away,' she finally responded.

'Not going to happen.'

She turned off the lights and the apartment went black.

'Son of a bitch.' He tried the handle, but the place was locked up tight. He stepped back to glance around the perimeter. Briefly, he considered going in by force. Instead, he did what he'd learned to do back when he and Bas had been young hoods with no direction. He picked the lock.

When he entered, she sprang off the sofa where she'd been sitting in the dark. 'What are you doing?' she hissed.

He kicked the door shut behind him and stalked towards her. She was outlined by the tiny light in the refrigerator door. Her hair was wet, her face was scrubbed free of make-up and she wore a loose T-shirt and shorts.

She'd taken a shower, but she was the classic girl-next-door. The embodiment of all his fantasies.

'You and I won,' he said firmly.

'What?'

'You said that nobody won, but you're wrong. You and I have something going, and I'm not going to just let you walk away.' Not without fighting for her.

She wrapped her arms around her waist. It was clear that she'd been crying, but she lifted her chin stubbornly. 'I was a mark, Remy. I get that. I was a way to take down your enemy, and you and Bas did a hell of a job. You dragged me right down into the dirt with you.'

His muscles bunched and he took another step towards her. 'Don't you use that sanctimonious tone with me. You did nothing that you didn't want to do, and I think it's been made crystal-clear that nobody is superior. We all have our secrets and our twisted sides. Some of us just refuse to hide them.'

Her hand shook as she pushed it through her damp hair. A piece of glitter reflected the light, left over from her halo, but she wasn't a fallen angel. She was a woman.

'You and Bas came after me, because you knew I was a dancer.'

'I came after you, because I wanted to fuck you.'

Her head snapped back. She was still so easy to shock.

She shook it off. 'You two planned the whole thing. Me, Paul, Steve ...' She flung her arms out at her sides.

344

'Was Samantha part of the game, too? Was she coaching from the sidelines?'

'You really want to point fingers at her?'

She looked away, chagrined. 'I suppose she's the real victim in all of this.'

That was it. He walked right up to her, and she retreated until the backs of her knees bumped against the sofa. 'You are not a victim, Leesha, and this was no game.'

She was on her toes, ready to flee, but she pulled back her shoulders and held her ground. 'Are you saying you had nothing to do with framing my fellow church members?'

'Framing them? I exposed them for what they are.' He jabbed his finger towards the top of the refrigerator where he'd found another of Paul's cameras. 'Are you telling me that Jeanne Young would be better off being videotaped in her own house? That you would?'

She paled, even in the dim light.

But he was just getting started. 'I don't give a rat's ass that Steve What's-his-face likes to dress up like a fairy godmother. What burns me is the way your entire church of righteous Bible-thumpers shunned him. Are you telling me that's right? That's holy?'

'I didn't shun him.' She tapped her fingers against her elbow. 'I just didn't like him.'

'Do you like me?'

The words hung out there, sinking slowly as she took her time answering. A flurry of emotions went across her face. Fury, outrage, wanting, tenderness. Her spine stiffened so fast, it was a wonder he didn't hear it snap.

'You pushed me at other men,' she flatly. 'You made me into a stripper and a whore.'

'Bullshit. You live for dancing, and you liked what happened in those back rooms.'

'Because I thought you were watching!'

That rocked him back on his heels.

'Oh, God.' She wrapped her hand over her mouth and turned away. 'And look, you've got me taking the Lord's name in vain like it's nothing.'

'It's not nothing.' He caught her and made her look at him again. Every muscle in his body was coiled. 'I was watching, and I hated that other men were touching you. What I loved, though, was the look on your face. I got off on the pleasure it gave you, and I'll stand by that. I wouldn't take any of that back. Would you?'

She pressed her lips together, just like she had that first day when he'd flustered her on the picket line. It made him want to toss her over his shoulder and carry her to the bedroom but, for once, that wasn't the solution. They needed to be upfront with each other if they were going to fix this.

'Are you going to deny that you enjoyed exploring your sexuality, Angel?'

'Don't call me that anymore.'

'But she's a part of you – a great part of you.' But she was right, he wanted Alicia. 'Damn it. Forget all the rights and wrongs, the he-said, she-said ...'

He raked a hand through his hair. 'Just be with me.'

Her breath caught, her mouth dropping open in surprise, and he couldn't resist. He ran his thumb deliberately over her lower lip. They didn't make any sense together – him, a guy who lived and worked in a seedy underworld and her, a bright and shiny-faced innocent. Only she wasn't so innocent anymore, and he wanted more than the boyfriend fantasy. Because together they clicked.

He wanted the real thing.

Her arms tightened around her waist, and her eyes glistened. 'You hurt me, Remy.'

The rasp in her voice cut right to his gut, but it was an opening. His heart started beating faster. 'I didn't mean to. I promise it will never happen again.'

She stared at him for a long moment and the silence got thick. 'What would people say?'

'That we're hot together. That we can't get enough of each other. Fuck, I don't care what people say. Do you?'

She licked her lips, and his knees just about unhinged. He shifted closer until their bodies brushed and speared his fingers into her soft hair. She was so beautiful, so ethereal. When he'd first seen her, she'd been unattainable, but now he could feel her flying just within reach. He wanted to grab her and reel her in, but he knew she had to come to him on her own. Anything else and he'd crush her. 'Are you still stuck there, Alicia? Or do you want a real life, with a real man? With me?'

She was trembling now. 'We can't. We shouldn't.'

'Isn't that when we have the most fun?'

'Oh, Remy.' She let out a shuddering breath and finally relaxed against him. 'You are not fun. You're scary and intense and protective and irresistible and …'

'And what?'

'And mine.' She laid her cheek against his chest. 'This is crazy.'

His heart jumped, and his knees threatened to do that funny thing again. 'I know, but it's right.'

Before he lost control of them entirely, he swung her up into his arms and turned towards the bedroom. He could hold on tight now, and he had no plans of ever letting go.

* * *

Alicia lay in bed with Remy, her head resting on his rippled stomach. Light was only starting to spill through the windows, and all was quiet. She trailed her fingers softly over his limp cock. She was still curious about some things and he'd let her experiment on him with her hands and her mouth.

She smiled softly. For such a big, tough guy, she knew now how to leave him weak and begging.

'Careful,' he grumbled above her. 'That's a dangerous weapon you're playing with.'

'Is it going to go off on me again?' She looked up at him, chin on his ribcage.

His fingers slid lazily through her hair. 'It just might.'

They relaxed back into silence, but her brain was whirring. Thoughts and concerns had been circling in her head all night long. Were they really going to give this a go? How would her father react? What about Bas and Samantha? She felt so miserable over that.

'I wish I'd known Bas was married,' she murmured. 'Nobody ever said anything. He always seemed so reserved and rigid. I really thought he might be gay or ...'

'Or what?'

'One of those leather-and-whip types.'

'A dom?' Remy gave a bark of laughter. 'Sam wouldn't let him take the reins like that. If anything, his lack of impulse control is what has got him into trouble in the past.'

'Like the accident?' She dropped her gaze and focused on tracing lines on his chest. 'My father said something about it. Was that what happened to her?'

Remy sighed. 'Bas was driving and Sam was in the passenger seat. He was going too fast, but there was a careless teen with a cellphone ... It was a bad time.'

'But they're still together?'

'In every way.'

She trailed her fingertips over his nipple. 'Every way?'

He cupped the back of her neck firmly. 'Every way. He didn't need to turn to you because he wasn't getting any.'

'I feel so guilty,' she whispered. Good and bad had flipped. Righteous and depraved had intertwined. Or was there no right and wrong? Maybe they were all part of being human.

'They'll get through it. They've gotten through worse.'

'So he'll tell her?'

Remy frowned. 'There are no secrets between them.'

And there weren't any secrets between them, either. In the whole world, he was about the only person who'd seen all sides of her. The good, the bad and the kinky – yet he wanted her, as is. He wasn't going to ask her to change. He wasn't going to bind her up with religion or make her give lap dances to his friends.

But what were they going to do? How were they going to make this work? 'What happens next? Where do we go from here?'

He wound a strand of her hair around his finger. It had dried wet and the curls were wild. 'Where do you want to go?'

That was the biggest question of all. She was at a turning-point in her life. She'd already decided she had to bring him with her, but which direction should she take? 'I don't know. I can't go back to my job at the church, but I want to get in touch with my faith again.' She grimaced. 'I know that might not make sense to you, but I feel adrift without it.'

'A person's relationship with God is personal.'

She raised her eyebrows. 'Are you religious?'

He rubbed the curl he'd captured between his finger-tips. 'My grandmother is. She raised me. I could quote scriptures to your father, if that would help.'

She considered that. There were so many sides to him she still didn't know. 'I'd like to meet her sometime.'

'You will. She lives down at the Green Meadows retirement home.'

Alicia cocked her head in surprise. 'The church does outreach work there. Bingo night and Bible classes.'

He smiled ruefully. 'You're not going to boycott my grandmother next, are you?'

She sighed. 'I don't think my father will be leading any more charges for a while. I think Samantha was right. After his empire started to crumble, he was looking for a way out. I hope he gets back to his faith, too.'

'Do you want me to talk to him? Because I will.'

She closed her eyes when he rubbed her ear. 'Not right now. I should talk to him first.'

'So what were your plans before you started working at the church? What was that business degree intended for?' he asked.

'A dance studio,' she sighed.

'So there you go. Why not do that now?'

She paused. She hadn't thought of that. It had always been her dream but, like so many dreams, she hadn't thought it could become a reality – especially after she'd given it up to help her father. Yet the bulk of her inheritance was still intact, and then there was the money she'd made at the Satin Club. 'I'd love that,' she mused. 'I could design classes for everyone, not just little girls. When I was looking for somewhere to train, I couldn't find any studios with that kind of programme.'

'I'm all for big girl dancers.'

She perked up, lifting her head off his chest. 'I could give pole-dancing lessons!'

He chuckled.

'No, I'm serious.' She pushed at his shoulder. 'Women are curious about them, and they're all the rage in the fitness world. It was even an exhibition event before the London Olympics. There are people lobbying for it to be included as an official sport.'

'Then do it.' He stroked his hand lazily over her bare bottom. 'Although does that mean you'd give up performing?'

She bit her lip. 'I love to dance, Remy.'

'I know you do, babe, and people love watching you.' He slid his fingers into her damp pussy, and Alicia stretched in delight. She'd sucked him off, and that had been enough for her. She arched when he found a particularly sensitive spot and started to rub. If he insisted, though ...

'Samantha said something about touring as a featured act,' she murmured.

His fingers stilled inside her. 'That's not such a bad idea. You could travel the country as a marquee name. That's where the real money is. You could be the next Gypsy Rose Lee. With the routines and get-ups you come up with, you're sure to be a hit.'

Could she really do that? Leesha's mind was spinning at the possibilities. There were strippers and burlesque performers who'd made the field an art form. Their names were thought of with enthusiasm – not derision. Could she be one of those select few? But what would she tell her father? Did he even need to know? 'I wouldn't even know where to start.'

'Bas would.'

She looked away. 'I couldn't ask him.'

'I can. He owes you that much.'

She sucked in a breath when her lover suddenly moved in that black panther way of his. She found herself on her back with him sliding smoothly into her. 'Remy!'

'That's better.' His black eyes turned onyx as he looked down at her.

He began an easy glide in and out of her. No rush, but all the heat.

She clutched at his shoulders. 'What about you? What are you going to do? I don't want to come between you and your friends.'

'You haven't. I'll still work at the club but, you know, I've always thought I'd be a great bodyguard – for the right body.'

'Ahhh!' She rolled her hips with his, matching his movements. He was the one who had the right body, and all the right moves. 'Remy.'

'I just want to be with you, Alicia.' He leaned down to kiss her. 'Be my private dancer?'

She groaned and wrapped herself around him. 'Just show me the rhythm.'

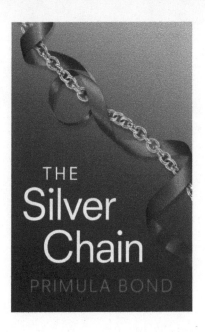

THE SILVER CHAIN – PRIMULA BOND

Good things come to those who wait…

After a chance meeting one evening, mysterious entrepreneur Gustav Levi and photographer Serena Folkes agree to a very special contract.

Gustav will launch Serena's photographic career at his gallery, but only if Serena agrees to become his companion.

To mark their agreement, Gustav gives Serena a bracelet and silver chain which binds them physically and symbolically. A sign that Serena is under Gustav's power.

As their passionate relationship intensifies, the silver chain pulls them closer together. But will Gustav's past tear them apart?

A passionate, unforgettable erotic romance for fans of *50 Shades of Grey* and Sylvia Day's *Crossfire Trilogy*.

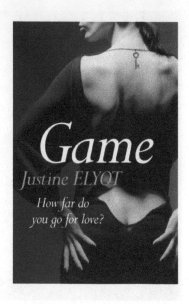

GAME – JUSTINE ELYOT

The stakes are high, the game is on.

In this sequel to Justine Elyot's bestselling *On Demand*, Sophie discovers a whole new world of daring sexual exploits.

Sophie's sexual tastes have always been a bit on the wild side – something her boyfriend Lloyd has always loved about her.

But Sophie gives Lloyd every part of her body except her heart. To win all of her, Lloyd challenges Sophie to live out her secret fantasies.

As the game intensifies, she experiments with all kinds of kinks and fetishes in a bid understand what she really wants. But Lloyd feature in her final decision? Or will th ultimate risk he takes drive her away from him?

Find out more at www.mischiefbooks.com

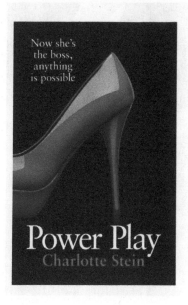

POWER PLAY – CHARLOTTE STEIN

Now she's the boss, everything that once seemed forbidden is possible…

Meet Eleanor Harding, a woman who loves to be in control and who puts Anastasia Steele in the shade.

When Eleanor is promoted, she loses two very important things: the heated relationship she had with her boss, and control over her own desires.

She finds herself suddenly craving something very different – and office junior, Ben, seems like just the sort of man to fulfil her needs. He's willing to show her all of the things she's been missing – namely, what it's like to be the one in charge.

Now all Eleanor has to do is decide…is Ben calling the kinky shots, or is she?

Find out more at www.mischiefbooks.com

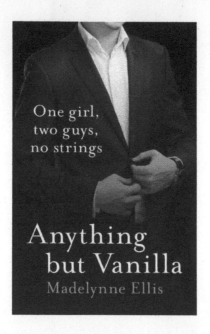